The Lady and the Mountain Man

The Mountain Series

Book 1

Misty M. Beller

This book is a work of fiction and any resemblance to persons, living or dead, or places, events or locales is purely coincidental. The characters are the product of the author's imagination and used fictitiously.

Dedication

To my family.
For your support, your encouragement, and your love.

Trust in the Lord, and do good;
Dwell in the land, and feed on His faithfulness.

Delight yourself also in the Lord,
And He shall give you the desires of your heart.

Commit your way to the Lord,
Trust also in Him,
And He shall bring it to pass.

Psalm 37:3-5 (NKJV)

Chapter One

Richmond, Virginia
March, 1874

"Are you going to poison her the way you killed your last

wife?"

Leah Townsend froze in the hallway, her right foot suspended midair as her breathing stopped. She lowered her toes to the floor, and then sidled closer to the closed study door—still not daring to breathe. The thick Persian rug muffled her footsteps. As she leaned forward, the strong scent of oil wafted from the mahogany wood door.

A throaty chuckle drifted out of the room. "I haven't decided yet. When I get tired of the nagging, I'll find a way to dispense with her. Assuming she's received her inheritance and her father's estates are legally mine."

Leah's blood ran so cold it froze in her veins. *Dispense with her?* Her brain repeated the words once, twice, and then took off like the hooves of a racehorse. Her blood began to move again, rushing through her so quickly it roared in her ears.

She'd recognize that voice anywhere. It held the suave tone of a man very sure of himself. The tone of the man she'd had nightmares about every night for weeks. The tone of the man her father had legally contracted her to marry in six days. Simon Talbert.

"You think she'll still go through with it? Now that her old man's dead?"

Leah strained to place the other voice. Her betrothed had left the dinner party to take care of a business matter, but she hadn't noticed with whom.

"She has no choice." Simon's voice again. "Unless she appeals to the courts to break the contract. But she won't do that. It was her father's dying wish. And after all, why wouldn't she want to marry a fine catch like me?"

A tingle ran down Leah's spine. Was he a murderer? Papa had been so excited about this marriage, surely he wouldn't sign her life away to a man who would kill her. Oh, why had she ever agreed to this crazy arranged marriage?

What had she heard about Simon's first wife? Only that the woman had been sickly and died at twenty-three.

A wave of fear started in Leah's stomach and welled up her chest until it almost smothered her. What had Papa said about Simon? She could hear his deep, comforting voice even now. *He has a fine reputation in the business community and will be able to care for you very comfortably.*

Money. This whole business of arranged marriages and betrothal contracts was about the money. And status. And what each person could gain. Except for the bride. The bride was the only person who lost in this game. Maybe not every arranged marriage was unpleasant for the woman, but this situation looked to be very dangerous for her.

She focused her attention again on the sounds drifting through the door. The men must have moved toward the windows, because their voices had lowered to an indistinct murmur.

Disappointed, Leah pulled away. She needed to get back to the drawing room anyway. Someone might question her absence, maybe even send a servant to help her.

Leah started down the hallway, but the door jerked open before she could take more than a step. She whirled, then froze, staring into the face of her betrothed, a man seventeen years her senior.

"Simon," she gasped. Did he realize she'd overheard? "I was just returning from the powder room. If you're finished with your business, perhaps you can escort me back to the drawing room." Leah extended an elegant hand, brows raised in the coy expression she'd learned from too many society parties. She didn't dare draw a breath.

Simon studied her, his tall form debonair in a dark tail coat and manicured black hair. At a glance, it was easy to see why the ladies flocked after him, and even more so when they learned of his extensive wealth.

But something about his posture now raised goose bumps on Leah's arms.

"My dear." His voice was too rich. Too smooth. Leah inched backward, but Simon stepped toward her. "Did you, uh... stand here waiting for me long?" As he neared, a whiff of spirits permeated the air, and red framed his dark eyes.

"No. No, I was just passing by." *Breathe.* She had to appear nonchalant.

Simon's eyes narrowed. Could he see through her façade? "My partner and I were just reminiscing. But many of our business dealings are highly confidential." Another man moved into the open doorway behind Simon. This man was shorter and leaner, but carried himself the same way Simon did.

His scrutiny smothered her.

"If you overheard our conversation, it wouldn't bode well for you." Simon's gaze bore a hole through her. "Of course, the last thing I would want is for anything to hurt you, my dear. Or hurt your close friends." Steel laced his every word. "Close friends like your Miss Emily."

Emily, her companion. Her dearest confidante.

Leah braved a glance at his face. His eyes had shrunken to black slits. Danger radiated from every pore.

3

He took another step forward, his hand tightening like a vise over her fingers. His words clamped down her chest. Her lungs wouldn't fill.

"The good news is..." He breathed hard air in her face. Leah forced herself not to react as the alcohol assaulted her eyes. "...I have many influential friends. Friends in the police force. In the courts. Friends who will believe my word without question."

He placed Leah's hand on his arm, then tightened his grip over her fingers, holding her securely in place. "It's fortunate for you, dear Leah, we'll be wed this week. I wouldn't want your life to end in a...painful and unfortunate manner."

A chill forced its way through Leah's body.

Simon turned toward the main corridor and began walking, his hand ensuring Leah stayed with him each step of the way. The other man receded into the room and closed the door.

Leah's heart beat so wildly her stomach ached. What should she do? She was walking on the arm of a murderer. How could she get away? Had he really meant he'd kill her if she said anything about what she'd overheard?

They were about to rejoin the party now. She had to compose herself until she could determine what to do. She couldn't allow Simon to see anything he said concerned her.

Deep breath. Shoulders squared. Chin up. Pleasant expression. Now float forward, full of poise and grace. The actions were ingrained, habit from many years of drilling and constant reminders, mostly from Emily.

"Ah, Mr. Talbert. Miss Townsend. We were just discussing the wedding gowns for the season." Mrs. Troutman cooed. "Miss Townsend, I'm sure you've become quite an expert on the topic with your wedding close at hand. Perhaps your fiancé can spare you so we can hear the details." She patted the settee next to her while gazing expectantly at Leah.

A conversation about wedding gowns, her own in particular, was the last thing she could handle right now. But it would get her away from this man. Although, maybe she should be discussing the gown she'd like to be buried in instead.

4

Leah slid her hand from under Simon's grasp and glided to Mrs. Troutman. Out of the corner of her eye, she watched Simon offer a stiff bow, then stride toward a group of gentlemen. Leah had an urge to hug the snobby woman beside her.

She endured a few minutes of the woman's gushing about the fashion plate in the front of this season's Godey's Lady's Book, but Leah's mind fidgeted. She had to get away from this house or she just might lose her poise. And Emily had always taught her a woman *never*, under any circumstance, loses her poise.

Leah smiled at Mrs. Troutman and tried her best to sound genuine. "I'm so sorry, ladies, but I'm afraid I must retire early this evening. I'm not feeling well. I will look forward to joining the discussion at another time."

"Oh, dear." Mrs. Troutman spoke in a cultured tone that reeked of condescension. "And you're practically the hostess of our little party, since you're betrothed to the host. Whatever will we do without you?"

She sounded as if she knew exactly what she would do with the loss of Leah's company. Most likely take the opportunity to thrust her own spoiled daughter under the notice of Simon Talbert, as she'd done so many times before. And she could have him. If Mrs. Troutman only knew what the man was really like, she would run far away from this tainted mansion.

But then remorse pricked Leah's chest. No woman deserved what Simon had in mind.

Leah gave the ladies another manufactured smile. "I'm sure my absence won't stunt the evening's enjoyment in the least. In fact..." she leaned forward conspiratorially "...I'll rely on you to make certain of that."

Mrs. Troutman preened like one of the peacocks Leah had seen in the park off Central Avenue. "Of course, dear. Now do go and take care of yourself."

Leah glided across the room toward Emily, her companion, former governess and—since Leah's mother had died six years ago—her dearest friend and mentor. Emily, elegant in her long, slender cuirass bodice, stood with the Lindsey cousins. Next to her, the younger ladies looked silly in their too-bright and childish Dolly Vardens.

"But, Emily, he has the croup. Do you really think that will help?" asked Olivia Lindsey.

Emily nodded, then looked up, her eyes studying Leah. "Aren't you feeling well, love?"

How did Emily do it? Leah had been sure she'd had her high-society mask in place. "I have a bit of a headache, and wondered if you would mind leaving a little early?"

Emily's eyes crinkled at the edges into a soft smile. "Of course not. I'll go call the carriage now."

"Please don't." Leah said the words a bit too quickly, but she had to get away before Simon saw her leave. "I'll do it and meet you in the foyer."

Twin lines of concern formed between Emily's brows. "All right, then." Emily turned to her two companions as Leah made her escape. "Olivia, I'll be praying your little Henry heals quickly..."

Emily was so kind. One day if Leah ever finally grew up—which didn't seem to have happened yet at twenty-two—she wanted to be as good and kind and caring as Emily.

Leah wound her way around clusters of acquaintances and society friends, almost to the wide double doors open to the foyer.

"Miss Townsend." The suave baritone voice stopped her cold. Leah didn't turn, forcing Simon to come around to face her. His eyes were black...cold.

"You're not leaving, are you?" Something hard glittered in his gaze.

"I, uh, I'm not feeling well." His scrutiny was too much. Leah dropped gaze. "I thought I would retire early."

Simon touched her chin with a forefinger, raising her face to his. He rested his thumb on the other side of her chin, in what would have appeared to anyone else as a tender gesture among sweethearts. But the pressure with which he gripped her chin left no doubt in Leah's mind of his message.

"I trust you're too ill to have a chat with anyone. I'll come visit early tomorrow to check on you." He dropped his hand but stepped nearer, drawing himself to his fullest height. Less than a foot of space separated him, and Leah could see every damp pore on his face. "I'm sure no one would begrudge me spending every moment possible with my bride-to-be."

His posture relaxed and Leah didn't wait for a better opportunity. She turned and fled the room.

Emily, always the thoughtful one, waited until they were safely tucked into the carriage before she turned to Leah. "What in the world is wrong? I've never seen you so pale."

Leah fidgeted with the silk ruffle on the hem of her coat. Should she tell the authorities? Tell anyone? Would they believe her over Simon? Papa had signed the contract with the man over six months ago, just before his death. Leah had always been convinced Simon was most interested in her wealth. Not the modest dowry she would bring to the marriage, but the vast amount of money and holdings kept safe in a trust until her twenty-third birthday—next February.

With Simon's money and extensive connections, not a soul in Richmond would believe a twenty-two-year-old woman over a respected business man like him. Why, at least fifty women in Richmond would switch places with her in an instant to have an opportunity to marry such a rich widower, despite the age difference.

Even Emily would be skeptical. She always had trouble believing the worst in people. But she would believe Leah. And maybe she could help.

"What happened, love?" Emily's gentle voice was prodding.

Leah took a deep breath. "When I was leaving the powder room, I heard voices coming from one of the hallways. I was curious, so I walked a short way and heard Mr. Talbert speaking with another man. They were…talking about me." She steadied her voice and told her friend about the tête-à-tête, and Simon's reaction to her presence.

At the end of it all, Emily was speechless.

"Do you remember hearing how the first Mrs. Talbert died?"

Emily's forehead wrinkled and her eyes grew distant as she rubbed two fingers over her jaw. "She always seemed healthy when I saw her. About a year or so after they were married, though, she stopped coming to most of the social events. I didn't hear much more about her for a while, but about six months later I heard she had passed away. I always assumed it was complications from being…in the family way."

Emily turned her attention back to Leah, eyes piercing. "Is it possible you misheard the conversation or misunderstood Mr. Talbert's meaning when he spoke to you?"

Of course, Emily would be reluctant to believe such a horrible thing. Leah could hardly believe it herself. How could Papa have trusted this man?

Her jaw tightened with conviction. "I'm positive I heard them correctly. And Simon made himself very clear." She turned to grasp Emily's hands, choking fear rising in her chest again. "What am I going to do? I can't marry him! I don't think I can even stand to be near him again. He said he would call early tomorrow to check on me. I'm sure he's planning to make sure I don't go to the authorities." Would Simon go as far as kidnapping her? But why not? A man who was plotting murder wouldn't think twice about a little kidnapping in the process.

Emily freed herself from Leah's hands only to wrap her arms around Leah's shoulders and rock, just like Mama used to do. "Leah, love. I don't know what we need to do just yet, except I know we need to pray. God will show you. He has a plan even in this, but you have to seek it. Seek Him. He loves you even more than I do."

Leah fought the sting of tears as the warmth of Emily's hug soaked through her fear.

Leah blew out her breath in a frustrated stream. Flipping through her Bible, she tried hard to fight the feeling her life was falling apart. Curled in a warm flannel nightgown against the late March chill, she sat tucked in bed, searching for direction.

Father, please speak to me. Do you have a way for me to escape this?

But was escape right? Hadn't God said to honor her father and mother, that her life would be long in the land the Lord would give her? But obeying her father's wishes appeared to be at direct odds with living a long life, in this case. Was God planning to save her through some miraculous act? Like he did with Daniel in the lions' den?

Mind rambling, she opened the Bible again and began reading in First Samuel. The early days of the Israelites always fascinated her. No matter how many times they wandered, no matter how many really bad choices they made, God always brought them back. He always forgave them when they truly humbled themselves before Him. Leah found herself absorbed in the story of young David and how God used him to calm King Saul when the distressing spirit would come upon him.

"And David was playing music with his harp. Then Saul sought to pin David to the wall with the spear, but he slipped away from Saul's presence, and he drove the spear into the wall. So David fled and escaped that night."

Goose bumps covered Leah's arms, and a little chill shot down her back. She kept reading.

"Saul also sent messengers to David's house to watch him and to kill him in the morning. And Michal, David's wife, told him, saying, 'If you do not save your life tonight, tomorrow you will be killed.' So Michal let David down through a window. And he went and fled and escaped."

When Saul was trying to kill David, David fled and escaped.

Escape.

That's what she had to do.

Chapter Two

*L*eah breathed a sigh of relief when she entered the breakfast room early and found Emily already seated at the long mahogany table. A faint shadow under Emily's eyes was the only sign in her otherwise impeccable appearance that she may not have had a restful night's sleep.

Leah, on the other hand, knew from a glance in her mirror earlier that she looked like she may have slept an hour at the most. And that was fairly accurate.

After she'd received God's direction for her to flee Richmond, Leah had spent an hour packing four trunks with the personal items she might need on her journey. Then she'd spent another hour unpacking two of the trunks, after deciding she should travel light so as not to raise suspicions with the bellboys and luggage handlers wherever she went. So now she was down to a minimal amount of clothing, toiletries, books, and the five hundred dollars she had saved from her spending money. Most of Papa's money was in the trust held for her twenty-third birthday, except the monthly stipend she received for personal expenses.

She waited impatiently for the housemaid to remove the covers from their full plates, and then fill each of their mugs with warm coffee. Even after Papa was gone, Emily had insisted they continue to eat formal meals so Leah wouldn't lose the habit.

"Thank you, Amanda." Emily was always full of grace and

kindness. The servant girl curtsied and scurried from the large dining chamber. As soon as she was gone, Leah leaned forward to place a hand on the table.

"We're leaving Richmond. You and I. Today. God directed me to flee and escape, so we have to leave this morning."

Emily dabbed at her mouth, not looking as shocked as Leah had expected.

"And where do you plan to go?"

Leah had given that a great deal of thought, but hadn't come up with a good answer. "I don't know, really. I don't have any family left, and we never did much traveling, so all of my friends are in Richmond. I guess I'm thinking we should go to Charleston for a while, since we used to vacation there and I know the city a bit." She frowned. "I'm not sure what I would do there, though."

Emily shook her head. "No, you need to go to St. Louis. It's in Missouri, and I have family there...of sorts. My sister's husband came from that area, and I know his family will help you. Their name is Barnett, and they're good people. I'll send them a wire after you leave, so they'll be expecting you."

"But you have to go, too."

Emily's eyes shone—with kindness or unshed tears? "No, I think this is also the opportunity God's given me to spend some time helping my sweet sister. It's been hard on her since her Robert died, and I think it would do her good to have someone with her right now."

"But don't you think you should leave town?" Panic welled in Leah's chest as she thought about getting on a train by herself. Walking away from the only friend she had left—the only life she'd ever known.

Emily's face dissolved into that gentle look of affection. "Leah, love. I spent many hours last night praying, too. God told me He has a special plan for you, and this is the way He wants you to start. He has other plans for me."

Leah's heart filled with both relief and panic at Emily's answer. "Are you sure?"

She patted Leah's cheek in a motherly way. "God has you safe in His hands, love. And you can know for sure I'll be praying for you every step of the way."

And then Leah did what she'd been trying not to do all night. She cried.

In less time than she had thought possible, Leah stood in front of a Richmond, Fredericksburg & Potomac train car. The observation car's exterior may once have been a cheery yellow, but the harsh sun and the layer of ashen soot from the steam engine had rendered it a murky beige. She felt like a stranger in the simple homespun dress—gray, with no frills, lace, or bustle—and only a faded carpet bag in her hands. Not a soul would recognize her as a Townsend in this depressing—and scratchy—costume.

When Emily got an idea in her head, there was no one save the Lord Himself who could stop her from acting on it immediately. She had inspected Leah's trunks and approved of most of the items inside, but changed out a few of the gowns for more 'serviceable' dresses. Then she'd found the homespun wool dress from who-knows-where so no one would recognize her at the train station, sent for a hired hack so no one from Townsend Manor would know where she'd gone, and had Cook pack a lunch to put in Leah's satchel. On the way to the train station Emily had given so many instructions that Leah's mind was exhausted already. And it was only nine o'clock in the morning.

Emily had kept their goodbye short and hopeful, pressing several papers into Leah's hand. "Please send me a note as soon as you arrive in St. Louis to let me know you're all right." It was the first time Emily had shown any kind of reluctance for Leah to leave. "Do you have the letter for Mr. Shelton?"

"Oh, that's right." Leah reached into her reticule and pulled out the sealed stationery addressed to her father's steward, Mister

James Shelton, Esquire.

Emily reached for it, her eyes meeting Leah's. "You didn't tell him where you're going, did you?"

Leah shook her head. "Only that I was leaving town and would contact him next year after my birthday to arrange my inheritance. And then I detailed the conversation I overheard between Simon and that other man, and also the things Simon said to me. I asked him to inform someone in the police department—someone he trusts."

Emily's mouth pinched in a grim line. "I hope he believes you. And I hope he finds the right person to help investigate. Simon has an impeccable reputation and the money to sway any decision."

"I know." Urgency washed through Leah. "We have to get out of here. Simon's probably already called at home."

Emily pulled her into a final fierce hug. "I'll be praying for you. Remember, I love you." And then she turned Leah around with a hand on each shoulder and practically pushed her toward the train.

After boarding, Leah made her way down the narrow aisle in search of an empty seat. She finally found a vacant bench, and collapsed onto the hard leather next to the window. She peered through the murky glass to get a final glimpse of Emily, and saw the woman waving and blowing kisses from the wooden platform. Leah waved back wildly, feeling her world slip away as the train jolted forward and her friend faded into the distance.

Leah leaned into the seat, and her heart ached like it was in a vise. What was she doing? She was leaving everything she knew and the best friend she'd ever had. And for what? Safety? How did she know where she was going would be any safer than staying with Simon Talbert? Sure he was *planning* to kill her, but who knew what menace she would meet on a trip halfway across the country to a strange city in the middle of an even stranger state.

Leah gazed out the window for a final glimpse of the Richmond train station. Why hadn't she *forced* Emily to come along? As far back as she could remember, she had been her dearest friend and confidante. Emily was fifteen years older than Leah, but that had never mattered. Mama died when Leah was sixteen, and Emily had stepped in to fill the void. A tear trickled down Leah's cheek as she sank into self-pity.

"Oh, you poor thing. Is this your first time travelin' by yourself?"

Leah looked up to see a short lady carrying as many bags as would fit in her wrinkled hands. The woman's hair had likely been blonde at one time, but it was now mostly white with a few golden strands mixed in, and her lined face radiated a kind soul.

Leah sniffed and made an effort to pull herself together, beginning with her poised smile. "Uh, yes, it is. Can I help you with those?"

With effort, the woman managed to set some of the bags on the bench, and then leaned over to place others underneath the seat. For a second, she swayed like she might topple with the rocking of the train. Leah reached out to grasp her arm, surprised at how bony it was, then moved the bags from the seat and helped the older lady sit.

"Ah, thank you, dear. These trains can knock my old legs over some times. I didn't used to be so unsteady on my feet, but gettin' old can be rough." She patted Leah's arm.

Leah couldn't help but smile at the likeable woman. "Do you travel often?"

Her clothing didn't appear lavish, but neither was it ragged. She wore a clean brown taffeta dress with a strip of lace around the high collar and long sleeves.

"My youngest daughter lives in Richmond with her four little ones. I try to visit a couple weeks each year to lighten her load a bit. Her oldest is barely in school and the youngest has started walkin' now, so she has more than a little on her plate. They're all smart as chickadees, though, and the two oldest can already read and recite sums."

She finally stopped to take a breath, then added, "I'm Louise Mathers, by the way, but everyone calls me Gram. And what might your name be?"

Gram was too bubbly to allow sadness to hover, so Leah relaxed against the cracked leather bench. "Leah."

"Ah, what a lovely name for a lovely girl. It's a pleasure to have your company. You remind me a bit of my Rebecca. She's my oldest grandbaby and has your pretty caramel-colored hair. She's a bit stouter than you, but she can sing like an angel. She'd like you, I'm sure…"

Gram chattered for another hour, then closed her eyes for a nap. When soft snores sounded from the older woman's open mouth, Leah took the opportunity to look at the papers Emily had given her.

Two scraps held addresses. One for the Barnett family in St. Louis, and the other for Emily's sister outside of Richmond. Next, she found a copy of the Richmond Enquirer. That was odd. Emily had always said it wasn't seemly for a young lady to be interested in newspapers and worldly affairs. The paper was open to one of the pages near the back, where rows of advertisements filled the space.

Her eyes wandered through the listings. In the "Lost.— Found." section, someone offered a five dollar reward for a missing lady's gold watch. The "Wanted…Situations …Females" took an entire column, but she couldn't bring herself to read too deeply. No doubt she would need to study those types of advertisements in detail when she reached St. Louis.

An advertisement in the "Personals" section just above the "Wanted" ads caught Leah's eye.

An intelligent young rancher of 25 years, 6 feet height, red hair, green eyes, seeks a wife in the Montana Territory. The young lady should be between 18 and 25 years, pleasant, and God fearing. Please send telegram or letter to Helena, MT addressed to Abel Bryant at Bryant Ranch, Butte City.

How curious! She'd heard of men placing advertisements for

mail-order brides, but she'd never actually seen such a listing.

The snores beside Leah ended with an unladylike snort, and Gram raised her head from the seat back. She licked her lips and looked around, taking in the landscape still flying by outside the windows.

"Nothin' like the rockin' of a train for a good nap."

Chapter Three

By the time the train pulled into the station in Washington, D.C., Leah had to try hard to remain amiable. She was tired, her spine and bottom ached from the unforgiving seat, her legs were cramped, and she wanted nothing more than to walk straight to a hotel with a warm bath and soft bed.

But as Emily had instructed, she disembarked the train and made her way into the depot.

"I need passage on your next train to St. Louis, please."

The thin man behind the spectacles was clean-shaven and balding, and he perused her with an air of condescension. "That would be the next Baltimore and Ohio, scheduled to arrive in about..." he peered at the watch hooked to his vest "...thirty minutes. You'll need to be ready to leave within ten minutes of its arrival."

Forty minutes. That would barely allow time for a quick meal, not a bath or a night's sleep. "Is there another train leaving tomorrow?"

His scowl made her almost wish she hadn't asked. But it would be heaven to crawl under warm covers and sleep. Leah pulled her shawl tighter around her shoulders. The sun was beginning to set, bringing on another cold March evening. She wished she had her wool coat, but at least it was packed in one of the trunks.

The man's whiny voice brought Leah back to the present. "The next train traveling to the western states arrives on Tuesday."

Tuesday? That was five days from now. Leah mentally groaned. "I'll need a ticket for today's train, then. Are there sleeping chambers available?"

The man's chest puffed out like she'd just thanked him for saving the President's life. "Yes, indeed. This train has one of the famous Pullman cars, with both upper and lower berths."

Leah sent up a silent prayer of thanks for little blessings.

By the end of six more very long days, the Pullman car proved to be much more than a little blessing. It was the only thing that made this trip endurable. When the car attendant announced the St. Louis Depot, Leah almost jumped to her feet to hug him. Her craving for solid land was palpable, tightening her muscles into knots. She could imagine a warm bath with scented soaps, silk sheets, and a soft feather bed that didn't sway through the night. And clean clothes. *Her* clothes, that didn't itch or stink.

Leah peered out the window, but couldn't see much through the small square of dingy glass. She stuffed her book into her carpet bag and rose as the train quivered to a stop. She filed behind the other passengers, shifting from foot to foot as they inched forward. Even in her exhausted state, she was too giddy to stand still. She'd arrived in St. Louis, and her new life was about to begin. Would this city be as large and cultured as Richmond?

Stepping from the train, Leah twisted her head to take in the sights, but what she saw brought her up short.

Water.

She stood in front of a vast lake. Not as large as the bay in Charleston had been, but close. On the other bank, far in the distance, a city rose from the murky depths like an Irish Sea monster.

"That's a lot of water." The baritone voice came from just behind her, and Leah whirled to find herself staring up into the emerald eyes of a man unlike any she'd ever seen. A full beard covered his face, making it hard to distinguish most of his features. Except those piercing green eyes. He looked to be a few years older than her, but probably not over thirty. His blue work shirt was clean and pressed, and accentuated the breadth of his shoulders.

The man didn't meet her gaze, but stared out over the water as if he were seeing far beyond. Then his comment registered in Leah's awareness.

"Yes, I suppose it is. Do you know what it's called? I thought we were far away from an ocean or any of the Great Lakes."

"The Missouri River." His voice was rich, and he still didn't look at her.

Leah arched a brow, then turned back to study the water before her. "It's a river? I've not seen one so wide. Is that St. Louis on the far shore?"

"Yep. The ferry's loading up now." He took a step, then motioned for her to precede him. The other passengers were moving forward, too, pressing toward the flat boat at the edge of the water.

"This way to the Wiggins Ferry," called a man with an official-sounding voice. "Only five cents to ride the ferry across to St. Louey."

The strong presence of the tall, green-eyed man stayed close as the crowd swept them onto a wooden pier and forward, toward a mustached man collecting fares at the entrance to the boat.

Just then, she remembered her trunks, which she hadn't seen in several days. "Excuse me, sir," she said to the attendant. "Will my luggage be brought across on the ferry?"

"Yes'm. You can pick 'em up at the yonder dock."

"Thank you." She dipped a slight curtsey and was pushed forward by the crowd boarding the boat. The rocking of the craft in the water was like being on the train again. Leah turned back to mention it to the man with the emerald eyes, but he wasn't behind her. Why did that make her feel even more alone?

She took up a crowded spot by the rail where she could see both banks, but her eyes drifted over the other passengers. There he was, standing in a quiet corner away from the swarm of passengers pushing toward the boat's edge. The crowd pushed in on her, too, so Leah gathered her nerve and moved toward the empty space next to the man. It was a bold move on her part, approaching a stranger she'd only just met and didn't even know the name of. But something about him intrigued her. Maybe he'd think she was just moving to a less congested part of the boat's deck.

Leah stepped up to the rail in the empty space between the man and an elderly couple. He turned his green eyes toward her in a nod, then gazed back over the water. He certainly was quiet.

"Are you from St. Louis then?" She infused a casual air into her tone.

"No, ma'am. Montana Territory."

That might explain the wild aura that surrounded him. Leah wanted another good look at him, but couldn't risk being caught staring. "How interesting. And were you visiting the East for pleasure, sir, or for business?"

"Settling my wife's affairs."

Leah's heart plunged at the words, but she forced herself not to examine the reason. "Is your wife traveling with you?" She turned a casual eye to his face as she spoke.

His focus stared straight ahead. "She died." The richness was gone from his voice, leaving behind flat steel.

Leah swallowed, her chest tightening with the effort. "I...I'm sorry."

She swallowed again. All other words fled her mind, leaving behind the desire to reach out and touch him. Offer some kind of comfort or support. She knew what it was like to lose a parent. But to lose a spouse, the pain must be unbearable.

Before she could think of something else to say, some way to ease the somber mood that had sunk over him, the official-sounding voice called over the crowd. "Make a line, folks. Make a line an' we'll have ya off the ferry in no time."

The man with emerald eyes turned from the rail and touched a hand to his hat. "Good day, ma'am." He never once looked at her as he strode toward the line gathering at the edge of the boat.

By the time Leah found her own place in line, he was twenty feet or so ahead. As she stepped onto firm land, she watched his hat disappear into the crowd. Something inside Leah wanted to run after him.

But she didn't move. Just stood, watching the spot where he'd vanished.

Leah couldn't have said how long she stood there, but finally awareness sank back in. People surged around her, and she made her way toward the edge of the sidewalk to get her bearings.

She scanned the swarm of dock workers and passengers. What now? She was on the verge of asking someone—anyone—how she could find a decent hotel, when she spotted a row of wagons with uniformed drivers along the street. Most of them had hand-painted signs that read, "FOR HIRE." Leah approached the nearest.

"Sir, might I hire you to transport myself and my trunks to the closest reputable hotel?"

He took a long drag on his cigar, his eyes roaming up and down her person. Not in an indecent manner, but calculating. They surely took in her sooty face and hands, gray homespun dress with not a frill in sight, and wispy hair missing a few hairpins. Leah was suddenly ashamed of her appearance.

Finally, he removed the cigar and drawled, "I reckon The Southern is probably the closest, if'n they have any rooms left. How many trunks ya got?"

"Two."

He nodded. "It'll cost ya ten cents."

Leah would have paid ten dollars at that moment if she could just get to the hotel. "Let's go then."

He held out a grubby hand. "Ya need to pay in advance."

The audacity! She tried not to let her annoyance show, but it took every bit of her training to hold her poise and not throw the dime in his face.

Oh Leah, what's wrong with you? Show him grace. The prick of her conscience made her feel more ashamed than her pauper's clothing.

Gideon Bryant trudged toward Fourth Street, exhaustion weighing his bones like chains. He'd purchased a ticket on the *Far West* steamship that left at daylight the next day, so he only needed a place to lay his head. He'd have bedded down at the docks if there weren't so many people swarming. His soul craved the quiet majesty of the Montana mountains.

But he was almost there. The *Far West* was one of the fastest boats on the upper Missouri, so he'd be back home in less than two months.

It'd taken him two years after his wife's death before he finally worked up the nerve to go East and resolve her final arrangements. But it was done now. And he was going home. Back to where his brother and sister were holding down their ranch.

Gideon crossed over the streetcar tracks at the corner of Fourth and Walnut streets, then stepped into the double doors of the Southern Hotel. As he took in the lush interior and people milling about the lobby, the staircase pulled his attention. Or rather the person climbing the staircase.

The woman from the ferry.

She mounted the steps like a queen, poised and elegant, with her strong chin jutting at just the right angle for him to see her profile. She was stunning. Even in her homespun grey dress, every eye couldn't help but be drawn to her. A few rich brown tendrils escaped from under her hat, gracing her slender neck.

Gideon watched until she disappeared around the corner on

the second floor, but found he didn't want to turn away quite yet. Was he hoping she would reappear? He was off his rocker. The last thing he needed was to get involved with another city woman.

He forced his attention back toward the clerk's desk and strode that direction. But something had pulled in his chest when he saw this woman. Something that started a longing.

He should fight it, shouldn't he?

Chapter Four

St. Louis, Missouri
April, 1874

*I*t was amazing what a warm bath and a decent night's sleep could do for a person. Leah added a few more pins to her coif and examined her reflection in the mirror. It was wonderful to be in her dark green brocade with the fitted jacket. In this attire, she felt like Leah Townsend again. Heiress, and lady of poise and breeding.

A rumble sounded from her mid-section. Time to attend to other matters of importance. Grabbing her reticule from the side chair, she swept through the door and down the stairwell toward the dining room.

The large dining hall was well-appointed with gold drapes outlining the full-length windows around the perimeter of the room. Elegantly-clad ladies and gentlemen sat at round tables covered in white linens and scores of silverware.

Leah followed the host to a small table, mindful of her poise. It was improper and borderline scandalous for an elegant young lady to be traveling alone—without a chaperone or, at the very least, a servant. With her head held high, she did her best to present a confident appearance.

With a cup of coffee in hand and a copy of today's St. Louis

Republican, Leah scoured the paper for anything that may be helpful in her search for work. A position as companion would be ideal, or maybe a governess. She'd always done well in her studies with Emily and *loved* to read a good novel.

She still had much of the $500 from her savings, but that money wouldn't cover living expenses forever. And it would be too risky to contact her father's steward for money, too much chance word of her location might get back to Simon. Besides, it might be fun to see what life was like in the working classes—at the very least it would be an adventure. And quite honestly, she craved a life of purpose, more than just rising in society's ranks.

Reading the paper took much longer than she'd expected. The Republican was an overwhelming piece, with eight large pages of very tiny type. It seemed they were almost through with construction on the Eads Bridge, the skeleton-like structure she barely remembered seeing in the distance the night before across the Mississippi River.

On page three, she finally found what she was looking for: Wanted…Situations…Females. There were not as many listings as in the Richmond paper, but she analyzed each advertisement, and came away rather disappointed. If she were a "first-class cook" or "experienced scullery maid" or "skilled dressmaker", she would have been in luck. As it was, it seemed she was grossly inexperienced for any of these jobs.

Father, You've brought me this far. Please show me what You have for me next.

Leah thought of the address Emily had given which was tucked in her reticule. She should probably contact the Barnetts today. She wanted to hold off as long as possible, though. See if she could do this on her own. Call it pride or a foolish sense of adventure, but she wanted to make something of herself.

After leaving a letter addressed to Emily for the clerk at the front desk to post, Leah stepped out onto Fourth Street to continue her employment search.

Much of the traffic seemed to be heading in the same direction, including a curious carriage that ran on a track like a train. It was pulled by a single horse and had eight benches with both sides open. As she watched, the coach stopped every block or so to let passengers on or off. It seemed to be a passenger car that transported people for a fare. Stretching her legs felt so good, that Leah decided not to ride the car, but she noticed several of the same curious conveyances on other roads she passed.

The traffic grew thicker as she approached what appeared to be the business district. The buildings on either side stretched up toward the sky, with some spanning half a block. Offices were above and window shops or eateries at street level. Leah felt almost like she was strolling through downtown Richmond.

After weaving through several streets, she came to a massive four-story building that took up the entire block. A flag posted on the front corner of the ornately carved stone structure waved "Wm. Barr Co." in bold, scripted letters. Writing across one of the man-sized windows near the door read, "The William Barr Dry Goods Company: Fifty-one departments devoted to the sale of high grade merchandise." Now here could be some job possibilities.

After strolling through a number of departments on the first floor, then making her way to the second level, Leah wasn't quite as hopeful. The departments she thought she could work in, such as millinery (she'd always been good at designing hats), floral (she had a natural gift for arranging flowers), and even women's fashion, were not hiring. They were in need of seamstresses for the ready-made clothing, but the thought of sewing all day in a dimly-lit back room made Leah cringe.

"We're always looking for delivery boys and scullery maids," said the slender, middle-aged woman who had been introduced as the director in charge of hiring. The pale blue of her gown softened the tired lines around her eyes.

Leah's heart sank, but she forced a smile. "Thank you. I'll keep that in mind."

Exhausted, footsore, and discouraged, she came very close to riding a streetcar back to The Southern. Only a single rod of determination kept her walking.

Perusing the St. Louis Republican the next morning, Leah's vigor was renewed and she was determined to find a job. Unfortunately, the "Wanted...Situations...Females" section was just as disappointing as the day before.

Maybe because of the same tiny black type, her mind drifted back to the advertisement for a bride in the Montana Territory. She couldn't imagine doing anything so impulsive as to agree to marry a man, sight unseen. Her situation with Simon was proof that even when one thought one knew a person, it was quite possible to be deceived. And deception could have deadly consequences.

Leah forced that thought from her mind, gathered her reticule and the newspaper, then made her way out of the dining hall and up to her room to prepare for another excursion around the city.

Leah wilted into the upright back of the settee in the waiting area of the hotel's dining room. Her leg muscles ached, blisters assaulted both feet, and her hope had been beaten down by each snooty butler and no-nonsense housekeeper at the grand mansions of St. Louis. Right then, she would be happy if she never had to walk again.

She inhaled a deep breath, held it for a few seconds, and then released it, feeling the exhaustion seep from her bones with the spent air. Since her settee was tucked into an alcove in the wall, Leah allowed her eyes to close for a moment. She made an effort to focus only on the sounds and smells filtering around her, pushing back the frustration and anxiety that resulted from this second day of unfruitful search.

The strong murmur of conversation and clinking silver drifted from the dining hall, along with a barrage of mingled smells. With concentration, she was able to pick out the aroma of baked apples, something sweet that might be ham, and another with a definite vinegar undertone.

From the hotel's main lobby came the whoosh of a door, a rush of outside sounds, then quiet again as the door closed. Footsteps clicked across the tile floor, then a man's voice.

"I need a room."

"Of course, sir," an official-sounding clerk responded. "And do you know how long you'll be staying with us?"

"Not sure yet. A few nights at least, but maybe longer." The stranger's voice held a familiar tone.

"Of course, sir. We're pleased to have you stay for as long as your business allows. Let me just record some information and we'll show you to your room." The clerk's voice muffled a bit near the end as he must have been gathering paper and pen.

A long silence ensued.

"I'm sorry, sir, just let me refill the inkwell."

"While you work, perhaps you could answer a question." The stranger's voice niggled forcefully in the back of her brain. Where had she heard it before?

He must have received an affirmative from the clerk, because he continued. "I'm looking for an acquaintance who is also staying in St. Louis, a Miss Leah Townsend. Have you heard of her?"

Leah's heart plummeted and she held her breath. How did this man know of her? She sank deeper into the sofa, making sure she was completely hidden from view by anyone in the hotel lobby. Why hadn't she used a false name to register? Because she hadn't really thought anyone would come after her. What a stupid, naïve thing to do.

"Why, yes. Miss Townsend has been staying with us for several days."

"Excellent." The pleasure in the stranger's voice sent a chill·

down her spine. "Can you please give me her room number so I might pay my respects?"

"I'm sorry, sir. I'm not permitted to share her room number, but I can have a note delivered, if you'd like."

A moment of silence.

"No, thank you. Not at this time. I'll hope to see her in the dining area."

"Of course, sir. Now, if I could have your name, please?"

"Robert Talbert."

Chapter Five

Robert Talbert.

That had to be Simon's brother. Had he come all this way to find her? She knew Simon wanted her inheritance, but was he really that desperate? How had they been able to track her? She'd been so careful to appear as a common traveler.

Questions swirled through Leah's mind as she watched Robert climb the staircase, following the bellboy to his room. They continued past the landing for the second floor and disappeared around the wall as they climbed toward the third floor. Leah's room was on the second level. At least they wouldn't be on the same floor.

"Excuse me, miss, but we have a table prepared for you."

Leah turned quickly to see the waiter, bowing slightly, with his hand gesturing for her to precede him. She had completely lost her appetite. The last thing she wanted was to run into Robert Talbert at his evening meal.

"Um... I'm not feeling well at the moment. I believe I'll take my meal in my room, instead."

He dropped his hand to his waist and deepened the bow. "As you wish. I will send a tray to your room then, Miss Townsend?"

"Ah, yes. Thank you."

"Very good then."

As soon as the man turned away, she shot a furtive glance toward the top of the staircase. Seeing no one, Leah squared her shoulders and made her way upstairs, moving as quickly as a genteel lady was allowed.

For the next several hours, Leah paced the floor in her hotel suite. What now? She couldn't stay in her room for weeks until he went away. Finding work required getting out. But staying in the same hotel with the man meant he was sure to see her coming or going.

Should she find different lodgings? That was an option, but if he was able to track her from Richmond all the way to St. Louis, he would surely find her at a different hotel in the same city.

Should she try to find Emily's friends, the Barnetts? Leah moved toward the desk and found their address in the papers Emily had given her. Wash Ave. She didn't recognize that street name from her wanderings over the last few days. Maybe she could check out the area and find the address tomorrow.

Leah allowed a long sigh to escape. She really did want to make it on her own. Maybe she should move to a different city. Maybe south to New Orleans? Or she could find a new city on the East Coast. But the thought of another week-long train ride made Leah sink into the desk chair.

She absently rifled through the papers on the desk, picking up the Richmond Enquirer. Her eyes landed on the curious request for a wife in the Montana Territory. Wasn't that where the man with the emerald eyes on the ferry had said he was from? But it was surely a huge place with thousands of men.

She read the advertisement again. *An intelligent young rancher of twenty-five years, six feet height, red hair green eyes.* An image of an auburn-haired rancher came to mind. It struck her as interesting that he mentioned his green eyes. Age, height, and hair color seemed to be normal enough information for a man to use to describe himself, but eye color?

The young lady should be between eighteen and twenty-five years, pleasant, and God-fearing. This Abel Bryant must be God-fearing, as well, for him to seek that characteristic in a wife. What would make a man seek a wife through a newspaper advertisement? Were there really so few women in the Montana Territory?

Leah suddenly realized that she fit the description requested in the ad. She was twenty-two years old, tried her best to be pleasant, and sought God's will in every area of her life.

Guilt washed over her as she realized she'd not sought God's direction that evening, since finding that Simon's brother was in town, searching for her. With a penitent heart, Leah bowed her head.

After pouring out her heart and fears to her Heavenly Father, Leah finally changed to a nightgown and snuggled her weary muscles under the soft covers. She descended into an exhausted sleep.

Leah wasn't sure when the dreams began, but she found herself running through the darkness. The cobblestone street beneath her slippers tossed up rocks to sabotage her flight. Simon Talbert stood a stone's throw behind her. He just stood there, arms locked over his tailored suit, a greedy look on his middle-aged face. Even though he never moved a muscle, Leah couldn't outrun him. She pushed her legs faster, her side and lungs on fire. She could hear Simon's ominous laughter behind her.

Finally, the dream changed and she was standing near the top of a mountain, looking out at the most beautiful sight she'd ever beheld. A herd of cattle grazed in a distant valley, looking like brown and black dots on a pallet of green. Beyond them, more mountains rose up majestically, their sides covered with trees around the bases, but the color gradually changed to white caps of snow on the peaks. She stood there with the wind gently ruffling her hair, filled with the most amazing sense of peace.

Leah awoke from the dream with sunlight filtering through sheer curtains. The feeling of peace lingered as she stretched and sat up in bed. Memories of the evening before flitted through Leah's mind, when she rose and padded to the desk to retrieve her Bible. The recollection of Robert Talbert wasn't enough to completely steal her peace, though.

Underneath the Bible was the Richmond newspaper, and

Leah again saw the advertisement for a bride in Montana. She picked up both the Bible and paper, then moved back to snuggle cross-legged in her bed. As she fingered the paper, glimpses from her dream wandered through Leah's mind. Mountains, cattle in a valley, a sense of rightness.

Did God want her to go to the Montana Territory? Surely not. What was in Montana anyway? Ranches, apparently. She pictured a vast field with hundreds of cattle, a two story ranch house in the distance with a wrap-around porch and friendly lanterns in the windows, welcoming her home. The scene felt warm and homey—a place she would like to be.

But was she really thinking about marrying this man? A perfect stranger? Hadn't she learned her lesson yet? But the "God-fearing" part was a promising sign. She couldn't remember a time that Simon had ever brought up the subject of God.

But to agree to marry a man sight unseen? Maybe she could stay at a hotel for a few months while they became acquainted. She didn't have to commit to anything until she was sure he wasn't a secret wife-killer.

That sounded like the most reasonable plan she'd come up with yet, so Leah began her morning toilette. Now all she needed to do was find a way to get to Montana.

The further Leah walked down Walnut Street, the fishier the air became. Finally, the wharf stretched before her, with the mighty Mississippi expanding behind it. Lined along the river's edge were double-decker boats, chimney stacks rising from both sides like horns. Each boat had a large wheel on either side, at least those she could see. In addition to the ships lining the shore, a few more loitered in the middle of the river, as if they were waiting for an invitation to join the party at the shore.

Party may not be quite the right description of what was

happening on land, but it was definitely a large gathering of people and things. Wooden crates were stacked everywhere, some laying around haphazardly while many others were stacked in tall rows, creating formidable walls. Wagons and horses waited patiently along the road, while men moved between them, unloading and loading the wagons like armies of ants carrying crumbs of food. To add to the bedlam, Herring Gulls soared around the sky, occasionally floating down to land and waddle along the river's edge, picking at remnants of who-knew-what.

Leah turned onto Main Street, walking parallel to the wharves and trying her best to avoid the moving wagons, and the muck left behind by the horses that pulled them.

Not only was the place busy, but it was noisy, too. Men called commands or banter to each other, each one trying to be heard above the din of the others. The gulls screamed their part of the conversation, too.

Leah tried to appear inconspicuous as she made her way among the working men. She was glad she had worn a simple brown walking dress so she didn't stick out as much as she would have in a bright lavender or red gown.

Apparently she wasn't completely inconspicuous, though, because almost every man she passed either doffed his hat to her or, if his hands were full, nodded in greeting. Most seemed respectful enough, but a few stares had been coarse. Leah moved swiftly past them.

As she strolled, she imagined the adventures each man had experienced aboard the various ships. Two men talking on a dock caught her eye. They weren't in motion like most of the others, but seemed to be in the midst of intense conversation. The older appeared rather distinguished, with a full but trimmed beard and a sharp quick eye. He wore a well-fitting suit that didn't disguise his lean, muscular frame. His companion, dressed more like a ship's mate in shirt sleeves rolled to his elbows, was speaking with great animation. The man with the beard had his head bent slightly, listening to his friend's discourse. His piercing eyes caught Leah's and watched her while he listened to his companion. Something about the man's demeanor caused her to stop and wait while they finished speaking.

After giving a short answer—which sounded more like a command—to his friend, the well-dressed man moved toward Leah and presented her with a formal bow.

"Good day, fair maiden." His voice was deep and resonant.

"Good day, sir." She gave him a polite nod.

"It's not often our humble wharf is graced with the presence of a lovely lady amidst the cargo."

Wisdom had taught her to ignore a comment like that, even if the way he said it sounded more fatherly than crude. "Is that your ship docked behind you, sir?"

He turned to glance at the craft in the water. It wasn't the largest boat there, but his voice took on a hint of pride. "Aye, the De Smet. She's a strong little lass. Only been in the water a couple o' years, but she's earned her salt. Can skim the Missouri better'n any raft out there." He waved a rough hand in the general direction of the other boats.

Leah felt the edges of her mouth lift in response to his obvious adoration. "So you generally travel the Missouri river north? Do you journey all the way to the Montana Territory?" She felt her chest tighten as she awaited his answer. It was too much to hope the first ship captain she spoke to would be going to Montana...and have passage available for her.

"Aye. She's aimed for Fort Benton at daylight tomorrow. I've scheduled a regular supply run."

Fort Benton, Montana. The hotel clerk had said that was the farthest town that could be reached by boat on the Missouri River. Her heart picked up speed.

"Do you... also carry passengers?"

He gave her a slow perusal, not trying to hide his appraisal. What was he looking for?

"A few." He eyed her speculatively. "Who wants to go?"

Leah raised her chin and eyed him back, a move she'd seen her father make on many occasions. "I'm looking to purchase passage to Fort Benton."

His face was impassive. "And what's your business there?"

Leah wasn't sure that was any of *his* business. For a minute she wondered exactly what business she did have going to the Montana Territory.

"I'll be visiting a friend... near Butte City."

He seemed satisfied with that explanation. "Fare's $300. You won't find a vessel to get you there faster than the De Smet."

Leah's heart surged, but she tried to hide her excitement with a nod. "Thank you, sir. What time should I be prepared to leave in the morning?"

"Be here with your bags at six o'clock. We'll be wavin' goodbye to Louey by seven."

"Thank you, sir." Leah reached a hand to shake on the deal, as her father had always done. He seemed mildly surprised but reached out to clasp her hand securely.

"It's a pleasure, ma'am. I'm Captain La Barge, by the way."

Chapter Six

*L*eah skirted two boys playing jacks on the sidewalk and an elderly gentleman helping his silver-haired companion alight from a carriage. According to a street vendor she'd asked, the telegraph was located in the Post Office at the corner of Eighth and Olive Streets. Just a few blocks north and away from the water.

She was pleasantly surprised to find a new four-story granite building at that location. It was an impressive structure with the words *U.S. Court and Post Office* across the front.

The pungent aroma of fresh cut lumber and paint wafted to her as she entered. While the clerk helped a stout, middle-aged woman mail her letters, Leah pulled the now-worn newspaper page from her reticule, pressing the many folds firmly. When Leah approached the counter, she recalled Emily's many hours of instruction and looked the clerk in the eyes.

"How can I help you, miss?" The clerk looked exactly the way she'd imagined he would, slender and balding with a smudged apron and rolled up shirtsleeves.

"I'd like to send a telegram, please."

"Sure thing." He reached for paper and a quill, dipped the pen in an inkwell, then eyed her expectantly over the top of his spectacles. "Where to?"

Leah glanced at the advertisement in her hand. "The town of

Helena in the Montana Territory. The telegraph should be addressed to Abel Bryant at the Bryant Ranch near Butte City."

The man scribbled, nodding as she spoke.

"And what should the wire say?"

Leah took a deep breath. She'd practiced the message several times in her mind during the walk here, but hoped she got the wording right. "Mister Bryant. In response to advertisement in the Richmond Inquirer. I am twenty-two years, pleasant and God-fearing. Will be traveling to Butte City via steamboat to arrive late June. I will locate you upon arrival. Signed L Townsend."

The clerk didn't look up with surprise or scorn as she'd expected. She had carefully worded the message so it wouldn't be obvious she was responding to a newspaper ad for a bride, but he must suspect such a thing. Why else would she send a description of herself?

He counted the words and announced the total cost, then copied the information into his log. Leah paid him, surprised at how expensive the message was. When the clerk finally did look up to receive her payment, his gaze—cool and judgmental—bore into her. Still, he didn't speak to condemn, only took her money, nodded stiffly, and moved toward a machine in the corner.

"I'll send the message now. Have a good trip."

Leah's cheeks could have boiled water as she flew out the door.

The De Smet was more lavishly appointed than Leah expected. The porter led her first to her cabin, which was small but appeared to be clean. A narrow bed was tucked against one side of the room, while another wall held a washbasin and door to the outer deck. Leah's trunks had already been placed against a third wall, and the fourth held a small straight-back chair and the door to the interior hallway.

No closet or even a wardrobe. Where could she hang her gowns? Perhaps she could lay out the gown that she planned to wear next so any wrinkles would loosen...hopefully. She prayed the ship provided a laundry service. Since there wasn't much to unpack, Leah headed back outside to watch the ship leave land.

As she stood at the rail, the towering city of St Louis slid away until it was nothing but a memory on the horizon. Then a bend in the river obliterated the metropolis completely, leaving fertile banks covered in foliage of all kinds—flowering trees, bright green grass and an unfamiliar leafy vine that covered whole sections of land and brush. The scenery was mostly untouched by human hands, although every so often they would glide past a farm or two.

After watching the passing beauty for almost an hour, Leah decided to explore the ship. On the upper level, she found a long narrow salon in the center, surrounded by the ring of passenger cabins. Mahogany wood panels lined the walls of the salon, and the furniture consisted of brocade-covered chairs in rich colors, mahogany wood tables, and elegant light fixtures dangling from the ceilings. A handful of passengers were scattered around the room, either reading or talking in groups of two.

Leah's eye was caught by a man in the back corner, dozing with his legs propped on a nearby chair. He wore the uniform of a porter. Upon closer inspection, she found him to be the porter who had assisted with her own trunks. He was young, maybe not quite twenty, and his baby face sported a thin mustache, like he was having trouble getting it to grow in. Leah felt a tender smile as she turned to leave the room.

The outer deck that surrounded the passenger cabins formed a complete oval. She moved to the lower deck and found it to be a semi-oval, closed at one end. It supported extra cargo storage, with crates and bundles filling much of the space on the deck. Only a single walking aisle around the perimeter was open. The minute she made her way inside, her nose told her the purpose of rooms on the lower level—food. She stood in a long dining hall, with the most wonderful sweet and tangy aromas wafting through the room. A door at the far end of the room led to the kitchen and the origination of that wonderful fragrance.

Just then, that door swung open and a waiter charged through carrying a tray of dishes. He gave Leah a patronizing nod, then proceeded to set the tables. It seemed her cue to exit. The rest of the lower level appeared to be for the crew and more cargo storage, so Leah wandered back to the upper deck to enjoy the passing landscape. It reminded her a little of the Virginia countryside, but with a bit more tropical feel.

What a pleasant affair dinner proved to be that evening. Leah found herself seated at one of the round tables next to a Mrs. DeSchmidt and her husband. Mr. DeSchmidt was a merchant from St Louis who specialized in purchasing raw goods from towns along the Missouri River, then reselling them to factories in the city to be processed into finished goods. On this particular trip, he traveled to Glasgow to purchase tobacco and hemp, and his sweet wife had accompanied him.

Mrs. DeSchmidt was robust, with a motherly manner and chocolate eyes that sparkled when she spoke. Although their children were grown and settled with their own families in St. Louis, Leah imagined that Mrs. DeSchmidt was probably the ideal grandmother.

A younger man she guessed to be in his mid-thirties sat next to Mr. DeSchmidt. During introductions, Mr. Henry Crenshaw proclaimed himself to be a journalist traveling all the way to the Washington Territory to write a series of articles for his home newspaper.

"And where is home, Mr. Crenshaw?" Mrs. DeSchmidt inquired.

"Columbia, South Carolina, Ma'am." His strong southern drawl sent a ripple of homesickness through Leah.

"I traveled to Columbia for business a few years back." Mr. DeSchmidt stroked his white beard. "I remember the people there were quite friendly."

Mrs. DeSchmidt leaned across her husband to address their fascinating guest. "And which newspaper do you write for, Mr. Crenshaw? We'll make sure to watch for your articles when they're reprinted in the St. Louis papers."

"The Daily Phoenix, Ma'am, and thank you." His chest puffed with pride. "I hope to find some interesting stories to send back to our Eastern readers."

Leah's curiosity was aroused. "And what type of stories do you anticipate finding, Mr. Crenshaw? Tales of gold and wild Indians?"

His brown eyes widened and met Leah's, his serious manner exuding courtroom honesty. She was mostly joking, so his response surprised her. "That's entirely possible. A reporter from the Charleston Daily News traveled to the Montana Territory and was almost scalped by real Indians."

"Oh my," breathed Mrs. DeSchmidt. Her husband shook his head in awe.

Despite Leah's interest in the topic, especially as it included Montana, she almost giggled at the younger man. His luminous eyes and hair slicked to one side, along with his clean-shaven face, gave him a school-boy look, despite the faint wrinkles that were beginning to form around his eyes and forehead.

But Mr. Crenshaw wasn't finished. "They say the country out there is absolutely wild, with five Indians to every white man. And the Indians would just as soon scalp you as shake hands. Why, a reporter from the Savannah Tribune was traveling with a wagon train a few years ago when the whole train was attacked. Half the men were killed before the soldiers showed up."

And so the meal continued, with Mr. Crenshaw regaling them with stories of how other reporters had experienced the wilds of the Northwest. After each story, Mrs. DeSchimdt would exclaim in reverent wonder and Mr. DeSchmidt would shake his head in amazement.

For her own part, Leah didn't credit three quarters of Mr. Crenshaw's wild accounts. Still, the country did seem rather untamed. What exactly was she getting herself into?

The next two months were exceedingly pleasant for Leah. When the weather was nice, she spent most of her time on the upper Promenade Deck, reading and re-reading either her Bible or one of the dog-eared novels she'd brought from home. Over the weeks, the scenery changed from mostly forest to miles of tall grass with a scraggly tree tossed in for good measure. The air also shifted from the muggy feel of St. Louis to a cooler, thin atmosphere.

The passengers disembarked at the various stops, with new travelers taking their places. By the first week in June, though, the passenger count had dwindled, being replaced by supplies.

"Why do you need so many supplies if the trip is almost over?" she asked one of the crew. He was a tall, lean man, with a thick curly beard that reminded her of a wooly black sheep.

"Ta sell." He said it as if she should have known that bit of information. "That's where the Cap'n makes most o' his money, from sellin' goods to the Terr'tory."

"At Fort Benton?" It made sense, she supposed. Probably a lot of goods had to be shipped from the civilized states.

"Sure, then they ship 'em on down the Mullan Road to Helena and the rest o' the towns. They pay a purty price fer 'em, fer sure."

"I can imagine." Although, she really couldn't. She didn't have a good knowledge of how much supplies cost, even back East. She'd never had to purchase food or household goods. Those were the responsibilities of the housekeeper and steward. So naturally, she really didn't know how much more expensive things would be in Butte City. But logic predicted the additional freighting charge would increase costs.

Perhaps her money wouldn't last as long as she had anticipated. Especially since she'd spent so much of her cash on the steamboat fare. It would be more important than ever to find work soon when she arrived in Montana.

Or maybe Abel would be the man of her dreams, and they would marry right away. For a moment, Leah allowed herself to dream. She'd read the advertisement over and over until the words drifted through her mind even while she slept. She could picture a strong, lean rancher with curly red hair and laughing green eyes that sparkled like a jade ocean. *Did he have a good sense of humor? Did he like children? Did he want children?* That last thought made her stomach drop to her toes. Maybe she was moving into this way too fast.

Two days later, Leah stood at the rail as the De Smet floated into the dock at Fort Benton. From watching at the other ports, she knew it would be a few minutes before passengers were allowed to disembark, allowing her time to step back into the cabin to make sure her trunks were locked securely.

Satisfied with the trunks, she glanced around the room a final time to make sure she'd not forgotten something. Her gloves and reticule lay on the corner of the bed, ready to go when she was.

There was just enough time to slip out onto the deck and say a final goodbye to the gentle noise of water lapping against the sides of the boat. The sound was loudest when the paddle wheels were moving, but even now she could hear the quiet splashes. It was balm to her soul, and Leah reveled in the peacefulness.

Voices from the other side of the boat drifted into Leah's reverie, signaling it was time to go. She pulled her wrap more tightly around her shoulders against the chilly mountain air, then stepped back into the cabin to gather her gloves and reticule. Leah stopped to stare at the bed in confusion, letting her eyes adjust to the dimmer light. There, on the corner, lay her white gloves, but not the reticule. She began a frantic search underneath the bed and around the sparse room, but found nothing else. Her trunks had already been taken off the ship, apparently. Had the same porter taken her reticule along with the trunks? That would be strange, but maybe not impossible.

With a knot wound tight in her stomach, Leah picked up her gloves and hurried toward the docks. Men were everywhere, hiking up and down the gangplank loaded down with crates and bundles. Craning her neck, Leah finally spotted a small pile of trunks off to one side. She hurried over to a man standing near the pile, holding a paper and lead pencil in hand.

"Is this luggage from the De Smet?" As she said the words, Leah spotted one of her trunks and breathed a small sigh of relief. She needed her reticule, though. All the money she had left was folded and clipped in a small wad in that little black purse.

"Yep, just let me know which 'r yers an' I'll pull 'em out." He spoke slowly, dragging his words, then turned his head and spit a long stream of brown juice. It was amazing any of the mess made it through the thick curly layers of the man's beard.

She pointed as she spoke. "That one is mine with the pink ribbon, and also the one beneath it. And there should be a small reticule with them, as well. Do you remember seeing that?"

"Well..." The man stopped to think, tapping his jaw as if that would help him remember. "I don't reckon' I remember seein' anythin' but trunks."

Trying to maintain a grasp on the edge of her patience, Leah increased the strength of her southern charm. "Could you please help me search, sir? I really need to find it."

It worked. The old coot softened like butter. "I reckon' I could help." And with that he dove in and started un-stacking trunks and kicking them out of the way until they had a scattered mess. But no reticule...

"Sorry, miss." He wiped his brow, then looked around at the jumble. "Hate we couldn't find it."

Leah forced a smile through her gritted teeth. "Thank you. I'll send someone for those two trunks shortly."

She spun around to study the army of men still working hard to un-pack and re-pack the ship. She wasn't sure who to ask next, but she *had* to find that bag. She prayed it was misplaced and not actually stolen.

Just then, Leah spotted Captain La Barge across the shipyard speaking with two men who wore leather clothing. Squaring her shoulders, she marched toward the group.

The Captain had his back to her approach, but his two companions saw her. They stopped speaking and gawked as she strode up. The Captain turned and offered a slight bow.

"Miss Townsend, I trust you've enjoyed your trip. Have you found lodgings yet? I can arrange for an escort to one of the local hotels, if you'd like."

Leah took a breath to steady herself. "Captain La Barge, may I please have a word with you?"

Without skipping a beat, the Captain turned to his associates. "Gentleman, if you'll excuse me for now, I'll meet you down at Mill's Cafe for dinner."

The taller man nodded, then elbowed his partner and they strode away, Leah's eyes following them as they walked. Both wore long leather cloaks and leather pants, and the smaller man wore a fur cap over his long, loose hair. The effect made him look positively wild.

"Now, what can I help you with?" The Captain's words jerked Leah from her distraction.

"Captain, I'm missing my reticule from my room. I believe your porter may have taken it when he removed my trunks."

Leah watched his reaction, expecting to see either frustration or anger darken his eyes. Instead, his brows knit together in deep concern as he stroked his beard. He studied Leah for a moment, his eyes not revealing the direction of his thoughts.

"I'm assuming you've checked the area where your trunks were placed?"

Leah threw a quick glance toward the trunks then quirked a

brow at the Captain. "Yes, we examined the area around the luggage."

A sadness flowed into his eyes to join the concern there. Finally, he sighed. "Miss Townsend, of course I will check with all of my staff, but I'm afraid you have been robbed. That particular porter was new to my ship. He only signed on to work while he traveled to Montana. He collected his pay before we docked and left immediately after the trunks were removed. I don't expect to see him again."

The icy fingers around her stomach reached up to squeeze her lungs, as well. "So my money is gone? You're not going to find him and make him give it back?" She wanted to stamp her foot but knew that was out of the question for a lady.

He sighed again. "Miss Townsend, I'm very sorry about this. That young man is likely long gone, but the best thing for you to do would be to see the sheriff about it. He can handle the search and make an arrest if he finds the man. The sheriff's office is right down this street, about a block on the left."

Leah's heart sank. *Lord, please help me not to cry.* "That's the best thing I can do?" She knew her voice sounded weak, but she felt like her bones had been jerked from her legs, leaving only a mass of skin and jelly.

Captain La Barge nodded, the skin around his eyes pinched. "Yes. While you speak with him, I'll take a look around the ship and talk with my men. If I find anything, I'll be sure to let you know."

Her shoulders slumped, and Leah turned around to trudge down the street. For once, she didn't care that she'd lost her all-important poise.

Chapter Seven

𝒯he jail was a single-story wood building, rustic by St. Louis or Richmond standards, but not unlike the buildings that surrounded it. Leah almost knocked on the door, but finally decided to step in. This was a place of business, after all.

She paused for a moment inside the threshold, for her eyes to adjust to the dim lighting. Her nose was assaulted by the odor of unwashed bodies and alcohol. The room held two desks—one tucked into either back corner—with a man sitting behind each. A door in the wall between them must lead to the jail.

"Can I help you, miss?" The voice came from the man on the right, so Leah moved forward in his direction. His features were compact, with bushy black brows and a mustache that didn't leave much room between them for eyes and nose.

"Yes, sir. I'd like to report a robbery, please. Are you the sheriff?"

"I'm Sheriff John Healy." This deeper voice came from the man on the opposite side of the room, as he rose and came to join his partner. He was a tall man, with close-cropped hair, rounded features, and a long goatee.

Just then, a muffled groan came from the direction of the back door. Both men ignored it, so Leah attempted to do the same.

She shifted to address them both. "I've come to report a robbery, please. My reticule was stolen from my cabin on the ship when we landed. Captain La Barge feels that it may have been the porter who unloaded my trunks. It seems he's been released from duty, however, and no one knows where to find him."

The sheriff stroked his goatee. "Was there any money in this reticule?"

Leah swallowed, her mouth felt sticky. "Yes, sir. All of my funds were in that bag."

He eyed her quietly for a moment, then finally spoke. "And did the Captain have any idea whether this man was planning to stay in Fort Benton or move on?"

Leah hesitated. "I… don't think he knows for sure. He said the porter was not a long-standing employee of the ship, but had been hired in St. Louis to work while he traveled to the Montana Territory. Do you have an idea where a newcomer would typically lodge in this town?"

A look passed between the two men, and Leah's insides balled tighter at the wariness in their eyes.

Finally, the sheriff spoke again. "Yes, Miss…"

"Townsend. Miss Leah Townsend."

"…Miss Townsend. We'll check both hotels in town. I'll speak with Captain La Barge for a name and description of the man." His weary eyes reached up to meet Leah's. "I have to say that a freighter left town about an hour ago with a couple o' newcomers in tow. If this man has committed a robbery, there's a good chance he's on board with them." He added as an afterthought, "I'll check around, though."

Leah worked hard to keep her shoulders squared and her chin from drooping. "And do you know where the freighter was going?"

"Down the Mullan Road. Prob'ly toward Helena, then who knows where else."

"And can you tell me where the stage office is? Perhaps I can intercept them in Helena."

She had no idea how she'd pay for the stage ride. Would they give her credit with the promise to pay as soon as she reacquired her reticule? Or perhaps she could trade for something in her trunks. She scanned the contents in her mind. Dresses, undergarments, a few toiletry items, and her books. Maybe a dressmaker would be interested in purchasing some of her gowns? After all, they were the latest in New York fashion, with fitted bodice, high bustle, and slight train.

"No stage in these parts, I'm afraid." This from the man with the scrunchy face still seated at the desk. He gave a humorless chuckle. "We don't quite have all the luxuries ya'll do back East."

A stage hardly seemed a luxury, but Leah kept that thought to herself.

The sheriff spoke up. "The best way to get to Helena is to ride along with a wagon already headed that way, or else buy a horse yerself."

How was she supposed to do that with no money? Maybe it was time to go to plan B. Abel Bryant would just have to come and get her. After all, if she was willing to take a three month boat ride to Montana, the least he could do is come and meet her at the dock.

Feeling better with her new plan of action, Leah asked, "Then can you please tell me where the telegraph office is located? I'll need to send a wire to Butte City for my friends to come collect me."

The sheriff stroked his goatee again as he spoke. "I'm afraid you won't be able to do that either, ma'am. The telegraph line to Helena 'n Butte has been down for a couple weeks now. Had a bad storm in the mountains that took her down. We just haven't had a chance to put it back up yet. You could send a letter if ya like with the next freighter. Usually takes about a week to get there and the same to get a response back. Assumin' they can find yer friend to deliver the letter, that is."

Leah fought back tears of frustration. Why was this happening? She had really felt God was leading her to Montana, yet from the moment the boat pulled into the dock here, nothing had gone right. Now she was stuck with no money to pay for food or lodging or transportation to Butte City.

She forced her mind to focus on what she should do next.

Somehow she needed to get some money. Whether she were to sell her dresses or work for the money, a dress shop would probably be the place to start.

Leah straightened her shoulders and forced a polite smile. "All right, then. I do thank you both for your time and assistance. Before I go, though, could you please give me directions to the local dress shop?"

The men exchanged another glance. She'd had about enough of their secret looks. The sheriff spoke again. "Fort Benton don't exactly have a dress shop like you're probably thinkin', ma'am. What women are here usually buy their fabric and such at the mercantile. It's down this street a ways further on the left."

She took a deep breath and smiled sweetly through her gritted teeth. "Thank you, sheriff. I'll make my way to the mercantile then. Good day to you both."

And with that, Leah spun on her heel and made her escape.

As she had come to expect in this rustic town, the mercantile was also constructed of wood. A sign above the door painted in bold black letters read "T. C. Power and Co. Mercantile".

The door jingled when Leah opened it, and she paused for a moment inside to get her bearings. Rows of merchandise extended to her right, flashing a wide variety of items—from sharp metal objects to barrels of food and bolts of wool. To her left, a circle of old men relaxed in ladder-back chairs. In the middle of the group stood a table which held a scattering of dominos.

Leah focused her attention on the counter straight ahead, and made her way toward it. The first thing she noticed about the man who stood behind the counter writing in a book, was that he had very little hair on top of his head and a great deal of hair across his face. He wasn't that old—not as old as Papa had been, anyway—but was almost completely bald. He must have been trying to make up for that, however, by his great wooly beard. He was not tall for a man, about the same as Leah's own medium stature. When the man looked up, though, he had a pleasant enough expression on his face.

"Well, bonnie lass, with what can I be helpin' ya today?" His accent was unmistakable and charming, and gave a softness to his manner.

"Good day, sir." Leah dipped a polite curtsey. She took the opportunity while her head was lowered to fortify herself with a deep breath, then raised up to her most competent, shoulders-back expression. "I've come to inquire whether you're hiring in your store. Perhaps you have need of a sales clerk or someone to stock the shelves?" She paused, trying to gauge his expression, and found it to be curious.

"You're the lass lookin' for work, ye say? If ya don't mind me sayin' so, ye look to be a proper upper-class lady. Not exactly the workin' kind." His words were spoken in kindness, but heat flooded her face.

"I... I'm afraid my reticule that contained my funds was stolen when our ship docked in your fair town." She tried not to taint the last words with the sarcasm she felt. "I'll need to find work for food and lodging until I can get word to my friends in Butte that I've arrived."

He cleared his throat rather loudly. "Well, lassie. I've no need for another clerk just now, I'm all set for the summer boom. Go and check with Mill's Café and the hotel, to see if they'll hire ye on. If they send ye back, well... That be God tellin' me to hire ye on for a couple o' weeks."

Leah could feel the heat all the way to the tips of her ears as she curtseyed again and thanked the man. This asking for a job was not a fun thing to do.

The jingle faded as Leah closed the door behind her. Her shoulders sagged and a bench beside the door beckoned. She sank into it, thankful for the chance to gather her thoughts. There must be something she was missing here. Hadn't God brought her this far through His direction? Leah closed her eyes tightly in an effort to shut out this crazy dream she was living.

Lord, I know you have a plan in all this. You are who You are, no matter where I am. Proverbs chapter three says trusting means that I cannot lean on my own understanding. So God, I'm going to sit in this place and wait for Your direction.

The peace that wafted through Leah was like a gentle aroma.

Just then, the bell on the door beside her clanged and Leah opened her eyes to see one of the old men that had been seated around the domino table. He wore long shirt-sleeves with no jacket, showing the leather suspenders that attached to his black wool pants. His scruffy grey beard covered much of his face, but Leah could see the skin around his eyes and forehead was a wrinkled leathery brown.

He didn't seem to notice Leah sitting on the bench, but removed his floppy leather hat from his oily grey hair and proceeded to sit down beside her. She was more than a bit surprised at his curious behavior, but as the smell of sweat and body odor wafted in her direction, Leah forced herself not to scoot away from him.

"See here, missy. My name's Ol' Mose. Leastways that's what people've been callin' me long enough I forgot what the rest of it was. Anyways, I heared what you was sayin' to ol' Johnny in there about how you was robbed and tryin' to git to yer friends in Butte City." He stuck a thumb through a suspender. "Well I got me a freight wagon I run back n' forth 'tween here and there. You'd be right welcome to ride along if'n ya like."

Leah was a bit dazed by the rush of completely unexpected information from the old chap. Was he offering her a ride to Butte? Did he really run a freight wagon? Why the old chap wasn't much bigger than Leah, and looked to be a few years past his prime.

She finally realized he was looking at her expectantly, waiting for an answer. Leah opened her mouth to respond, but she had no idea what to say.

"You're… offering me a ride? In your wagon?" Her voice squeaked like a schoolboy.

"Yes'm. Plannin' to leave out at first light tomorry."

Leah surveyed the man, realizing he was serious about the offer. But was he trustworthy? How would she determine that?

"I…uh…I have two trunks I'll need to take with me."

He reached a nubby finger to scratch through his beard.

"Reckon' that'll be fine. We can tie 'em on top."

He dropped his hand to his lap and cocked his head as if pondering something. "I don't usually carry folks with me as a rule, but God kept a'nudgin' me sayin', 'Ol' Mose, you go on an help this girl now, ya hear?'" He threw up his hands. "So, here I sit."

When Ol' Mose flashed a slightly-toothless grin, Leah wanted to reach over and hug the man. Instead, she smiled. "Thank you, Mr. Mose. I would be honored to ride in your freight wagon."

"No, ma'am. The name's Mose or Ol' Mose. No mister about it. My Pa, he was a mister but not this young son of a gun." And then he flashed his toothy grin again.

Chapter Eight

Near Butte City, Montana Territory
June, 1874

*W*oosh. *Thwak!*

Gideon heaved the ax back over his shoulder, then slammed the blade forward into the ice.

Woosh. Thwak!

He was close to water, he could feel it in the softness of the ice.

Woosh. Thwak!

A mighty crack split the air as his ax sank deep into liquid.

The lowing of the cattle behind him grew louder and more insistent as the animals smelled the water. Gideon hacked the edges to widen the hole, then jumped to the side as the cattle surged forward.

Leaning against the ax, he stopped to catch his breath and watch the animals jockey for position. Winter had lasted longer than normal this year, with the final snowstorm a couple of weeks before. Hopefully, he wouldn't have to break ice for the cows much longer before summer heated things.

He kept a careful eye on the latest calves, still wobbly on their feet. It would be easy for one of the little guys to get knocked over and trampled as the cattle pushed forward to the water.

The Bryant Ranch was up to about fifty head of cattle now. Not anything like the big ranches he'd heard about in Texas, but their little herd was growing. If at least most of the calves came with no problems this year, they would have close to seventy head.

How will I take care of seventy head of cattle by myself, now that Abel's gone?

The now-familiar ache cut his breath short. Scenes from the horrific grizzly attack that had killed his brother the week before flashed through Gideon's mind. He scrubbed a hand down his face in an effort to clear them. He couldn't get bogged down in this now. He missed his baby brother with a physical pain, but that wouldn't bring him back. It hadn't brought any of the others back.

He needed to deal with reality for now. He could manage the work, at least for the summer months. He may need some help with the haying, but that would be it. Especially with Miriam taking on most of their brother's chores around the cabin.

His baby sis had always worked her fair share. Like when Pa died. She had shouldered much more than her half of the housework. Then when Ma took sick and died, too, Miriam took over everything.

As much as he hated to admit, he'd married Jane partly in hopes she would help Miriam with the house and garden and cooking. Jane had tried, really she had. Deep down, though, he knew she'd hated mountain life. She was afraid of it, with the harsh winters and wild animals constantly lurking about. And maybe her fear had been well-founded, because it was one of those wild animals that finally took her life. Then Miriam had gone back to running the household on her lonesome.

Gideon picked up his ax and headed back to the little barn he'd built in the valley to store hay and animal supplies. He needed to check on the broodmares, too. The grey mare looked to be within a week or two of foaling.

He now understood how Miriam must have felt for all those years, shouldering the load by herself. Abel had always been his partner with the ranch. The brothers had worked together so long, they could read each other's minds, not to mention reading the weather and the animal signs.

Abel was the one who'd first found the gold on their property, too. They never mined much of it, just enough to restock supplies every few years. The gold allowed them to keep most of the cattle and build up the herd. Someday, they would have a vast herd with hundreds or even thousands of cattle. Someday...

Which led him back to his original conundrum—what he would do when the winter months hit again? It would be a challenge, for sure, to keep the cattle watered and with enough food in the deep snow. With no garden through the winter to supplement their food supply, he would need to hunt more. The constant snow on the ground made work harder and slower.

Should he start panning for gold again as soon as the weather warmed? He'd probably need the dust to pay a hired hand. But if he was mining, he really would need someone else to help with the cattle and haying. "Grrrrr..."

The dog at his feet whined and inched forward on his belly until almost touching Gideon's boot. He reached down to scratch behind a black ear.

"Sorry, boy. Didn't mean to say that out loud."

Drifter accepted the apology by licking Gideon's sleeve.

Every muscle, bone, and joint hurt beyond what Leah had ever felt, as she half-climbed-half-fell from the wagon. She dragged herself toward the tree line bordering the road in search of a little privacy.

"Jest don't wander off too far. An' can ya bring some logs and sticks back fer the fire?" Ol' Mose called as he started pulling things from the wagon. Riding for ten long hours in the jolting, creaking wagon didn't seem to bother him in the least.

Leah nodded, her need too great to stop as she stumbled through the trees until she was a safe distance from the campsite. She needed a necessary house, but of course there wasn't anything like that in this primitive wilderness.

On her way back to the wagon, Leah picked up some logs as Ol' Mose had requested. With her arms loaded down and her hair mussed from the pull of branches, she stepped through the tree line into the clearing. Ol' Mose was hunkered on his hands and knees over a pile of sticks. He appeared to be blowing into them as a thin stream of smoke curled up into the sky.

Leah dropped the logs in a heap nearby, and Ol' Mose leaned back to reveal a small flame. He surveyed the logs she'd brought, then looked up at Leah with a twinkle in his faded brown eyes.

"You ain't never picked out logs fer a fire 'afore, have ye now?"

Her face grew warm. *Was it that obvious?* "No, sir."

"Well, then." He rose to his feet more gracefully than Leah would have expected for a man his age. He appeared thin and frail, but he must have muscle by the way he was able to maneuver around the wagon and camp.

Ol' Mose stopped in front of the heap at Leah's feet. "See here." He picked up some small sticks. "These are good for when the fire's little. They're nice and dry and small, so they'll catch easy-like. That one over there is too wet to use for anythin'. An' the big'uns there." He pointed to the thick round logs she'd struggled with. "These have a few strikes against 'em. They're green so it'll be hard for 'em to catch, they won't put out much heat, and they'll smoke like the devil 'imself is sittin' with us."

Leah was trying to follow him, but he'd lost her when he said the wood was green. Those logs were as grey in color as the sky before a storm. *Is Ol' Mose color-blind?* She supposed it was possible.

Suddenly the old man let out a cackle and slapped his thigh. "I bet I stumped ya when I said the wood was green, didn't I? That means it was just growin' and didn't have a chance to dry out yet. The dry stuff is what we want fer a fire. Oak and maple make good fires, not too many sparks but plenty o' coals for cookin'."

Leah nodded, locking that tidbit in the back of her mind for later. Thankfully, Ol' Mose didn't require much from her as he unhitched the mules, and grabbed a few items from the wagon. But dread settled in when Ol' Mose returned with two leaf- and dirt-covered blankets.

"Fer your bed," he said, tossing them at her.

She could do this, she just had to set her mind to it. Still, the thought of her goose-down mattress back in Richmond flickered unbidden through her mind.

When the old fellow began cooking their dinner, Leah tried to pay close attention. She'd loved the times as a girl, when she could sneak down to the kitchen to help Cook make dinner or bake desserts. Cooking and baking had always fascinated her, although she'd rarely been allowed to practice. Thankfully, Mose liked to chatter, and talked through everything he was doing.

"We'll get these beans a'started right off, since they take the longest to cook. Then, once some o' the coals get white hot, I'll mix up cornbread in yonder skillet and we'll have a real feast on our hands." He apparently believed his statement, too, from the grin showing in his eyes.

"Ere you a good cook, Miz Townsend?"

"No, I'm afraid I've never had many opportunities to cook. I've enjoyed it when I was given the chance, though."

"Pshaw. I figure a pretty little lady like you would have all the opportunities ya wanted."

Leah didn't have the energy tonight to explore that statement completely, but it sounded wrought with irony.

"Ere ya from the East, then?"

"Yes, sir. From Richmond, Virginia."

He let out a low whistle. "Yer parents must be awful worried about ya travelin' so far. And methinks it's a mite rougher here than what yer accustomed to."

"Both of my parents have died, sir." Tears didn't immediately spring to her eyes anymore, but it was still hard to talk about them. She missed Mama and Papa so much it ached.

Ol' Mose was quiet for a moment. "Awful sorry to hear that, ma'am."

Leah cleared her throat, ready to change the topic. "So tell me about yourself. Have you always run a freight wagon?"

"No, ma'am. Used to be a trapper back in the day. Ran with the best o' the mountain men, I did. Jedediah Smith, Jim Clyman, an' that ol' coot Hugh Glass. Now there's a story worth tellin'. D'ya ever hear it before?"

Leah shook her head, never having heard of any of the men he mentioned. But she knew from the tales he'd told in the wagon that Ol' Mose was a master story-teller. So she settled back against one of the *green* logs and prepared for a good one.

"Well, ol' Hugh was on one of Mr. Henry's trappin's." His eyes came to life. "Hugh had gone on ahead and got in a tussle with a she-bear protectin' her cubs. He finally got the upper hand with only his knife, but by the time the she-bear was layin' on the ground, so was Glass. He was knocked out an' bleedin' an' on his last breath when the rest found him.

"Well they kept awaitin' fer the ol' coon to die, and the Injuns was gettin' closer. Finally, Mr. Henry asked fer a couple men to stay with Glass and bury him proper once he finally expired. Said he'd give them an extra six month's pay. Bridger was just a young tike then—seventeen I think—so he and Fitzgerald volunteered.

"The Injuns got closer an' those boys got nervouser an' ol' Glass just kept on barely breathin'. They went ahead an' dug his grave and finally decided to lay him in the hole, cover him with the bear hide, and save their own necks."

Ol' Mose positioned a skillet on the rocks at the edge of the fire, then poured a thick batter into the pan.

"When ol' Hugh woke up, he found hisself under that hide without a stick o' clothes or gun or knife, either. He had a broke leg and was missin' so much skin ya could see clear through to his rib bones in spots.

"He was awful sick, too. But ol' Hugh didn't let that keep 'im down. He set his own broke leg and wrapped hisself in that hide and started crawlin'. Took him six weeks, but he crawled all the way to the Cheyenne River. Ate berries an' roots an' whatever meat he could scare t'other animals away from. Said the only thing that kept him goin' was the thought of gettin' back at those two varmints that left 'im in that grave to die. Anyways, when he made it to the river, he sailed right down to a Sioux camp, an' they doctored him up. Finally made it to Fort Kiowa a bit later."

Silence settled over them. In the pan, the batter began to turn golden. Finally, Leah asked, "Did he ever find the men that left him for dead?"

Ol' Mose breathed a soft chuckle. "Funny thing that. He found both the men separately, but didn't end up killin' either one of 'em. He gave reasons why he didn't, but I'd like to think it was God workin' on his heart, softenin' him up for forgiveness."

Leah glanced at her new friend. He'd mentioned God a few times through the day, but this was the first time he'd said anything overtly religious. She gently prodded, "You sound like you have some experience with forgiveness."

"Yes, ma'am. I ain't always had the nicest things done to me, but I ain't always done 'em to others, neither. God gave me an awful lot o' forgiveness, then softened me up so's I could learn how to pass it on."

For a few minutes, they stared at the fire in silence. Then Mose reached to pull the frying pan from the coals and began dishing out plates of beans and cornbread. He didn't speak again until he handed Leah a tin plate and spoon.

"So you said you're here to stay with some friends, did ye?"

How much should she tell him? She trusted this man, and something about him made her suspect he wouldn't think badly of her for answering a newspaper advertisement for marriage. She might as well be honest.

"In a way. I've responded to an ad for a young rancher seeking a bride." She found herself rushing through the words to get them over with.

Ol' Mose looked thoughtful as he munched a mouthful of beans. "What's his name? Might be I know him an' can tell ya if he's a good sort."

Not only did he not judge her, but he was offering to help. Relief washed over her. "His name is Abel Bryant of the Bryant Ranch. Have you heard of him?"

Ol' Mose's beard split into a grin. "Sure do. Gideon an' Abel run the ranch now that their pa's passed. Couldn't find better boys in the whole Montana Territory." He nodded with a certainty that made Leah release a breath she didn't know she'd been holding. She even felt her own face answer his grin.

Chapter Nine

The mules plodded into the clearing as Leah absorbed her surroundings with wide-eyed interest. In the evening dusk, she saw two wooden structures. One was obviously the barn, with fences fanning out on three sides. A well-worn path ran from the barn to the other building, which looked like a log guest cottage. A covered porch spanned the front, but neither the porch nor the steps had a handrail, only occasional log posts that supported the roof. White ruffled curtains could be seen in both of the windows that flanked the front door.

The door opened and a little blonde wisp of a woman stepped out. She wore a bright smile and wiped her hands on the greyish apron at her waist. As the wagon pulled to a stop, the woman hurried forward, and Leah realized she was actually no more than a teenager, fifteen or sixteen at most.

"Oh, I'm so glad to see another woman I could just hug you." For a moment it seemed the girl might actually follow through with her words, as the little magpie bounced around to Leah's side of the wagon.

"Please do come in and have supper with us." She looked over at Ol' Mose. "Gideon will be back from the cattle any minute, and he'll be pleased to see you."

Leah's heart skipped a beat. If Gideon would be coming back from the cattle, surely Abel, her possible future husband, would be with him. Ol' Mose had said they worked the ranch together.

Leah climbed carefully from the wagon. Her muscles had toughened after five days of jolts and jarring. She pressed both hands to her skirt, inhaled a breath for fortitude, and turned to face the girl with her most pleasant expression.

"Hello, I'm Leah Townsend. I believe Mr. Abel Bryant is expecting me."

Leah waited for the look of recognition to come over the girl's face. It did, sort of. Recognition mixed with... horror? Her eyes widened big as silver dollars, the green illuminated in the centers. Her face became deathly pale. Within seconds, those green eyes clouded and, for a moment, Leah thought she would break into tears. Or swoon. Leah impulsively reached forward to slip a gentle hand around the girl's shoulders.

She seemed to catch herself quickly, and pulled the dirty apron up to wipe her eyes.

"I'm sorry, I..." She looked up at Leah with the most mournful expression in her wide emerald eyes. "Abel died about two weeks ago. Gideon sent a wire tellin' you not to come, but I guess you didn't get it..." Her voice drifted off with the last few words.

It took a moment for the words to register, then they released a torrent of emotion in Leah—shock, disbelief, and sadness for the man she had come to appreciate in her imaginings. But at the pain etched on the young girl's face, Leah forgot her discomfort as a deep sympathy flooded her.

On another impulse, she leaned forward and embraced the girl. Leah knew all too well what it was like to lose someone she loved. She felt the girl's slender arms wrap themselves around her as if she was starving, and human touch the only thing that could feed her. Leah couldn't define what passed between them during that hug, but she felt a connection with this girl she'd never felt with anyone except Emily.

Finally, the girl stepped back, wiping at her eyes again. She looked at Leah, suddenly shy. "I'm Miriam, Gideon and Abel's little sister."

Leah smiled through her misty vision. "It's a pleasure to meet you, Miriam."

Miriam seemed to recover herself a bit then, and looked up at Ol' Mose, still seated in the wagon watching them.

"If you'd like to put your mules in the barn, there's plenty of hay and water there for 'em. Then, come on in the house. I have coffee on and dinner should be just about ready by then."

Leah marveled silently at the way the girl pulled herself together and suddenly became the lady of the house, as rustic as that house might be.

Ol' Mose nodded. "Yes'm. I'm awful sorry to hear about your brother, Miz Miriam."

Before she could respond, he slapped the reins and rumbled, "Giddup!"

Miriam turned back to Leah, her shy smile returning. "If you'd like to come on in now, I'll fix ya a cup of coffee. I'd like it if you'd tell me all about yourself. I don't get to visit with other women much, so you comin' is a real treat."

"Of course." Leah followed her into the cabin.

If she'd thought the outside was rustic, the inside was close to primitive. They entered a large open room that appeared to be both kitchen and drawing room. On her left in the sitting area, a large fireplace dominated the wall, with a wooden mantel above and a few miscellaneous chairs placed in a semi-circle around. One of the seats was a rocking chair, reminding Leah of her favorite rocker in her childhood nursery.

Straight ahead and dividing the sitting area from the kitchen, were two closed doors, with a ladder between them that climbed the wall to an open area below the ceiling. How strange.

Leah turned her attention to the right where Miriam was scurrying between an iron cook stove and a work table. A few open shelves lined the wall, along with several barrels and leather sacks. Taking up most of the space, though, was a wood plank table with six ladder-back chairs around it.

"Please sit down." Miriam gestured toward one of the chairs at the table. A mug graced the table in front of one of the seats, steam wafting from the liquid inside. "You're probably worn out from the trip from Fort Benton." She grimaced. "Although you may not want any more sittin'."

"Thank you." Leah moved forward to accept Miriam's hospitality. "I don't mind sitting as long as the chair doesn't bounce around." She smiled slightly at her own attempt at humor.

Miriam's face broke into a wide grin, her shy smile gone and the magpie Leah had first seen fully returned. As Leah arranged her navy skirt around the chair, Miriam began cutting some kind of green leaves on the work table.

"I think your dress is the prettiest thing I've seen in years. Is that the style they're wearing back east now?"

Leah frowned at her demure traveling suit. "This is the style of a traveling gown. Most day dresses and especially the evening gowns are much lovelier than this, with bright colors and heavy ruffles, especially over the bustle."

Then she noticed the faded brown calico work dress Miriam wore, suddenly ashamed of her rambling. "But none of them are nearly so practical as the gown you're wearing."

She tried to think of another nice comment to make about Miriam's dress—gown was really too strong of a word for the woebegone piece of material. Its length was almost too short both in the skirt and in the sleeves, even for Miriam's petite body.

She didn't seem embarrassed, though, and waved off Leah's comment. "This ol' thing has seen better days for sure. I need to make a new one, just haven't found the time to go all the way to Butte for new calico."

Leah was saved a response by the thump of boots on the porch and the light squeak of the front door. Ol' Mose shuffled in, followed by a true, honest-to-goodness mountain man. He turned to shut the door, then hung his hat on the wall. Something about him struck her as familiar. His profile showed him to be a bit younger than the mountain men she'd imagined. He had a full beard and wavy brown hair that just covered his neck.

Then he turned toward them, and Leah saw those deep emerald eyes. Her heart leaped.

He was the man from the ferry, when she'd first arrived in St. Louis.

Butterflies flipped in her stomach as Leah looked again into his green gaze. Those eyes were an even deeper shade than Miriam's, and the long green work shirt he wore accented them perfectly.

He was taller than she remembered. Next to Ol' Mose, he looked like a giant. But he didn't carry himself hunched over like most tall men she'd seen. He stood straight and confident in his own masculine skin.

There she was.

Was this a vision? Or was the woman from St. Louis actually sitting at his kitchen table? If he hadn't lost his marbles, then how did she get here?

She sat poised and elegant, with a little hat perched on her head that would do absolutely nothin' to protect her from the sun. Just like she'd come out of a New York City parlor room. And she was looking at him as if he had two heads and three arms.

"Gideon," his baby sister piped up from the cook stove where she stirred something in the big pot, "I'd like to you meet Leah."

He nodded a greeting in the general direction of the woman, and turned to hang his leather hat on the peg behind the door.

"Leah, this is my big brother Gideon."

"It's a pleasure to meet you, Mr. Bryant."

Now there's something he hadn't been called in a month of Sundays...Mr. Bryant. Especially not in a voice that reminded him of the lullabies Ma used to sing when Miriam was a little tike. Just then, his traitor dog Drifter strolled right up to the lady, sniffed her outstretched hand, then wagged his tail wildly as she rubbed the sweet spot behind his ear. Gideon knew what that dazed look on the dog's face meant. He'd found a soul mate.

He tried to keep his "harrumph" to himself, but by the warning look on Miriam's face, it must have slipped out. Moving toward the shelf to grab a bowl, he motioned for Ol' Mose to do the same. He stepped toward the stove and filled his dish almost to the brim with the beef stew, and was about to turn toward his usual place at the table, when Miriam put a hand on his arm to stop him.

"Gideon," her voice was low, urgent. "Leah is the one who responded to Abel's advertisement. She sent the telegram."

Gideon froze, trying to make sense of what his sister had just said. "But...I sent a message telling her not to come." Of all the nerve. She must be desperate for sure. He'd warned Abel not to place that silly ad.

The sadness was stronger in Miriam's eyes than it had been the last few weeks. "She didn't receive the message." Then the sadness was joined by a glimmer of hope. "I want her to stay, though, Gideon. Can she stay?"

He knew if he said what he wanted to, it would crush his baby sister. Instead, he brushed her off with, "I'll think about it."

Leah sat silently, eating occasional bites of the watered-down stew. Her mind was too busy to join the conversation volleying back and forth between Miriam and Ol' Mose.

Now what? This had been her one real plan. Even though she'd thought to find a job in Butte City in case the marriage with Abel Bryant didn't work out, deep down she'd really thought it *would* work. God had clearly opened the doors for her to come here. Why would He bring her to this obvious dead end?

She cautiously glanced at the older brother while the others were enamored with one of Ol' Mose's stories. Did he remember her, too? His face hadn't shown any recognition, just shock, partially concealed by the thick brown curls covering the lower half. What did he look like under that thick beard? Was he handsome as his strong cheekbones suggested? The thought took her by surprise, but she told herself Abel would likely have looked the same. She was just wondering what might have been. Still, that kind of thinking would get her nowhere, at this point.

Leah dipped her spoon into the bowl again and pulled out a chunk of meat. The soup was definitely not the best she'd eaten, but better than nothing. It wasn't even as good as Mose's campfire cooking, which had been surprisingly flavorful considering the limited supplies he used. She lifted the spoon to her mouth.

Uggh. This bit of meat was the toughest bite yet. Leah forced her mind back to what she should do next. She had no choice at this point but to continue on to Butte. Maybe there would be work for her there, or maybe she would head back to Helena or Fort Benton. Ol' Mose had mentioned staying the night in the Bryant's barn, since it was still a few hours to Butte. Maybe they wouldn't mind if she stayed out there, as well. Or maybe it was possible they might have an extra room with a real bed? It was too much to hope.

Leah glanced at Miriam, her green eyes glowing as she hung on the old trapper's every word. Leah felt a tug in her chest. Even though she really didn't know her, she would miss this young woman.

After dinner, Leah helped Miriam wipe out the dishes, a task she'd done for Ol' Mose while they were on the trail. She took the opportunity to pose the question she'd been contemplating.

"Miriam, I think Ol' Mose said he usually stays the night in your barn when he comes through here?" She stopped for a response.

"Yep, we try every time to put him up in the house in one of the extra beds, but he won't hear of it. Says he can't sleep on a soft mattress."

Leah loved the way Miriam's eyes sparkled when she talked. She seemed to have a zest for life. Unlike her stoic, silent brother.

"Would it be all right if I sleep in the barn, too? I'll be leaving with him in the morning, of course."

Leah watched Miriam for a response. The girl's eyes flared and she rose to her full height, which was still a half-head shorter than Leah.

"Absolutely not." Miriam dropped the tin dish and rag on the counter, and placed a fist on each hip.

"First of all, you will *not* sleep in the barn. You'll sleep in our spare bedroom like any other guest. And second, there's no way I'm letting you leave after just one night. I haven't had a woman's company in years, and I plan to keep you as long as possible." Her shoulders sagged a bit, and her smile returned. "You need to stay a few days, at least, until we figure things out. You came here at Abel's request, and he'd turn over in his grave if he knew we threw ya out."

Leah couldn't help but love the little fiery magpie in front of her. She reached for Miriam's nearest hand and gave it a squeeze. "You're a kind soul, Miriam Bryant. Thank you."

Chapter Ten

A distant clatter pulled Leah from the comfortable dream that clutched her. She sat up, trying to place her surroundings. The room was small and the cotton sheets were worn soft, cozier than the silk bed clothes she was accustomed to.

At last it came to her. Montana Territory. The Bryant Ranch. She sank back with a groan. She had finally made it—and there was nothing here for her after all. She needed to move on with Ol' Mose today.

Leah threw back the covers and rolled over to place her feet on the cool floor. The small movement caused her muscles to scream so much she had to bite her lower lip to keep from crying out. Before leaving Richmond, she'd never known she could hurt like this. And just from riding in a wagon...it was amazing.

Through sheer determination, she forced her muscles to go through the process of dressing in her navy suit again and pinning up her honey-colored tresses. It would be so wonderful to have a hot bath and fresh clothes, but that was not to be if she was to leave with Ol' Mose right after breakfast. All her other clothes were still packed in trunks, tied down in the freight wagon.

He was usually ready to pull out of the campsite by the time the sun crested the tops of the trees. Leah could already see the sun shining through the pale blue curtains over the window, so Mose was surely chomping at the bit. Probably just waiting to eat breakfast with Miriam and Mr. Bryant.

She checked her reflection one more time in the small oval mirror over the washbasin, then picked up her hat and pulled open the door.

In the cabin's main room, Miriam greeted her with a smile as she scraped white goo out of a frying pan. The kitchen held a medley of smells, but not anything Leah expected. No crackle of bacon or spicy aroma of cinnamon toast. Instead, it smelled of charcoal and grease and…maybe bread.

"G'mornin'." Miriam looked as fresh as a flower this morning. Her cream-colored hair was platted in a long braid and wrapped in a knot on the back of her head. Today, she wore a faded blue dress, but her apron was clean and white, if a bit frayed. Her green eyes shown, even in the dimness of the cabin.

"Good morning," Leah murmured as she moved toward the kitchen. "I'm sorry I wasn't up to help you get started on breakfast. Is there something I can do now?" She looked around for an extra apron.

"Not a thing." Miriam wiped the goo from the frying pan into a tin jar. "I left you a plate of food and a mug on the table. The coffee on the stove is still hot."

Leah's mind jumped to alert. "You mean breakfast is over? Why didn't you wake me? Is Ol' Mose ready to go? I need to help him load up."

Before her flurry of questions was half finished, Leah had pinned her hat in place and moved toward the door. Ol' Mose would be itching to leave if he had finished eating.

"Leah, wait!"

Leah ignored the call as she hurried out the door and across the yard to the barn.

"Leah!"

She jerked open the big barn door, and stopped for a moment in the shadowy building to get her bearings. A row of stalls stretched down the right side, and a wagon stood in front of hay piled on the left—an empty wagon. No sign of Ol' Mose's freighter or the two tired mules.

Leah spun around to face a breathless Miriam. "Where is Ol' Mose? Has he taken the wagon with your brother somewhere?"

Miriam shook her head, panting from her wild dash to catch Leah. "That's... what I was... trying to tell you." She swallowed, her labored breathing slowing a little. "Ol' Mose left for Butte City this morning. Said he'd give us a chance to sort things out, and he'll stop on his way back through to check on you."

"Nooo..." Leah slumped against the side of the barn, thoroughly frustrated with the way things were going. He was supposed to take her *with* him. She needed to get to Butte and find work there.

Miriam tentatively stepped toward Leah, placing her hand on Leah's arm. "We can't just let you show up and leave again so soon, Leah. It wouldn't be right. We want you to stay on for a few days, at least, until we figure out what to do next."

Still slumped against the barn, Leah raised her head and saw the earnest expression in the girl's eyes, knowing desperation probably showed in her own. "But you and Mr. Bryant don't owe me anything. You didn't ask me here, and it's obvious your brother doesn't want me to stay. I need to make my own way, and the best place to start, at this point, is in Butte."

A mischievous look came over Miriam's face. "If I could have asked you here, I woulda. I've wanted a friend for so long now, you're like a gift from God, Leah Townsend."

Leah's desperation softened a bit at that. "My trunks?"

"They're in the cabin."

Finally, Leah let out a sigh. She supposed another day or two wouldn't matter too much. Pushing away from the barn, she wrapped a hand through the crook of Miriam's arm. "All right then, I'll stay until Ol' Mose comes back through. But then you needn't worry about me any more after that."

"Oh, I'm so glad." Miriam rested a hand over Leah's, and the two women continued that way back to the house.

Leah couldn't believe how quickly the morning flew. As much as her body craved a warm bath and relaxation, she needed to earn her keep and not be a burden. So, she swept out the cabin while Miriam kneaded the bread dough for dinner. As they worked, the younger woman quizzed Leah about her trip on the steam boat. Then Miriam showed her how to clean out the barn and restock the hay and water in the stalls.

"We don't keep most of the animals in the barn at night during the summer months. Just Bethany, the milk cow, and Gideon's riding horse. The rest of 'em run with the cattle, except the wagon team that stays in the corrals. We try not to feed hay any more than we have to. It's *awful* hard work to cut and store it." Miriam rolled her eyes to emphasize that last point.

Leah brushed hay from her gown. Her whole body ached, but she dared to ask, "So what do we do next?"

Miriam linked arms with Leah and led her out of the barn. "Now we go check the garden to see if my tomato plants are surviving. I just moved them to the ground last week so I want to make sure they took root. And while we walk, you can tell me all about where you grew up. I think you said it was Virginia?"

"Yes, in Richmond."

Miriam's eyes twinkled with a faraway, dreamy look. "Is Richmond a big city? Like New York and Chicago? With balls and parties every week?"

Leah's lips curved a little. "Yes, I suppose Richmond is a big city, but not as big as New York. And yes, we had balls and parties—more often than I liked."

Miriam's eyes grew wide. "Did you wear those big hooped skirts and have servants to help you dress?"

"Well, I did wear hoops when they were the fashion. Now most of the skirts are slender through the sides but gather over big bustles in the back."

Leah stopped speaking when they reached a large garden plot with little green plants in long neat rows. Miriam scanned the entire section, then made her way to some leafy green shoots about ten inches tall.

"And did you have servants to help you dress?"

Thinking about the simple life the Bryant's lived, Leah reluctantly nodded, hoping Miriam wouldn't press for more info.

"And did you have servants to cook and clean for you? And drive your carriage? Did you have a carriage?"

Leah suddenly saw how excessive and unnecessary that lifestyle had been. Had they really needed fifteen servants to keep house for herself and her father? But, it would have been unseemly for the Townsends to keep anything less.

"Did you, Leah?" Miriam looked up from where she was crouched by the plants.

Leah chose her words carefully. "Yes, we did have servants. And honestly, they were my closest friends. I used to giggle and play dolls with the housemaids when I was little. Then as I grew up, Emily was my companion and closer than a sister to me."

"I've always wanted a sister." Miriam sighed wistfully. "I sort of had one a few years back, but she's gone now."

Leah raised an eyebrow, and Miriam explained. "Gideon took a wife a couple years after Pa and Mama died. But Jane died about a year after Gideon married her. I liked havin' her around, but she always wanted to stay cooped up in the cabin. I think she was afraid to be outside or somethin'. I'm not real sure why, though."

Poor Gideon. He'd lost everyone close to him except his baby sister—parents, wife, and now his brother. Is that why he was so quiet and somber? Despite their almost instant friendship, Leah didn't feel she knew Miriam well enough to ask such a personal question.

Thankfully, Miriam rose to her feet and motioned for Leah to follow. "And speaking of Gideon, we'd better get some lunch on before he gets back or we'll have a grumpy man on our hands." Miriam's tone was light, but Leah could certainly imagine the man she'd seen last night might be grumpy—hungry or not.

Gideon did come in a short while later, with the dog trotting by his leg. Miriam flashed her brother a warm smile as she poured white gravy over slices of bread.

"There he is. Ya hungry, big brother?"

He nodded, hanging his hat on the wall peg. "Yep."

Leah stopped pouring coffee into the mugs on the table when the dog trotted up to greet her. She bent down to stroke the animal, his tail waving like a flag.

"What's his name?" When she didn't receive an immediate answer, Leah looked back and forth between Miriam and her brother, waiting for someone to respond. Miriam seemed to be purposely ignoring her.

Finally, Gideon spoke. "Drifter." His voice was deep and clear, but the man surely didn't mince words.

Leah focused again on the sweet animal who pressed his face into her hand, eager for more scratching. His body was covered with a sort of flea-bitten bluish-grey fur. His face was a black mask, divided down the forehead by a strip of grey. He seemed to be intelligent by the way he kept his ears focused with the sounds of the room.

"Hey there, Drifter," she crooned, rubbing the spots behind his ears with both thumbs. He responded by sharing a sloppy kiss which caught Leah right on the tip of her nose. A giggle sneaked out of her before she could stop it. "You're a lover, I see."

Just then a sharp, short whistle sounded, and Drifter lunged away from her, parking himself at Gideon's side.

"Stay." The sound came out so much like a growl, Leah almost missed that it was a word.

The room became silent, and Leah wasn't sure what had just happened. She glanced up at Gideon, who had seated himself at the table and lounged as if nothing was out of the ordinary. A quick look at Miriam showed a seething scowl aimed directly at her older brother.

Miriam broke the silence by carrying a tin plate of gravy over to the other side of the kitchen, farthest away from the table. "Come'on, Drifter. I've got a treat for ya, boy."

Leah turned back, expecting the dog to trot eagerly toward the yummy stuff. He didn't, though. Despite his longing gaze toward the plate on the floor, he kept himself planted beside his master.

With a frustrated grunt, Miriam planted both hands on her hips and glared at her brother. "Gideon."

The unspoken dressing down seemed to work, for Gideon relented. "Go," he growled. The dog jumped to his feet and bounded across the room.

Despite the inherent insult to Leah in Gideon's behavior, she found the entire exchange to be rather amusing. Drifter was obviously well-trained and devoted to his master. But he seemed to like Leah, too, and that didn't sit well with Gideon. When all was said and done, though, the big brother loved his baby sister and just couldn't say no to her.

Chapter Eleven

*T*he prayer was said by Gideon in his usual to-the-point, no-extra-words-spared style. "Bless us, Lord, and these Your gifts. Make us grateful. In Christ's name, Amen."

After the blessing, lunch was a silent affair, with each of them focused on their white gravy poured over beef and bread. Again, the beef was almost too tough to eat, and very salty. What made it so tough? Had Miriam cooked it too long?

To her surprise, Gideon was the one to break the silence. When his plate was almost half empty, he spoke without looking up.

"Well, I reckon the only thing for ya to do is go back to where ya came from. St. Louis or Richmond or wherever that is. I can help arrange for travel and such."

It took a moment for Leah to realize he was speaking to her. He wasn't looking at her when he spoke, an action which would be considered quite disrespectful in proper circles. She tried to overlook it, but felt her hackles raise, just the same. To be safe, she counted to five before speaking.

"Mr. Bryant, I thank you for the kind offer, but I won't be going back to St. Louis, Richmond or any other place in the Southeast."

For the first time, she saw a flicker of emotion as he raised his very green eyes to look at her.

"Ma'am," his tone was measured, controlled, "you will have to go back to where you came from. There is nothing for you here. My brother is dead." The words were flat, then he dropped his eyes back to his plate.

Compassion nudged her, and the need to clarify her statement. "Mr. Bryant. I understand I cannot stay here. I *am* planning to leave. I simply am not able to go back to St. Louis nor to Richmond, which is the city from which I originally hail." There. That should help explain her position.

A blue vein appeared on Gideon's forehead that hadn't been there before.

"And why is that, if I may ask?" He spat each word as if he were expelling cat hair from his mouth.

"Because, sir, when I arrived in Fort Benton, the gateway to your *fine* Territory, I was robbed of my reticule and all funds. Therefore, I have no money with which to pay for a ride back to that same Fort Benton, nor the expensive ship ride to St. Louis. Nor train fare for the *five days* it would take to travel from there to Richmond."

She could feel both her voice and body temperature rise with each sentence. "And not only that, but there is a man in Richmond who is seeking to marry and poison me for my inheritance. I last saw his agents when I was in St. Louis, so I will *not* be going back to that city.

"However, Mr. Bryant, you need not fear I will impose my presence upon you any longer than absolutely necessary. If you will kindly tell me the way to Butte City, I'll leave posthaste."

Feeling a little spent after her outburst and more than a little embarrassed, Leah picked up her fork and began to spear a piece of soggy bread. She refused to meet either of the Bryants' eyes, and the silence that ensued cloaked her like a suffocating blanket.

Miriam came to her rescue. "Well, I for one say going to Butte City is *not* an option. With all those out-of-work miners in town, it's not safe for a woman to walk by herself in daylight, much less live there alone. There's no way I'm letting a friend of mine stay there by herself with no protection."

Leah looked up to see her sweet little magpie friend with arms crossed and eyebrows raised. Even though she disagreed with Miriam's opinion, tears sprung to her eyes at the emotion behind the words. It felt good to have someone care about her. Emily's face flashed through Leah's mind, and she wondered how her dear friend was doing. Miriam's next words obliterated that thought.

"I know what you should do, brother. Since Abel's not here to marry Leah, why don't *you* do it?"

Leah choked on the bread she was swallowing. Through her breathtaking coughs, she heard the clatter of a fork on the table, boot thuds on the floor, a sharp whistle, and the slamming of a door.

"I'm sorry I embarrassed you, Leah, but I still think you should marry Gideon."

Leah tried her best to ignore Miriam while slicing the ham with a long thick knife. If she got this done without chopping off a finger, or at least drawing blood, it would be a miracle.

"You came here to marry a Bryant, right? It's the perfect solution. You didn't know Abel, but you were going to marry him. Why not Gideon?" Miriam's voice dropped to a stage whisper as she leaned toward Leah. "And I never said this to Abel, but Gideon's the better looking between the two."

Leah gasped, bringing a giggle from Miriam. "Your face is as pink as that ham."

Heat rushed through her body. To be honest, she hadn't seen enough to know if Gideon was handsome. Sure he was tall with broad shoulders and alarming green eyes. But that bushy beard and loose brown curls covered most of his face, making it hard to distinguish the features beneath.

Not that handsome is the only thing I'm looking for in a husband.

Maybe she should share that thought with Miriam. Let her see how unsuitable Gideon really was.

"Miriam, I can't deny I was hoping Abel would be handsome, but what drew me to his advertisement is the fact that he wanted a God-fearing wife. It's most important that my future husband be a devout Christian who knows God and seeks His will. On top of that, he must be kind and considerate to others, honest, loyal, and trustworthy. Someone I could respect."

Miriam's eyes were bright and she almost hopped from excitement. "Do you know you just described Gideon exactly?"

Leah gave her a look she hoped said she'd easier believe President Lincoln had come back to life and was knocking at their door.

"Honest. He just doesn't know what to do with himself around you. Once you get to know him, you'll see what I mean."

Leah shook her head, then placed the plate of ham on the table.

They worked quickly to finish the meal. With twilight dusting through the window, Gideon would be back soon. What would he have to say about Miriam's outlandish suggestion? It would be nice if she knew a little more about the man.

"What does he do all day?" Leah asked, as she placed three sets of plates and forks on the table.

"Usually he works with the cattle or horses. Some days he goes hunting. We eat the meat and tan the hides to sell, so he hunts a good bit. Would you put those preserves on the table, please?" Miriam nodded toward a jar on the shelf closest to the window.

Just then, the sound of boot thuds echoed from the porch, followed by the squeak of the front door. Leah grabbed the coffee pot from the stove using her apron for protection from the hot handle as she'd seen Miriam do, and began filling mugs while Miriam carried the sliced bread and green beans to the table. It was amazing how comfortable it felt to work with Miriam in the kitchen. The day had been busy, but fulfilling in a way, as if she were contributing toward a common goal.

"Hi, big brother," Miriam called out. "You're just in time for the food."

Leah forced herself not to look up at Gideon, but when Drifter jogged over and pushed his muzzle in her skirt, she couldn't resist giving the dog a quick head rub. He seemed disappointed when she stopped, but finally turned back to his master and settled himself next to Gideon's chair.

When they were all seated, Gideon again spoke a succinct prayer before they loaded plates and began eating. This time, Miriam tried to keep up a steady conversation, first with Gideon. But after a series of nods or one-word answers, she gave up and turned her questions toward Leah.

"Did you have any pets back in Richmond, Leah?"

"Not really. I had a horse I always rode—an Arabian mare named Dove—but no real pets. Not for lack of asking, though, I assure you."

Gideon set down his fork, and leaned back in his chair. Both young ladies turned to look at him expectantly.

"Miss Townsend, I've given it a lot of thought. You came here with an understanding, in response to my brother's request. Since it's not possible for him to honor his side of the agreement, I'd like to pay your fair back to St Louis or wherever you'd like to go."

"But—"

Gideon held up a commanding hand, and Leah ceased her argument.

"My sister's right. Butte City is not a place for any proper lady to stay. Fort Benton's not much better, especially for a lady unescorted. It'd be much safer for ya if you'd head back toward the eastern states. I'll send you with enough gold dust to cover the cost of your trip out here, and your fare back to St. Louis."

That was the most she'd heard him speak in the two days she'd known Gideon Bryant, and Leah found herself caught by the deep emerald of his eyes as he finished. A girl could get lost in them if she wasn't careful.

She was able to keep just enough of her wits to hear his words, and when they sank in, gratitude washed through her.

Leah hated for him to put out so much money, but it was true she wouldn't be here in the first place if it wasn't for his brother.

"I thank you, Mr. Bryant. That's generous of you. I am willing to accept your offer, with the exception that I can't go back to the eastern states. The danger is too great the man seeking my life would find me. I'll go to any city in the western territory, though, you deem suitable."

Gideon nodded and picked up his fork again. "I'll give it some thought."

And that's what he appeared to do for the next ten minutes or so as they finished the meal. He finally looked up again, which seemed to be his sign that he was about to speak.

"I think Helena might be as good a place as any for you to start. It has a few respectable hotels and cafés. Might find a position in one of those. I'll still refund your fare out here so you have some money to live off for a while."

Yes, the three hundred dollars she'd spent on the steam boat ride would buy room and board for a gracious while. Leah nodded and offered a half smile. "Thank you. And do you know when Ol' Mose was planning to come back through here? I'll see if he can take me to Helena, or at least a place where I can hire a driver."

Gideon leaned back in his chair, appearing to mull over this. "No need. We can take you down to Helena. Miriam's been itchin' to go to the mercantile, and I have some leather for the harness shop. We'll leave tomorrow after breakfast."

Leah breathed a silent prayer of thanks. For the first time, things seemed to be looking up. God really was guiding her steps.

As Leah swept the kitchen floor after breakfast the next morning, she tried to make some sense out of her emotions. Why this feeling of melancholy that had shadowed her all morning?

She felt as if she were leaving her home and family again. True, Miriam was like a long lost sister, but they had only met two days ago. And she would miss this peaceful cabin secluded in the mountains. Something about the clear air as it filled her lungs, and the ambiance, so quiet except for the twitter of birds. She could easily see why someone would never want to leave this place.

But that was not to be her lot this day. She needed to move on and find God's place for her.

Having gathered all the dust and crumbs in a pile, Leah swept them toward the front door the way she'd seen Miriam do the first night. Out the door and off the side of the porch they went. At first, Leah had thought it curious the porch had no rail, but now she saw at least one benefit—dirt could be easily swept to the side and not down the stairs where people would tromp it right back into the house.

She stopped to admire the view before returning to the house. Miriam was changing into her town clothes, and Gideon had gone to hitch the wagon and team. Both of Leah's trunks were packed and by her bedroom door, so she had time to enjoy her peaceful surroundings one last time.

By standing on the far left corner of the porch, she could see a mountain range far away, peaks still covered in snow. What would it be like to live in a place that still had snow in June? Having grown up in the Southeast, such a phenomenon seemed foreign. Perhaps she could travel to those mountains now, too.

A motion to her left caught Leah's eye and she leaned over the edge to get a better look, holding to the corner post for support.

A deer? Yes! A chestnut brown deer stood alert just inside the yard, watching Leah with bright, wary eyes. She barely dared to breathe, afraid the animal would dart into the trees and disappear forever. Inch by inch, Leah reached out a hand toward the animal, wishing she could get a little closer.

Bang!

A horrendous boom sounded, and the deer dropped at the same time she herself was falling. Her grip on the post slipped, and she reached for something—anything—but came away empty. She heard a scream in the distance, just as the ground collected her with a bone-jarring thud.

Chapter Twelve

*L*eah couldn't breathe. She tried and gasped, but couldn't force air into her lungs. Her chest might explode any minute. She clawed at the ground, trying to push herself onto her knees, anything to get some air. With that movement, came a shot of pain through her right leg and a flash of light in front of her eyes.

"Ahh!" It was all she could say. Her leg hurt so badly, she couldn't think or speak. At least her breath was coming a little easier now.

"Easy now. Don't move just yet." A voice crooned above her, while big hands gently rolled Leah onto her back. Was that God? The voice didn't boom like she'd always imagined God's would, but was a mixture of strength and honey, both manly and gentle. She allowed the hands to work as the agony shot bullets up her spine. Maybe if she were perfectly still, she would lose consciousness and leave this searing ache behind.

"Can you tell me where it hurts?"

Leah squinted up, trying to find the source of the voice.

Gideon. His emerald eyes were pools of concern.

The question he'd asked finally registered, and she took a quick inventory of her body. It was hard to tell with the pain shooting up her leg and overflowing through her other limbs.

"Just...my leg and...my chest...I think."

"Leah." Miriam's face came into view beside her brother's.

Gideon didn't acknowledge his sister, but studied Leah's skirts with a wrinkle between his brows.

"I'm going to need to move your skirts a bit." His gaze went to Leah's face. "Is that all right?"

"Yes," she gasped. If he could make the torture stop, he needed to get on with it.

He eased the bottom of the skirt up on her right side until she saw a flicker of ache in his eyes. He sucked in a breath.

"I'm going to carry you into the house now. It's going to hurt, but we have to get you inside so we can splint your leg. You can scream or squeeze the life out of my arm, whatever you need to. All right?"

He looked at Leah like he was waiting for her consent. What else was she going to do? The pain was excruciating, but she instinctively knew Gideon would do everything he could to make it bearable.

Miriam's gentle hands propped up her shoulders as Gideon's large arm slipped behind her. His other arm went under the bend of her knees, and the touch seared like fire in her bone. Leah sucked in her breath and grabbed his shoulder, trying to claw away from the agony.

"Easy there. I've got you. Easy now." His steady cadence and the smoothness of his movements helped calm her a bit. His chest was strong, like a shelter from the raging torment. Leah buried herself in it. Was this what it felt like to hide under the shadow of the Almighty's wings?

Too soon, she felt herself being lowered into a bed. Again, the touch of her foot on the mattress sent a jolt of fire through her leg.

"Miriam, I'm goin' to get supplies from outside. Need you to gather a long bandage to wrap the splint and some clean cloths."

"All right, and I'll put on some Willow Bark, too."

Leah heard the exchange from far away. The misery inside her was the only thing that would hold her attention. She tried reciting Scripture under her breath.

"The Lord is my Shepherd, I shall not want. He maketh me to

lie down in green pastures. He leadeth me beside still waters. He restoreth my soul." She wanted to scream, it hurt so bad. "Yea, though I walk through the valley of the shadow of death, I will fear no evil for Thou art with me."

A cool cloth covered Leah's forehead and a gentle hand smoothed the hair away from her face. Leah opened her eyes to Miriam's sweet smile.

"Gideon will be back in just a minute, and he'll get you fixed up."

Leah's mind was so foggy. "Is the doctor on his way?"

Miriam's voice was sad. "I'm afraid there's not a doctor in Butte or anywhere close. The closest is in Helena, about five hours away."

Leah tried to sit up. "Is he going to take me in the wagon then?"

Miriam gently pushed Leah back against the pillows. "Shhh… Lay back down. The wagon ride would be harder on you than anything, and probably mess your leg up even more. 'Sides, Gideon knows what to do. He always was the best at doctoring people and animals. He's splinted more legs than I could count on both hands."

Just then, the man himself entered the room, with two flat boards in one hand and a small leafy branch in the other. He moved around to the foot of the bed near Leah's injured leg and placed the boards on the floor.

He looked into Leah's face. "How're you feelin'?"

She tried to form a smile, but wasn't sure her features made it. "Hurts."

A wave of sadness washed over his expression. "I'll be honest, it's gonna hurt a bit more when I start workin' on it, but then you'll feel better." His eyes met hers with an intensity. "Do you think you can make it?"

Leah could only nod. If she could look into his deep emerald eyes the entire time, she just might be able to do this. He seemed satisfied with the nod and turned to his sister.

"Is the tea ready? She needs some before we get started."

Miriam disappeared from the room, and Leah watched while Gideon tore the long cloth into strips about the length of his arm. He eased the skirts up again and, making sure nothing touched her leg, he positioned the boards on either side of the broken bone and the cloth at regular intervals along the wood.

"Here you go. This'll help with the hurting." Miriam entered the room with a steaming mug and a spoon. She ladled the bitter stuff slowly into Leah's mouth until Leah finally shook her head.

"I can drink. Just help me." If this stuff would make the pain go away, she wanted it down as quickly as possible.

When the mug was empty, Miriam stepped back and Gideon took over.

Standing by her leg, he looked into Leah's face again. "I need you to stay as still as possible, all right? Even when it hurts."

Leah nodded, biting her lower lip. "All right." Her voice sounded as small as she felt.

She watched as Gideon rested her leg on the cloth bandages, tucking some of the leaves from the branch against her skin. He wrapped both hands around her calf, and she forced her mind to focus on the feel of his callused hands instead of the burn inside her limb.

And then, with a flick of his wrists, he squeezed and jerked her leg in a single excruciating movement. An explosion of white fury shot through Leah's body. She moaned and clutched Miriam's hand, unable to contain the torment inside.

A gentle hand stroked her hair, and tears streamed down her face. But she was too miserable to care.

Gideon positioned the boards and tied strips of cloth around them about every six inches. He used the remaining fabric to tie her foot up so her ankle made the shape of an "L".

When he finally looked up at Leah, the torture on his face matched what radiated through her body.

"I'm sorry." He almost whispered the words, but Leah understood his meaning. She answered with a nod, hoping he understood her own silent message. He hadn't wanted to inflict so much pain, but he had to so the leg would heal correctly. She understood.

Miriam appeared at Leah's side with another steamy mug before Leah realized she'd gone.

"Here. Drink one more cup of the tea and we'll let you sleep."

Leah was too exhausted to do more than swallow as the warm liquid poured down her throat. When it was finished, she sank against the pillows and was asleep before Miriam left the room.

Gideon stood in the bedroom watching Leah sleep. She looked so small and fragile, surrounded by pillows with her leg cinched between two planks. She *was* small and fragile. What was she doing out here, anyway? This country was wild and tough — not for the delicate.

He couldn't shake the feeling of her snuggled in his arms as he'd carried her. It had been so long since he'd held a woman that close. It made him want to protect her, to shield her from all pain and danger. It had been harder to splint her shin bone than any other he'd had to fix. Knowing the agony he was inflicting had almost sent him storming out the door and far away from the cabin.

How had he let this happen in the first place? It was that blasted porch. If he'd put a rail around it like he'd thought about doing so many times, this never would have happened. Well that was something he could fix now.

But then a niggling of responsibility kicked in. He'd fix the porch right after he gutted the deer. No sense in wasting good meat.

The pounding wouldn't stop.

Bang, bang, bang, bang.

"Oohh... Come in." It was more of a moan than a call. She needed to make the pounding stop.

Bang, bang, bang, bang.

"Leah?" Miriam poked her head in the door. "I thought I heard you awake. How do you feel today?"

"Oooohh..." She wanted to clutch her hands over her ears. Between the fire in her right leg and that awful racket, she could just scream.

Miriam's head disappeared from the doorway, then reappeared again with the rest of her body, hands carrying a wooden tray.

"You're probably hungry, and ready for some more tea, huh?" She set the tray on a bedside table and reached for the mug. "Let's start with the tea, though."

Leah nodded. "What is that banging?"

The corners of Miriam's mouth lifted. "Gideon."

Leah gave her an annoyed what-are-you-talking-about look. She didn't have the pain tolerance for word games right now. "You mean Gideon's tearing the house down?"

Miriam giggled as she held the cup to Leah's lips. "No, silly. He's building it. Adding a rail around the porch, that is."

Leah felt her brows arch, taking the cup from Miriam's hands. "He is?"

Miriam looked so proud of herself. "Yep," she sank onto the bed and leaned forward like she had a great secret to tell. "He felt *terrible* about you falling. He's been out cuttin' wood half the night and should be done with the porch in just a bit."

Leah took another swig of the bitter drink and sank back against the pillows. "But it wasn't his fault. I lost my balance, that's all. It was my own mistake for leaning over so far."

Miriam's green eyes lost their vibrancy for a moment. "Oh, Gideon always takes other people's problems on himself. Blames himself for everything bad that happens around here."

Leah reached for Miriam's hand. "Please tell him my accident was not his fault. He needn't feel bad about it."

The twinkle reappeared in Miriam's eyes as she reached for Leah's empty cup and replaced it with a bowl of mush. "You tell him that yourself. Now, eat a little bit before the tea puts you back to sleep."

Leah wrinkled her nose. "I can't sleep all day. I need to be helping you with your work. Is there something you can bring me to do in bed? Sewing maybe?"

"Hush now." Miriam rose from the bed as if to escape the talk of Leah working. "You need rest to help your leg heal. But maybe I'll bring in potatoes this afternoon and you can help me peel them for dinner." She held up a finger. "If you rest all morning and are feeling better by then."

Miriam leaned forward to plant an affectionate kiss on Leah's forehead. "Just put your bowl on the tray and I'll be back for it in a while. Sweet dreams."

It wasn't until after Miriam had left the room that Leah realized the hammering on the porch had stopped. She felt a smile touch her lips. Maybe Miriam was right. Gideon—the mountain man—*could* be kind and considerate.

Chapter Thirteen

*L*eah stretched and shielded a yawn, careful not to move her lower body. Miriam's light tap sounded on the bedroom door. "Come in."

The sweet, perky face appeared in the doorway, framed by blond wisps that had escaped the knot on her head. "Are you up for some company?"

"Oh, yes." Leah didn't even try to hide her eagerness.

Miriam pushed through the doorway with a leather sack, a bowl, and two knives. "I need to peel potatoes for dinner and thought you could keep me comp'ny if you're up to it?"

"I believe your offer earlier was for me to *help*, so I fully intend to hold you to that. I feel like a lazy bum lying in this bed all day when you're both so busy."

As soon as she finished speaking, Leah realized the irony of her statement. Three months ago, she wouldn't have thought twice about lying around all day. Her life had been full of leisure and reading, with a party thrown in here and there for spice. What a different person she was becoming. A better person.

Miriam didn't sit until she settled Leah comfortably against the stack of pillows, knife in hand, a rag in her lap to catch the peelings, and the bowl in between them.

Leah picked up a potato and looked at the knife, trying to determine the best way to go at this. Finally, she held the underside of the potato in her left hand, and the knife in her right, blade facing away. She skimmed the top of the potato with the knife, stroking away from her body. After the first slice, only a few small brown strips of potato peel had been removed. Leah frowned at the potato. This might take longer than she'd thought.

"What are you doing?"

She looked up to find Miriam watching her, curiosity smothering her face.

"Trying to peel this potato." She worked to keep annoyance from sneaking into her voice.

"Did you bump your head when you fell?"

Leah gave her a dark look. "No."

Understanding flowed over Miriam's face, and she covered a giggle with her hand. "You've never peeled potatoes before, have you?"

Leah pushed down her defenses. "I've never had the opportunity to peel them before, but I'm sure I can do it."

Miriam nodded. "Of course you can. Here, hold your knife like this." She demonstrated turning the knife so the blade faced toward herself. "And peel the potato toward you, but watch your thumb. You want to take just the top layer off and not get very much of the white meat."

Leah studied as Miriam peeled a continuous strip that wrapped all the way around the potato almost two times before breaking. That looked easy enough. She tried the same and came away with a peeling about the length of her thumbnail. Maybe it was a little harder than it appeared, but she would get the job done.

They worked in silence for a few minutes before Leah felt she had the hang of it enough to talk while she worked. She was dying to know the story that had brought the Bryant family to such a remote part of the country. Besides, it was probably better for the potatoes if Leah asked the questions and Miriam did most of the talking.

"So, have you always lived in the Montana Territory?"

"No, we moved here when I was five." Miriam kept her eyes

on the potato zipping around in her hands. "We used to live in Kentucky, on a little farm near Lexington. But Pa and Mama came out west to claim land under Lincoln's Free Homestead Act."

Leah had a faint memory of her father talking about the Free Homestead Acts. He'd said they weren't a good idea, that they would encourage Europeans to come to America to claim the free land. It was good that hadn't been the case for the Bryants.

Miriam continued. "We just had ten acres back in Kentucky, and Pa was a tobacco farmer, but he always wanted to raise cattle and horses on a big ranch. He finally had the chance to make his dreams come true."

Leah smiled. "Not everyone gets that chance, but I'm glad he was able to. He certainly picked a beautiful place to build a ranch."

Miriam flew through the potatoes, peeling at least three to Leah's one, despite the fact she was doing most of the talking.

"Yep, it is a pretty place. Pa got the ranch started and taught the boys how to tend to things. Winters are hard, though, and we lost him in a snowstorm almost six years ago."

"Oh, Miriam, I'm so sorry." Having lost her own father eight months earlier, Leah knew what her friend had gone through.

The girl shrugged. "Yeah, it was hard. Hard on us all, but especially Mama. She loved Pa so much, she never was the same after he died. She took sick the next fall and died of a fever, but I think it was really a broken heart that took her."

"And how old were you when she passed?" Leah asked quietly.

Miriam sighed. "I was eleven."

"Oh, Miri... You were just a girl." Leah laid the potato in her lap and released her own sigh. "I was sixteen when my mama died, but I had Emily to help me through things."

"Who's Emily?"

"She was my governess growing up, but she stayed on to be my companion after Mama died. I don't think I would have made it through those years without her." Not ready to keep the conversation on herself, Leah redirected the topic. "So do you raise both cattle and horses here?"

Miriam nodded, not seeming to mind the switch. "Mostly cattle, but we have three broodmares now. Gideon likes the horses best, even though they're a lot of work to raise and train before they're ready to sell."

Leah hesitated to comment on the man, but finally said, "Gideon seems like a hard worker who can do most anything."

Miriam looked up from her potato long enough to flash a proud smile. "He's amazing, all right. A natural born leader. I think that's why he and Abel always got along so well. Gideon was the leader and Abel was the doer. They both had a sixth sense when it came to animals, too. I think that's why it was such a shock about the bear." The tenor in Miriam's voice dropped with her last few words.

"The bear?"

Miriam swallowed. "That's how Abel died. He tangled with a grizzly, we think, but we never saw the bear. Gideon found him in the woods after his soul had already gone to be with Jesus."

Miriam's voice grew husky, so Leah allowed silence to settle over them, except for the scrape of knife against potato. She looked up to check on her friend a few times, and when a tear rolled off the end of Miriam's button nose, Leah leaned over to stroke her shoulder. Anything she could say would only make it harder for her friend.

A few minutes later, Miriam set the last of the peeled potatoes in the bowl and rolled her shoulders, reaching to massage her neck. Her lips curved into a timid smile through the mist in her eyes.

"Leah, in case I haven't said it enough, I hope you know how excited I am you're here. I haven't sat and peeled potatoes with another woman in years. It's good for the soul, I tell ya."

Curious, Leah decided to ask one more question. "Don't you have any female neighbors close by?"

"Nah, most of the spreads around here are 160 acres or more, so the houses aren't very close together." She began gathering the potato bag full of peelings and the knives. "To the east is John

Stands-alone and his son. John's half Sioux and they keep pretty well to themselves. On the other side is a trapper fellow we call Skeet. He comes over for dinner every now and then." She flashed another smile, this one brighter than before. "If we're lucky, he brings his fiddle."

Miriam dropped a kiss on Leah's forehead. "I'll bring you some more Willow Bark tea in a minute, then you get some rest, all right?"

That sounded like an excellent idea, as Leah sank back against the pillows. It was relieving that her leg didn't hurt so much when she visited with Miriam, but it ached like crazy now. And she was so tired...

Everything hurt. Her head. Her underside from lying flat in this infernal bed for two days. And most especially her leg.

Leah reached for her Bible and ruffled the pages without much direction. She needed to pull herself out of this mood, but it was hard to make herself do anything with the continuous throbbing in her leg.

Not for the first time, Leah bemoaned the fact that there wasn't a doctor anywhere in the vicinity. Gideon seemed to know what he was doing when it came to splinting her leg, but surely a doctor would have also given medicine for the pain. The Willow Bark tea helped, but it also put her to sleep. It seemed like she'd been asleep for a week now.

She heard a thud from the other room and glanced toward the door. What was Miriam doing in there?

Leah forced her eyes on the pages and flipped to Psalm chapter twenty, one of her favorites. Before she'd read more than the first line, Miriam's light knock sounded on the door.

"Come in, Miriam. You don't have to knock, you know." *Bad Leah. You are a guest in their house and she is doing everything possible to make you comfortable, including waiting on you hand and foot. Don't take the misery from your own silly mistake out on this sweet girl.* The internal reprimand seemed to help, because Leah was able to force out a small smile as Miriam almost skipped into the room.

"We have a surprise for you, Leah."

Behind the little magpie came her brother, and Leah was taken once again with how tall and muscular Gideon was. His broad shoulders tapered down to a trim waist, and he didn't appear to have an inch on him anywhere that wasn't covered in lean muscle.

Miriam stared at her like a puppy eager to run outside and play, and even Gideon had a sparkle in his emerald eyes.

"What's the surprise?" She was more than a bit curious.

"You'll have to come in the other room to see it." This from Gideon as he moved closer to the right side of the bed. "Do you think you can manage that?"

She regarded him, hoping the shock didn't register too strongly on her face. "I don't think I can walk yet, if that's what you mean."

Was that a mischievous sparkle in his eyes? "No need. I can carry you, I reckon'."

She shouldn't allow it, but she did want to see the surprise. Since Miriam was there, maybe it would be acceptable for him to touch her. But only because she couldn't walk herself.

Leah bit her lip as she nodded. "All right."

As Gideon neared, his presence surrounded her. Good thing Miriam had helped her with a sponge bath that morning.

Gideon slipped a gentle arm under her shoulders, and another under her knees. The splint on her leg kept it sticking out at an awkward angle, and Leah bit her lower lip hard to keep from crying out at the fire in her bone. She forced herself to focus on Gideon's arms. She'd never been so close to anyone this strong before. The men whose arms she'd daintily touched as they escorted her in the ballroom were like twigs beside Gideon's massive trunks. And his chest was strong enough to shield her from anything.

From the shelter of Gideon's protection, Leah saw the familiar surroundings of the sitting area and kitchen. He stopped for a moment while Miriam fussed with something, then he gently set Leah on a soft...bed? She looked around, and found they had, indeed, brought a bed into the main room.

A glance at Miriam's face showed pure enthusiasm. "Now you don't have to lay in that bedroom all by yourself. You can talk to me while I work, and take your meals with us and everything."

Thankfulness overflowed from Leah's chest. What kind people these were. She returned Miriam's smile through the mist clouding her eyes. "It's perfect. Thank you."

Gideon shuffled his feet for a moment behind Miriam, then turned toward the front door. "Reckon I'd better check on the animals." He glanced toward his sister. "Be back for supper."

Leah watched while Miriam straightened the kitchen and swept the cabin floor. The younger woman did most of the talking, with Leah asking questions about her childhood and what it was like to grow up with siblings. As much as she enjoyed the conversation, Leah still felt guilty she wasn't able to help with the work. When they settled into a comfortable silence, an idea came to her.

"Miriam, do you get to read much?" The girl looked up from scrubbing a grease mark on the floor.

"Sometimes I do in the evenings. We don't have many books, but I've read the Bible an' Pilgrim's Progress so many times they're fallin' apart."

Leah smiled. "Have you ever read *An Old Fashioned Girl*? It just came out a few years ago, but it's one of my favorites."

Miriam's forehead wrinkled a little. "I haven't heard of that one."

"If you'll go look in my smaller trunk, you'll see a stack of books. Bring that one and I'll read to you while you work, if you'd like."

Her green eyes grew wide. "Oh, that'd be like heaven. That'll make even cleaning out the stove a treat."

Miriam returned a few moments later with the leather-bound

book in her hand and an expression of awe on her face. "Leah, you have so many books. I've never known anyone with all those books that weren't for schoolin'."

Leah held back a chuckle. "Miri, you are welcome to read any one of them any time you want. Once I can finally get out of this bed, I'll do some of the work and let you lie around and read all day."

Miriam's face was almost giddy as Leah opened the book and began the adventures of Polly, a girl not so unlike Miriam herself.

Chapter Fourteen

Leah watched Miriam wipe each damp plate with a towel before placing it on the shelf. Dinner that night had been beans and cornbread—Ol' Mose's favorite campfire meal. Miriam had added bacon to the beans, though, and fried the cornbread in bacon grease, which deepened the flavor for both.

Leah released a dramatic sigh. "Miri, I'm going to grow out of my dresses if I lay here much longer and eat your good food."

Miriam's cheeks blossomed into a grin. "I imagine you'll be up before ya know it, and wishin' you could lay around again."

"It couldn't be soon enough for me." Leah was determined not to grumble, so she decided to change the subject. Before she could think of another, the thump of boots sounded on the front porch and Gideon appeared in the doorway, shadowed by Drifter. Upon entering the room, the dog headed straight for Leah, propping his front paws on the bed to reach her. Gideon seemed to have made peace now with the love affair his dog held for her, so she didn't worry as much about encouraging the animal's affection.

"How ya doin' boy? Did you work hard today?" His tongue lolled to the side as she found the good spot behind one of his ears.

While she petted the dog, Leah watched Gideon in her peripheral vision. He carried two long sticks to his chair in the sitting area. Even though the weather was too warm for a fire, Gideon and Miriam still gathered most evenings around the big fireplace to do hand work, read, or just wind down. Miriam usually curled up in the rocking chair, while Gideon took the ladder-back chair closest to the hearth.

Gideon sat, working on one of the stick ends. Her curiosity finally made her turn full attention to watch him. He had attached a short piece—no longer than her hand—perpendicular to the long pole like the shape of a "T", and was wrapping strips of leather around the short wood.

He didn't seem to notice her watching him, or didn't say anything. That was his nature, though. Most of the time, he never acknowledged her presence, except the occasional nod when he first entered the cabin. He was a little more vocal with his sister, but never said more than needed to get the job done.

What made him so quiet? Was it because he'd lived in such a remote place for the last eleven years? That could contribute to his lack of need for words, but surely it wasn't the only reason he rarely spoke. Was it due to all the trauma he'd endured with so many loved ones dying? Perhaps he blocked himself from getting to know or care about people, because he was afraid of losing them.

She shook herself mentally. Now she was really overanalyzing things. She needed to get out of this bed and away from her own crazy mind for a while.

Leah refocused her attention on Gideon as he laid one stick on the wood floor and reached for the other. Then it occurred to her what he was making. Walking sticks! Crutches, a doctor back home had called them. They would help her get out of this awful bed without putting weight on the broken leg.

Thank You, God, for Gideon. Leah wanted to cheer out loud, but kept it to a silent prayer for now. She felt herself grinning from ear to ear.

She watched as Gideon wrapped the last of the leather around the wood piece that would fit under her shoulder. From her position, she could see the lamplight flicker and dance in his deep green eyes. They shone like the richest of emeralds tonight, full of depth and wisdom. What she would have given right then to hear his thoughts behind that emerald mask.

At last, Gideon rose to his feet and carried the walking sticks toward Leah's bed. Her heart picked up speed as he approached. His eyes locked with hers for a moment, before he leaned the smooth wood pieces against the headboard.

"These should help you get around some. Just don't put any weight on your right leg."

"Thank you." It sounded like a paltry response when he'd just given her freedom, but Leah didn't know what else to say. She hoped he could read the rest in her smile.

Gideon held the colt firmly between his left arm and right leg, using his free hand to stroke the little guy's chestnut shoulder. This foal was close to two months now and showed definite signs of maturing into a high quality stud. He had the lineage to do it, and his confirmation was looking to be just what Gideon had carefully selected in his breeding stock—square stocky hindquarters, wide chest, broad forehead, and good height. Now, if he could just get the temperament right. That was the part that usually took time, but he was laying the foundation.

Would Leah like to see the foals? The question popped into his mind unbidden. Thoughts of their female houseguest had been doing that a lot lately. He wasn't sure how she felt about horses, but she seemed to like dogs. He was pretty certain she'd fall in love with these guys, too.

He released the colt and stepped back to rub its faithful mama. Rosie was a good broodmare, and had thrown two fine fillies in past years. Now she'd more than outdone herself with this leggy, chestnut colt.

"How about it, Rosie girl?" He scratched the mare's jaw as

she leaned into his hand. "Would you like to take a visit to the barn tonight? There's someone special I want you to meet, and she'll probably give you some of Miri's carrots if I let her."

The mare reached up to blow into Gideon's hair, which he took as her agreement on the scheme. He couldn't help but imagine the light in Leah's eyes when she saw the colt for the first time. When she got excited, her pale green eyes shimmered like early morning dew on spring grass.

He reminded himself again he only felt sorry for her. The broken leg was his fault completely. The image of her sparkling eyes stayed with him as he mounted his own horse and led Rosie back toward the cabin. Drifter and the colt scampered behind, playing the animal version of a game of tag between the trees.

When they entered the yard, Gideon tied off his mount at the hitching rail in front of the barn, then led Rosie to the house. The colt stopped to sniff out a patch of dandelions, but at Gideon's whistle he gave a mighty leap sideways. Landing on all fours, he stood snorting at the fire-breathing dragon that was surely hiding inside the yellow flowers.

"You are a rascal." Gideon chuckled, as the colt scampered to the safety of his mama. Now to get the girls outside.

"Miriam!" he called loud enough for his voice to carry through the wooden door.

His answer came shortly in the form of Miriam's cheerful smile in the doorway, framed by blonde wisps. Her apron was splattered with occasional red spots and charcoal smudges.

"Oh, you brought up Rosie!" Miriam squealed. "Leah, you have to come see this."

Miriam disappeared inside the cabin. Gideon stroked the velvety muzzle of the broodmare as he listened to the sounds of shuffling and women's voices drifting through the open door, then a slow thump of wood upon wood. Leah seemed to be moving slowly on the crutches, but that was probably a good thing. She needed to take it easy and not push herself yet.

When Leah appeared in the doorway, with Miriam hovering beside her, Gideon's stomach did a little flip. There was no denying their guest was beautiful. Her honey brown hair was pulled back in several twists, revealing streaks of caramel here and there that drew out the light green of her eyes. Her skin was paler than it had been when she'd first arrived at the ranch. Was that from staying inside the cabin for so many days? Or from the pain that surely still radiated in her leg? Not once had he heard a complaint, though. For a city girl, she was pretty tough.

"Ohh..." Leah breathed as she stepped out onto the porch. "It's so little."

The colt stood on the near side of his mama, alert and watching these new two-legged creatures curiously.

"Look at how long his legs are." Miriam's voice held a giggle.

Leah kept hobbling on her crutches toward the stairs, and Gideon finally realized her intent. He dropped the mare's rope and strode forward to slip his right hand under her elbow while she tried to descend the first step. "Careful there."

She turned sideways to maneuver the three steps. No matter how she turned, though, she couldn't find a way to lower herself without bending or putting weight on her right leg. She finally let out a little frustrated huff.

She was so blasted cute, he hated to deny her. But still... "It's probably better you stay on the porch anyway."

He was about to turn back to Rosie, when Leah looked up at him with the saddest puppy eyes he'd ever seen. Drifter at his hungriest moment had nothing on her beseeching expression.

Something fractured in his chest, breaking the ties that held him in place. His hands moved of their own volition as he wrapped them around Leah's so-tiny waist, lifted her from the stairs, and gently lowered her to the ground.

He had the insane urge to pull her close and wrap his arms around her. He caught himself just in time, jerked his hands away, and turned back to face the horses. His breathing was strong as he fought to bring himself under control. What was wrong with him?

Gideon stepped around to the other side of Rosie where the colt peeked under the mare's neck. Maybe the little guy had the right idea to watch from a safe position. Still, he'd brought the colt up for the ladies to see. Gideon wrapped both arms around the little body and half-led half-pushed him out of hiding and toward Leah and Miriam.

Leah held out a hand, palm up, as they approached. The colt sniffed, ready to dart back at any moment. But he seemed to approve of her, for he took another step forward, this time close enough for Leah to reach out and scratch the base of his neck.

"There's a boy. You're a cutie, you know that?" The colt sidled closer, pushing into her hand as she scratched.

As the colt moved, Gideon released him, Leah's nearness radiating like heat from a roaring fire. He had to admit, though, she impressed him with the way she handled herself around the horse. She didn't try to pet the colt's sensitive head, but started with a favorite itchy spot on the shoulder.

Miriam spoke up. "He's adorable, but I'd better get back inside or the meat will be tough as boot leather. I'm glad you brought him, big brother." She caught his gaze and Gideon could see the approval in her eyes. But when she threw a glance toward Leah, then winked at him, heat climbed up his neck.

"What's his name?" Oblivious to the silent exchange between the siblings, Leah raised her sea green eyes to meet Gideon's, causing the now-familiar flip in his stomach. He swallowed, trying to bring some moisture back to his mouth.

"Doesn't have one yet. Any ideas?"

She lowered her gaze to the copper-colored foal who sniffed his way up her arm. "Hmm... His coloring and thick body remind me of a painting I once saw of the Trojan Horse in Homer's *Odyssey*. Did you ever hear of it?" With that last question, Leah looked up at him, head cocked in innocent curiosity.

"I've heard it a time or two." Oh yes, he knew about the Trojan Horse, the one the Greeks used to sneak into the city of Troy and conquer. Pa used to tell that story when the family was gathered around the fire on winter evenings.

He studied the colt again. He did sort of look like the Trojan horse. A glance at Leah showed she was doing the same, her brows puckered and her head tilted a little.

Finally, she turned the force of her gaze on Gideon, and all former thoughts left his mind.

"So what do you think about Trojan?"

He felt himself nod dumbly. He really needed to get it together. "I think it fits him."

She turned back to rub the colt's silky neck and, for a moment, Gideon simply enjoyed the sight before him. Leah's face glowed in the light from the setting sun, the paleness now replaced with a rosy hue. She released a soft giggle as the colt reached up to sniff her chin.

"I think he likes you." Was that jealousy he felt? Pathetic. Who was jealous of a horse?

She flashed a delighted smile toward Gideon as she spoke again to the foal in a sing-song voice. "Hey, Trojan. Let's go see your mama, shall we? She's a good girl, but I bet she'd like some attention, too."

As Leah wobbled forward on the walking sticks, the colt scampered ahead to hide behind his mother again. Gideon fought the urge to step up and help her. The expression on Leah's face was grim determination, as if she were pushing through the pain, determined to make her body do what she wanted despite its complaining.

Just as Leah reached the mare, Miriam appeared in the cabin doorway. "You two about done playin' with the livestock? Dinner's ready, and if you come now, it won't be burned."

Did Leah's nose wrinkle before the mare shifted to block his view?

Chapter Fifteen

Leah squinted at the tiny hole of the needle in her hand. The mid-afternoon sunlight streaming through the open doorway glinted off the little metal cylinder, making it a challenge to poke the black thread through the miniature opening.

Miriam hummed "Holy, Holy, Holy" in the rocking chair beside Leah's bed, still stationed in the main room of the cabin. Her fingers flew as she crocheted a sock out of uncolored yarn.

"That hymn has always been one of my favorites," Leah confided. She'd finally gotten the needle threaded and created a series of knots to bind the loose ends of the thread together.

Miriam nodded agreement, but kept humming as she reached the chorus.

Emotion from the melody filled Leah's chest, and she lowered her voice to a secretive tone. "I once heard an opera soloist perform that song in my church in Richmond. It was one of the most beautiful things I've ever heard. That day, I decided that's the song I want sung over my grave when I die."

Miriam's humming ceased, as did her crochet hook, and her sea green eyes grew round as half dollars. "Leah, what a morbid thought."

A blush warmed her cheeks. "It's just such a beautiful hymn. And what better testimony after my life ends than to give praise to the One who put me here to begin with?"

Miriam's hands began to move again. "I suppose so. But I try not to think about death—mine or anyone else's."

Leah's heart went out to the dear girl. She really had been through more death than anyone her age should. It was amazing she could remain so positive and upbeat, always smiling or chattering away.

Her brother, on the other hand, was Miriam's polar opposite. Never a word unless it was absolutely necessary. And had she seen him smile yet? She couldn't help but wonder what the other brother had been like. Was he quiet and sober like Gideon? Dare she ask?

"Miriam?" Leah kept her face focused on the tear she mended in Miriam's jacket.

"Mmhmm."

"Would you mind telling me what Abel was like? Was he as solemn as Gideon is?"

Miriam looked up, a faraway look in her eyes and the hint of a smile touching her lips. "Abel wasn't solemn, not in the least. He loved to laugh and joke. He had Mama's red hair, so of course he could get riled if wanted. But he loved people."

She blinked and focused her dark green eyes on Leah. "Of course, Gideon wasn't always such a stick-in-the-mud either. He didn't joke around much like Abel, but he always had dreams and wanted to do big things. Once you got him talking about his ideas, you couldn't get him to stop." Her face held the rueful look only a sister could master.

"What kind of dreams?"

Miriam shrugged. "He carried on Pa's dream for the ranch, especially the horses. He's always wanted to breed the best horses in Montana. He's really excited about that colt he brought up a few days ago." She waved a hand dismissively. "You should ask him about the rest."

Hmm… Maybe she would.

"You said Gideon had a wife once. What happened to her?"

Miriam took so long before speaking, Leah began to think she hadn't heard. Finally, she answered, her attention never leaving the yarn and needle in her hands.

"Jane was a nice girl. Real pretty. Gideon met her down in Butte City when he'd gone for supplies. Her pa was a miner there, back when the mines were big business. I never could decide if he loved her or just felt sorry for her.

"Anyway, he brought her home and she settled in. Mama and Pa were already gone by then, and I was excited to have another woman around the house. She hated it here, though. I think mountain life scared her. Not that it was much tamer in town, but she hated the wild animals and the hard work and cooking without many store-bought provisions." Miriam stopped speaking, her eyes taking on that faraway look again. This time, though, the smile wasn't there.

"Did she run away?"

Miriam shook her head and released a sigh, dropping her eyes back to the half-finished heel in her hands.

"No, she was bit by a rattlesnake. She'd ridden out to take lunch to the boys, and I guess it spooked her horse. She made it back to the house on foot, but by then the poison was in her blood. She died that same day."

Leah's throat tightened. How awful.

"Gideon always blamed himself—for bringin' her up here in the first place, and then for not bein' there when she needed him."

"But it wasn't his fault. He couldn't have known a snake would bite her." What was this crazy need to defend the man?

Miriam shook her head. "I know that. We all tried to tell him, but he never would listen. That's about the time he stopped talkin' so much."

Leah wanted to cry. What a sad, sad story. In that moment, she wanted to make things better for this strong man who carried so much unnecessary burden. She wanted to show him the truth, help him shoulder some of his load. But why? She couldn't explain her desire, but it was so real her chest ached. Maybe she could start by helping him dream again...

Leah perched on the edge of the bed, watching Miriam scurry around the kitchen putting away dishes. She'd been up for breakfast, but her leg still ached enough it was hard to spend too much time on the crutches. Her body tired quickly these days.

"So what's on your to-do list for today?"

Miriam didn't stop to look at Leah, but kept flitting from table to counter to shelf as she answered. "I need to go out and do some weeding in the garden. The grass is almost as tall as my green bean plants. It'll take over soon if I let it."

Outside. A bit of sunshine was exactly what she needed to get her strength back.

"If you'll help me change dresses, I'll work in the garden with you."

Miriam shot a skeptical look over her shoulder as she lifted the stack of tin plates onto the shelf. "I don't know if you're ready for that yet."

"Please? I can sit between the rows and scoot along as I pull weeds." Leah tried to add a touch of sweetness to the pleading in her voice.

Miriam released a short laugh. "Leah Townsend, a member of Richmond's elite, is begging me to let her crawl through the dirt in my little garden? Your friends would never believe it."

Leah wanted to stick her tongue out at the girl, but settled for wrinkling her nose. "They'll never know if you don't tell them."

Miriam laughed again as she wiped her hands on her apron and moved toward Leah's bedroom. "Which dress do you want me to get?"

"The grey homespun. It should be in the bottom of the smaller trunk. And thank you."

Miriam rolled her eyes as she walked from the room.

Two hours later, Leah was amazed at how much work a garden was. Not that she'd complain, though. The sun was glorious on her back and she'd never known how much fun it was to crumble dirt in her hands. If only Emily could see her now. She'd either sit down and cry, or hug her sides from laughter.

Leah braced her hands in the dirt behind her, and scooted back to reveal another section of grass to pull. Her splinted leg drug in the dirt, and Leah frowned at the brown streaks on the bandages. After this little escapade, the cloth would need to be changed for sure.

She blew out a breath, hoping to clear her face of the wispy brown tendrils that had escaped her bun. They fell right back in her eyes, so she raised an arm to wipe them away.

Before reaching for another hunk of grass, she stopped to survey the four long rows of green beans, peppers, and lettuce they'd weeded. Each row was about fifty feet long, so they'd made good progress this morning. Of course, Miriam had done three to Leah's one, but it felt good to be doing something productive.

She'd better get moving again to finish this row. Miriam had already gone inside to put lunch on the table, so Leah would need to hobble in soon. She reached for a clump of grass, but a motion at the top of her vision caught her attention.

From that moment, it all happened so fast. The snake slithering toward her, its head raised not a foot from her leg. A scream. A mighty blast that was loud enough to be from a cannon. Pieces of the snake flying in all directions.

Gideon's heart pumped like the hooves of a stampeding herd as he let his gun slide to the ground. His hands balled into fists to keep from shaking as he charged toward the woman on the ground. He was pretty sure he'd gotten there before the snake struck, but his mind kept throwing images at him—Jane lying on the bed, the dress torn off at her shoulder to reveal the arm swollen three sizes too big. He saw it all again in vivid detail. Black skin seeping up to her shoulder. The look of sheer agony as tears freefell down her cheeks.

He reached the woman on the ground, and it took a moment for his mind to register what he saw. This wasn't Jane. It was Leah. Her face didn't wear the crazed fear and pain Jane's had. He crouched for a better look and drank in the trust in her eyes. No fear, just strength there. He wanted to cry.

"Are you hurt?" He heard the huskiness in his voice, but had no control to change it.

"I'm fine. Except…"

His chest picked up speed again. She *had* been hurt.

"Except what? Did it bite you?"

Her lips tipped up then. She was smiling?

"No, no. I'm fine, except…you're cutting off the circulation in my arm."

Gideon looked down at his hands. By golly, he was clutching her arm like it would save his life. He loosened his grip and rose to his feet.

"Sorry," he mumbled.

He was about to step away from the beautiful creature that had just cut ten years off his life, but a glance at his feet showed he was dangerously close to squashing a green bean plant. That would never do.

Anyway, he needed to get Leah out of the garden and back in the cabin where she'd be safe.

"C'mon. Let's get you inside." He bent down again to help Leah stand, but a look around revealed her crutches at the other end of the row.

"If you would be so kind as to bring my crutches, I can take it from there."

But when he looked into Leah's face, he saw the pain lines around her eyes and the weary expression that clouded them. It looked like she'd more than overdone it for the day.

"It'll be easier if I carry you in."

"But Mr. Bryant –"

The moment he scooped her up, her protest ceased. Once again, he was amazed at how well her petite frame fit in his arms. He carried her the thirty yards or so to the front of the cabin, and felt her head rest against his shoulder. A wave of warmth flowed through his chest, a balm to the dull ache he'd carried so long.

Miriam met them on the porch, a hand shading her worried eyes from the sun.

"Is she all right? What happened?"

"I'm fine." Leah's voice was patient, motherly. "There was a snake in the garden, but Gideon shot it before anything happened."

Gideon slipped sideways through the doorway so he didn't bump Leah. When he reached the bed, he eased her down onto it. His arms and chest immediately felt the loss.

The expression Leah turned on him though, brought the heat back into his body. Her pale green eyes shimmered and a soft smile played with her lips.

"Thank you, Gideon, for rescuing me again."

He knew he needed to say something, but with her looking at him that way, his brain just wouldn't work. He finally forced out "You're welcome" before turning away. He had to get out of here and regain control.

"Need to get my gun," he mumbled as he escaped out the door. It wasn't until he was walking toward the garden that he realized Leah had used his Christian name. Did she know she'd done it?

Chapter Sixteen

Leah sent Miriam a thankful smile as the young woman approached the bed with a pot of water and a rag.

"Thank you, Miri. I'm afraid my hands are in need of a bit of fresh water." She glanced down at her dirt-streaked dress and bandages. "I probably need to get the rest of me cleaned up, too."

Miriam flashed a sly smile, "You might also want to work on your face." She set the pot on the bed linen. "Hold on a minute, and I'll get you a mirror."

One look in said mirror brought a gasp to Leah's lips. "Oh, Miriam. Why didn't you tell me?" Dirt streaks lined both sides of her face, across her forehead, and under her left eye. She looked like the pictures she'd seen of Indians on the advertisements for a Wild West show that had come through Richmond last year.

And her hair looked like she'd ridden through a windstorm. Stray wisps stuck out around her face in every direction. Her bun sagged several inches lower than she'd pinned it that morning.

Leah looked away from the mirror to see Miriam watching her with crossed arms, amusement sparkling in her teal eyes.

"Well don't just stand there, help me." Leah dipped a corner of the rag in the water and rubbed it across her forehead. Gideon would be back in the cabin any minute, and she didn't want to be in the middle of her toilette when he entered.

Miriam rolled her eyes dramatically as she moved around to

work on Leah's hair, landing a playful swat on her shoulder in the process. "Don't worry, we'll get you all prettied up again before Gideon gets back."

Leah didn't have time to correct her, but it was a good thing the dirt covered the pink that rose to her cheeks.

By the time Gideon came back in, Leah had washed and straightened her hair. She may not qualify as *pretty*, but at least she was cleaner.

From the bed, Leah bit into her cold ham sandwich. Across the room, Miriam and Gideon ate their lunch at the table in silence. She longed to sit with them, but after the morning's events, her leg throbbed. It felt good to lean back against the wall of pillows.

She found herself sneaking glances at Gideon throughout the meal, often catching him watching her, as well. His expression could best be described as brooding. Creases formed on his forehead, and his brows came so low she couldn't see the deep green color that always captivated her.

As soon as his plate was empty, Gideon rose and whistled for Drifter, then stalked out of the cabin.

Leah heard a heavy sigh and turned her attention to Miriam, who rose to follow him. "I'll be back in a minute."

What was wrong now? Was Gideon mad at her for being out in the garden today? Or just worried? His wife had died of a snake bite. It made sense that any interaction or even a sighting of a snake would shake him up.

Finally, the click of Miriam's heels sounded on the porch. She appeared, carrying Leah's crutches, but the usual perky smile was missing from her pinched lips.

"Miriam, what's wrong with Gideon? Is he angry with me?"

Miriam's face took on a touch of bewilderment. "No, he's not mad at *you*." She shook her head and picked up Leah's tray from the side of the bed. "Don't worry about him. He just needs to work out a few things." Her lips pursed in amusement. "I think it threw him for a loop when he realized it was a harmless old garter snake."

"You mean the snake wasn't poisonous?"

"Nope." Miriam began stacking dirty dishes from the table.

Leah sank back against the pillows, all the energy sucked out of her. It wasn't poisonous. She felt a grin spill onto her lips. Poor Gideon.

It was happening all over again.

Heave. *Thwak!* Two chunks of wood sailed off the stump, landing in the piles that had already gathered.

Gideon had told himself he would never bring another woman to this place again. Ever. With another log on the stump, he heaved the ax back over his right shoulder. *Thwak!*

He'd told Abel not to do it. Women were trouble, every last one of them. And Easterners were the worst. Had Abel listened? No. And now look what had happened.

Heave. *Thwak!* His muscles griped, but Gideon pushed harder.

Heave. *Thwak!* Too hard this time. The ax lodged itself deep in the stump.

He stopped to wipe his face with his sleeve. With that woman around, he couldn't even strip off his shirt anymore.

While his muscles rested, his brain wouldn't stop. The image was seared in his mind from earlier that day. Leah, sitting between the green bean plants, her splinted leg extended, hair mussed in the cutest way.

And then, in an instant, that cute little expression turned to fear. He'd followed her line of sight to the snake and his heartbeat froze. His body reacted automatically. Before he knew what he was doing, he sighted the Winchester and squeezed. It wasn't until the striking snake dissolved into pieces, that he'd relaxed.

Why was death following him? How many people did he have to lose before it was enough? Ever since they'd moved to this wild territory in '63, people he'd loved had been picked off like a sniper's target.

But he didn't fault the land. No, the land never promised to be gentle or make things easy. It was hard and completely untamable, but gave you the feeling you'd really accomplished something. You were proud to have the chance to live another day in this fierce country of unimaginable beauty. No, the land never promised to take care of them. It was God who had made that promise…and failed.

The scissors sliced deliciously through the lavender fabric. Even though they were rusty and snagged often, these shears could get the job done. Leah didn't normally consider herself to be the destructive type, but watching the ruffles fall away gave her a little thrill.

A gasp from the doorway brought her attention up.

"You're cutting your dress?" Miriam rushed forward to pick up the long strip of lavender frill that had dropped to the wood floor. She raised mournful eyes to Leah's. "Why?" Leah would have thought she'd just kicked Miriam's puppy.

"Oh, these dresses are not very practical." She waved the scissors casually over the mass of lace and ruffles. "I only have the one wool dress I can really work in. The rest of these require bustles and extra tight corsets, and the trains are impossible to move around in. I'm going to break my other leg if I don't do something about it." She kept her tone light and teasing.

Miriam still fingered the cut fabric as if it was a dearly departed friend. "But they were beautiful."

And compared to Miriam's dingy brown garb, they were. Miriam's dress was not just an old style, it had *no* style. The high neck and straight bodice did nothing to enhance any curves. The skirt flared a little more than the bodice, but didn't gather in the back or have room underneath for more than a petticoat or two, certainly not a crinoline or bustle. The dress had obviously been made for function *only*.

Seeing the mound of ruffles in Miriam's hand gave Leah an idea. "Miriam, go get the grey dress you wore yesterday."

"What?"

"Quick, I have a wonderful idea. Is it clean?"

Nodding, Miriam moved toward her room. Leah finished cutting the ruffle from the lavender train, then snipped the layers that would have rested on the bustle. She'd need to do some hemming, but then her gown would look fine and be so much easier to work in.

"Here you go." Miriam laid the drab grey gown on the bed next to Leah.

"See here. If we start the ruffle at the top of the skirt in the back, then cross it down to the bottom around the front, then back up in the rear. It'll add fullness in the back like the current styles, and give some length to the bottom."

"Wow..." Miriam breathed.

Leah continued, "Then we can add some tucks to the bodice, maybe put a piece of this lace at the neckline to make it all blend." Leah held up the dress and lace in an attempt to illustrate her designs. "It'll be lovely."

Miriam bounced on her tip-toes and squealed like a young child on Christmas morning. "Do you mean it? Really?"

It was impossible not to grin at such a picture. "Of course. You'll look amazing." Leah barely had time to brace herself before Miriam tackled her in a hug.

"Oh, thank you. Thank you."

Leah returned the embrace, then laughed as she extracted herself. "No need to thank me. Do you want to help with the stitching or are you too busy in the garden?"

Miriam plopped down with a bounce on the bed. "I've picked everything that was ready, so I can help until it's time to make lunch." She jumped up again like a cricket. "I'll get my sewing things."

While they worked, Leah offered suggestions for Miriam's gown and continued to remove the extra trim and yardage from her own. She'd start with these three, and alter some of her other dresses later if she needed them.

"There." Miriam held up the dress, displaying a finished skirt.

"Wow, it's amazing how the ruffle brings it to life."

"Ooh, I can't wait to try it on." Miriam clutched the gown to her bosom.

Leah felt a smile spill out at the joy on her friend's face. "Finish the bodice first, though."

Miriam giggled in response.

Just then a shadow fell across the light from the open doorway, pulling the lighthearted mood from the room. There stood Gideon, his face shadowed so Leah couldn't make out his features. His broad shoulders were strong and straight as he removed his hat and turned to hang it on the hook.

When he moved out of the doorway, Leah could see the tightness of his profile—the part not covered by the mountain man beard, that is.

"Oops." Miriam jumped up and scooted toward the kitchen. "Sorry, big brother. Lunch'll be ready in two minutes. We were sewing, and I lost track of time."

Drifter padded to the bed and whined, eager for his usual greeting. She reached down to scratch behind his ear and under his chin, only removing her eyes from Gideon for a quick glance at the animal. His long tongue caught her wrist in appreciation.

Gideon didn't respond, only sank into his chair and crossed his arms, his face stoic. Of course, was that any different from his normal expression? Still, something felt different about his demeanor now.

Miriam didn't seem to notice, and kept on chattering. "You should see what we've done to my dress, brother. It's the prettiest thing you've ever seen. And it was all Leah's idea. She gave me the material, too. Cut it off of her own dress."

As Miriam chirped out those last few comments, Gideon

turned to examine the heap of fabric on the bed. Then he raised his gaze to Leah. She didn't drop her eyes or pretend she wasn't paying attention. Instead, she met his piercing gaze head on.

Was he angry? It was hard to tell from this distance. Was he just upset about the lunch? Or was it a bigger issue. Maybe he didn't want Miriam to have anything more than practical dresses. Could that be because of his experience with bringing his wife from the city to this wild country?

Leah tried to hide the apprehension that rose at the intensity of his stare. She offered the hint of a smile, trying to show him it was fine. She waited, holding his gaze, her heart wondering what he would do next. And then he did the last thing she expected. His eyes softened into a gentle smile.

Chapter Seventeen

Leah braced her weight against the work counter as she draped the thin strip of crust over the rich burgundy of the blackberry pie filling. Despite the ache when she put weight on her leg, over the past few weeks she'd learned how to move around without too much pain. It was easiest in the kitchen, where she could lean against the counter while she worked.

And who would have thought she would enjoy cooking and baking so much? Miriam always made it seem like a chore, but Leah was learning to look at it more as an art form. Especially the baking part. Now that she was beginning to understand what each ingredient added to the outcome of the dish, it was fun to experiment with flavors and textures. And since they were right in the middle of berry season, Miriam was always bringing in a basket of raspberries or blackberries or currants from the valley. Leah couldn't wait for the day when she could be the one out riding through the mountains, picking berries and helping with the animals. Patience, though.

She shot a quick prayer heavenward for continued healing. *Father, thank You for Gideon's skill when he splinted my leg. And thank You for mending the bones.*

While in this prayerful attitude, Leah's mind drifted to her new friend. *Lord, I pray You'll guide Miriam in Your path for her life. I think she feels trapped here on the mountain, with almost no interaction with other people. Help her know You haven't forgotten her. Help her trust that You have the best plan in the right timing.*

And then there was Gideon. Leah's heart ached for the man, strong and attractive, yet obviously hurting underneath his mountain man façade. *Lord, please soften his heart. Help him to heal and forgive.* She wasn't sure who he needed to forgive most, God or himself. But God knew.

Her prayer was interrupted by a clatter of steps on the porch. Miriam's blonde curls popped through the doorway and she began chattering almost immediately.

"I got a whole basket full of red currants on my way back from taking lunch to Gideon. See how big these are? We should get a bunch of jars if we make jam from these. How's everything coming for dinner?"

Leah felt a smile come on as the younger woman finally stopped for breath. "The last two loaves of bread just came out of the oven and this pie is ready to go in now. The potatoes are peeled, so there's nothing left to be done until later."

"Good. I suppose we should start on this jam then." Miriam's face pulled into a grimace. "I hate to spend the afternoon in this hot kitchen when it's so glorious outside."

Leah felt a bit of sympathy for the young woman. "If you tell me what to do, I'll make the jam. You can take the afternoon off. Get one of my books and find a cozy spot outside."

Miriam nibbled her lower lip, but then finally sighed. "No, jam is too hard to just tell you what to do. I'll have to show you the first time."

And so, they set to work. Leah watched carefully every step of the way so she would be able to do the job herself next time. She truly felt bad for Miriam, like she was caging a wild bird who just wanted to fly about and sing, making the world a lovelier place.

"You know what I always imagine when I'm stuck in the kitchen?" Miriam said as she poured sugar into the pot with the currants. She didn't wait for Leah to answer. "I imagine I'm a grand lady in a New York mansion. I sit in my summer room all morning and sip tea and eat biscuits smothered with currant jam, while talking with friends about all the latest fashions." She sighed wistfully. "What a wonderful life."

Leah couldn't help but chuckle at such naiveté. "Well, your imaginings could be technically correct from a glance, but it's really not as wonderful as you make it sound."

Miriam blinked at her, coming out of the stupor. "I forget sometimes you used to live like that. You seem so *normal*."

Leah ignored that comment as she stepped forward to stir the currant and sugar mixture, but it brought her secret pleasure. She really wanted to be normal and hardworking and helpful. That old life of idle uselessness was behind her for good.

"It might sound fun to be a lady of leisure, but it's not really what it seems. Instead of being allowed to do *nothing*, it was more like I *wasn't* allowed to do *anything*. I could only read from a select group of books, draw, play piano, or do needlework, but that was about it. I couldn't go anywhere by myself, always had to maintain my poise, couldn't walk faster than an elegant stroll, and I've never, ever ridden a horse astride. That life was so confining."

Leah stared down into the bubbling red jelly, her mind drifting to another place and time. "When I was little, I used to sneak down to the kitchen in the afternoons. Cook would let me help her pour ingredients, or mix batter, or roll out crusts. I loved feeling useful."

She was drawn from her memories by a gasp from behind.

"Speaking of pie, I think we'd better check yours," Miriam said.

Leah turned, dragging her bad leg, to watch Miriam open the oven door and pull out the golden-crusted pie. The burgundy-black filling bubbled, sending a sweet aroma through the kitchen.

"Perfect." Miriam held the steaming concoction up for Leah to examine. "Gideon would be none too happy if we burned his favorite dessert." She winked at Leah before placing the pie on an empty shelf.

Turning back to look in the pot Leah was stirring, Miriam watched the gooey bubbles for a moment. "So tell me more about your life. Were you friends with the mayor's wife and special people like that?"

"Well...I did attend many of the same dinner parties as the mayor's family, but I'm not sure I would say any of those ladies were *friends*. We were all trained to be so proper and poised, never saying what we actually thought. And most of them were so snooty they wouldn't step out in the rain, even with an umbrella."

Miriam's eyes took on innocent confusion. "Surely you must have had friends. Weren't there girls your own age?"

Leah nodded. "I would consider those girls acquaintances, really. My dearest friend was my companion, Emily Alders. She was several years older than me, but one of the kindest people I've ever met." Leah gave Miriam an appraising look. "You would have loved her."

Memories of Emily brought a familiar sting to the back of Leah's throat. Time to change the topic. "Is the jelly supposed to have foam on the top like this?"

Miriam peered into the pot. "Yep, that's normal. We just need to scrape it off. And it looks to be ready to pour into jars now. Can you do that while I start the beef for dinner?"

"Of course."

As she ladled jam from the pot into jars, Leah watched out of the corner of her eye as Miriam extracted a hunk of beef from the barrel in the corner. She placed the meat in the other pot and added enough water to cover, before moving it onto the hot part of the stove.

Leah cringed at the sight. Surely there was a different way to cook meat that wouldn't make it so tough it would wear longer than the leather soles of her boots.

Her mind filtered back to those afternoons spent in the Townsend kitchen. What had Cook done with meat? She remembered seeing the maids pounding the stuff with an iron mallet, but what would that do? Shape the meat? She didn't remember seeing any beef dishes with unusual shapes. Maybe it helped to tenderize things. It was worth a try, right?

"Miriam, I remember our cook in Richmond use to pound on the meat with a mallet after it was parboiled but before it was fried. Would it be all right if we try that?"

Miriam raised her brows, but shrugged. "Fine with me, but I don't have a mallet in here. I could go see if I can find something in Gideon's tools."

Leah looked around the room. "What if we try a frying pan instead?"

By the time they'd pounded and fried the meat, boiled and mashed the potatoes, mixed gravy in the frying pan, and arranged all the food on the table, Leah was exhausted. But she was more than a bit anxious to see if their experiment would yield any benefit in the texture of the beef.

Miriam must have noticed Leah's fatigue, for she finally pointed to Leah's chair. "Sit."

It came across as an ultimatum, so Leah obliged, sinking into the chair with painful deliberation.

Gideon came in not long after and took his normal place at the table, only nodding in response to greetings from both women. Leah's chair was across from him, and she reached out a hand to offer Drifter her normal greeting.

After Gideon said a simple blessing over the food, then loaded his plate, Leah tamped down her apprehension as he began to eat. She casually moved the food around on her own plate, trying not to appear obvious she was watching Gideon for a reaction on the food.

After half the meat on his plate was gone, she finally received the hoped-for response. He raised his head to look at his baby sister.

"Meat's good, squirt."

Miriam dabbed her mouth with a napkin. "Why thank you, big brother. Leah actually taught me a new technique. Makes the meat tender, don't ya think?"

Gideon's glance flickered to Leah, then back down to his plate as he nodded. "Seems so."

And apparently that's all he was going to say, for his fork dove back into the beef, using it to sop up mashed potatoes and gravy.

Something about this man both frustrated and drew her. Why was he so reserved? Why couldn't he open up and talk to them like any other person? It wasn't as if either of them were strangers anymore. Maybe she should try an experiment.

Clearing her throat, she began, "So, Gideon. How were the animals today?"

"Fine." He didn't even look up, just loaded potatoes and gravy on a slice of bread.

"Have there been any new calves born in the last few weeks?"

"Two."

"Oh, I'll bet they're precious. All the babies and mamas are healthy?"

"Yep."

Leah wanted to shake the man, but kept her poise instead. Perhaps all of Emily's training had been for this moment.

She needed to make sure she phrased her questions so a one-word answer wouldn't suffice. Horses were his favorites, so maybe that subject would get him talking.

"So what are you working on with Trojan these days?"

Gideon stopped chewing and his head came up. She couldn't quite read the expression in his eyes, but it was guarded.

"Leading."

This man was impossible.

She kept her voice pleasant. "Walking on the lead line? Is he learning quickly?"

"Some. He's a stubborn little guy, though."

At last. More than one word. Leah tried not to let the victory show on her face, but her heartbeat raced with delight. "Yes, I would imagine most little boys are stubborn, even the four-legged variety, but his eyes had an intelligent look."

The shield in Gideon's eyes lowered for a split second and she caught a sparkle before he replaced it. His only response was "Yep" as he reached to spoon a second helping of beef onto his plate.

Leah relished the warmth in her chest throughout the remainder of the meal. To top it all off, Gideon pushed his empty dessert plate toward Miriam saying, "Pie was good. Prob'ly the best I've tasted."

Miriam's face took on a coy expression as she rose and scooped more of the sweet stuff from the pan on the back of the stove. "It was wonderful, wasn't it? Leah made the pie."

Leah missed Gideon's reply because she kept her face focused on the berries in her own plate. The best blackberry pie he'd tasted? Heat crawled up her neck and across her cheeks.

It took her a few minutes to regain composure, but Gideon's comment to Miriam that he was headed to the barn brought Leah's attention back into sharp focus.

"Gideon," she called as she stood and reached for her crutches. He was already putting on his hat, but turned to face her. "Do you think I could follow along and learn how to milk the cow? Now that I can move around more, I'd like to help out with more of the barn chores." His stance was reluctant, so she pulled her trump card. "I know it would take some of the load off Miriam in the mornings."

He hesitated for a moment, his gaze drifting down to her splinted leg. Finally, he acceded reluctantly. "As long as you do what you're told."

She let a grin split her face. "Agreed."

Gideon was patient as she hobbled across the uneven ground toward the barn. He ambled along beside her, picking at the stem of a weed, and acting as if it always took him five minutes to walk from one building to another.

Drifter, on the other hand, dashed off toward their destination. When he'd almost reached the barn, he stopped and looked back as if to say, "What's taking you so long?" He trotted back to them and began weaving back and forth behind them, making sure they made steady forward progress.

Leah smiled. "I'll bet he's good at keeping the cows in line."

"Yep, he's a big help when I move 'em from one pasture to

another. It used to drive him crazy that I wouldn't keep my horse inside the herd with the cows." He gave a short chuckle. "Now he's mellowed out some."

Leah had never seen this side of Gideon. And she'd rarely heard him speak so many words in a full day, much less in one conversation. She wracked her brain to think of something to keep him talking. "He seems like a great ranch dog. Where did you get him?"

Gideon tossed the stem he'd been picking at. "Found him when he was a puppy on another ranch near Butte. A good dog's almost as good as an extra man, especially on a small ranch like ours."

They reached the barn, and Gideon held the door open for her. After they entered, he stepped forward and strode toward the huge mound of hay in the left corner. "I just need to fork hay to the outside horses, then I'll bring in Bethany."

True to his word, he returned soon with a spotted cow in tow. She wore a rope halter and plodded steadily, her heavy udder swinging with each step. Leah picked up the empty tin pail from beside the barn door and hobbled toward Bethany's stall. On his way into the stall, Gideon grabbed a three-legged stool, then tied off the cow near the pile of hay and placed the stool next to her side.

Gideon met Leah at the stall door and took the pail from her hand. "It's probably best you watch for now. It would be hard to sit on the low stool with your leg splinted. If she starts to move around you won't be able to get back fast enough without getting hurt."

Leah opened her mouth in protest, but swallowed the words before they made it out. She'd promised to obey orders. She closed her mouth, nodded, and moved to lean against the wall. She would watch for now, but couldn't promise she'd be happy about it.

As Gideon settled into the comfortable rhythm of milking, it seemed her viewpoint really wasn't that bad. She had the perfect angle to watch the muscles flex in his arms and shoulders as he moved. The thin cotton of his faded blue shirt hid little of his strength, sending a warm tingle in her midsection. Around him she felt... safe.

Chapter Eighteen

A yawn stretched Leah's jaw as she fastened the last button at her neck. It was nice to have her bed back in her private room, across the hall from Miriam's. She could almost hear the coffee calling from the kitchen, and for once she wished she'd not requested to take over breakfast duties. It would be nice to walk into the kitchen and smell the coffee already brewing, ham sizzling on the stove, and buttermilk biscuits rising in the oven. Well, the least she could do was have all those good smells ready when Miriam and Gideon came in from their chores.

Leah reached for the crutch and thumped her way into the main room of the cabin. Her right arm was thankful she only needed a single crutch these days.

By the time she had the biscuits in the oven and her first pan of ham sizzling on the stove, Miriam fluttered through the front door.

"G'morning," she chirped, setting the bucket of milk and a basket on the table. "I think one of the hens is setting now, so we'll have some biddies in a few weeks."

Leah reached for the basket, and Miriam passed it to her. "Biddies?"

"Baby chicks." Miriam hoisted the bucket of milk and moved over to the work table. "While I get this milk strained, can you fry up extra ham for lunch? Gideon and I will be out with the cattle today."

"Of course." Leah shifted her things to make room for Miriam. "Are you doing something special with them?"

Miriam shot her a rueful look. "It's branding time. Gideon hired a boy from one of the other ranches to help us."

"Branding time?"

"Yes, I hate this part. We catch all the new calves and put our brand on them, so folks know which ranch they belong to."

"That sounds like work, but not so bad."

Miriam wrinkled her nose. "I didn't tell you *how* we put our brand on them. The boys have a metal poker in the shape of our brand. They heat it real hot over a fire, then press it into the cow's hide." She shivered, distaste souring her expression. "It's hard to watch and smells awful."

Leah felt the blood leave her face as she listened to the description. "Oh, that does sound terrible."

The sound of the door opening interrupted their conversation. Miriam called out her usual welcome. "Hey, big brother."

Leah turned to offer her own greeting, but froze at the sight before her. Gideon had just turned from the hat rack and was moving toward his chair at the table. At least she thought it was Gideon. The man before her had the same tall, muscled frame and the same piercing green eyes. But his face did *not* wear the mountain man beard she'd become so accustomed to. He was clean-shaven, with a square jaw, and his chiseled structure intensified the emerald of his eyes. Wow.

A jab in her ribs pulled Leah's attention from the sight before her. She turned to find Miriam covering a snicker, and realized her own jaw was hanging slack. She snapped it closed and turned toward the skillet of ham, mortification floating up her neck. She hoped in spades Gideon hadn't seen her gawking.

As she forked the fried ham onto a plate and placed freshly sliced chunks in the pan, Leah's mind reviewed the brief image she'd seen of the man. Nice features was an understatement. Without the bushy beard, his face came alive, but she wished the image in her mind were sharper.

Throughout breakfast, Leah had trouble focusing on Miriam's usual chatter. She stole regular glances at Gideon, taking in the finer details of his features. His jaw was square but his chin came to a strong point. His skin held a distinct difference in color between the tan around his eyes and the creamier shade of his lower face and neck. Her fingers itched to stroke his cheeks and see if there was a difference in the texture of the two colors.

But when she glanced at him and found his piercing green gaze watching her, Leah immediately dropped her eyes and pushed away from the table. "More coffee, anyone?"

She slipped the crutch under her arm and hobbled to the stove, returning with the coffee pot and making sure to keep her gaze far away from Gideon's face.

"Thanks, Leah, but I could have got that for you." Miriam offered a sweet smile as she refilled the cup in front of her.

"It's no problem."

When she turned to pour the hot liquid in Gideon's cup, he placed a hand on top. "None for me. Gotta head out." He wiped his mouth and rose from the chair. Leah couldn't stop her gaze from rising with him. "Miri, make sure you bring a rifle. I'll pick up Jim and meet you at the overlook."

When the cabin door closed and the latch clicked, Leah heard a giggle behind her. She turned to find laughter dancing across Miriam's face.

"What's so funny?"

"He looks a lot better with a shave, doesn't he?"

Leah shot her a disapproving look, hoping it would stop any further teasing. She stacked dishes from the table, while Miriam carried them over to the wash bucket.

"I'm still waiting for an answer, Leah dear."

Leah found her most innocent voice. "And what was the question again?"

"He looks a lot better with a shave, doesn't he? Gideon shaves about once a year when summer starts to get hot. I tell him every year he should get rid of that beard for good, but he won't listen."

Her voice took on a suggestive tone. "Maybe he needs to hear it from someone other than me."

"Well it's certainly none of my business." Leah hoped she didn't sound like she was trying to convince herself. It was definitely time to change the subject. "Miriam, would you mind if I come out to watch you saddle your horse? I'd like to learn how."

Miriam's head snapped up from where she scraped a plate over the compost bucket. "You don't know how to saddle a horse?"

Leah shrugged. "The groom always cared for my mare in Richmond. Nobody ever taught me how to do it myself. Ol' Mose taught me how to harness his mules, but that's all I know."

Miriam gave her a sympathetic look. "You poor dear. We'll have to fix that now."

Leah wiped the already-clean counter, just in case dust had settled when she'd loaded wood into the cook stove. She glanced around for something else that needed doing, but couldn't find a thing. She sighed.

She'd been alone at the ranch all day, and had cleaned the cabin, forked hay into the empty stalls, picked vegetables from the garden, prepared beef crepes to fry for dinner, and made cinnamon rolls with sweet cream for dessert. The spicy aroma had toyed with her for the last hour, making her restlessness all the worse.

She glanced out the window, trying to gauge how far past noon the sun had moved. Miriam hadn't said anything about them being out after dark, although Leah really didn't know what would be involved with branding. *Lord, please don't let them be late.*

Maybe now would be a good opportunity to catch-up on her journal writing. She usually tried to write weekly, logging the recent happenings and her thoughts about them. She grabbed her crutch and headed toward her room.

No sooner had she settled herself on her bed with the book and her fountain pen, splinted leg propped on the quilt, than a strange noise drifted from outside. It sounded almost like a flock of birds, or maybe the chickens. She placed her splinted leg on the floor, grabbed her crutch, and hobbled as quickly as she could out the front door.

The noise was definitely coming from the little shed that held the chickens, and stray feathers drifted through the cracks in the boards. What was in there? A fox? Her crutch would come in handy to scare it off.

The door was unlatched when she arrived, so she jerked it open and charged in, scanning the ground for a wiry red pest. As her eyes adjusted to the dim light, Leah found herself facing a man, knife poised over his head like an ancient warrior about to throw a javelin.

The glint in his eye and the leer on his face filled her with enough fear to paralyze. While the chickens squawked about in terror, the man advanced toward her, knife raised in attack position. The blade glittered in the sunlight filtering through cracks in the boards. He looked old enough to be her grandfather, with a scruffy beard, dirty clothes, and a floppy hat.

He spoke in a throaty growl. "Hold on there, missy. Looks like I found someone to cook my supper fer me."

Leah didn't move. What did he have planned? Her mind scrambled to find a way out of this. Away from this man. Could she lock him in the chicken coop and run for help?

He was close enough now to touch her, and he rested the tip of his knife at the base of her throat. She didn't breathe, but the sharp metal burned against her skin.

He snickered. "Where's yer menfolk?"

"Will...be...back." She put great effort into not moving her throat as she spoke each word, so they came out in a hoarse whisper. He never lifted the point of the knife from her neck, and the sting became stronger.

"I reckon you'll have time to fix me supper then, won't you, darlin'?" When he spoke the last word, he reached behind her and patted her bottom.

Cold, steely fire flooded Leah's veins. If he didn't have a knife sticking in her neck, she would have taken him apart one joint at a time, right there in the chicken shed. No man had *ever* touched her in such a place, and this dirty vagabond was the last man she'd allow the right.

He seemed to sense her hatred, because his smirk dried up. His voice was rough when he spoke again. "Get on with ya and fix me some food. But jest know me and my knife'll be with ya each step o' the way."

He pulled the blade away from her throat, but kept it hovering in front of himself like a barrier.

Leah turned away from the man and limped toward the house, as much to regroup her thoughts as to obey his demands. Who was he? Had Simon sent him? He didn't look like a man her ex-fiancé would do business with, but could he be a hired kidnapper?

What was she going to do? It would be hours before Gideon came back. She racked her mind for any weapons that might be in the cabin. Gideon and Miriam had the only rifles she knew of. They did have a kitchen knife, but it was due a sharpening. Unless she could get the drop on this man, it would be no match to his razor-sharp blade.

If he wanted her to cook for him, was there a way she could poison him? Leah dwelt on that idea for a while, but couldn't think of anything better than undercooked meat. And he'd surely notice that. Maybe she could get him near the fireplace and push him into the flame. Not to kill him, just injure him long enough for her to get the upper hand. She'd have to watch for an opportunity.

Inside the cabin, Leah stoked the fire in the cook stove, then heated grease in the frying pan for the beef crepes. While she worked, her assailant leaned against the wall in the little kitchen, his white knuckles revealing a firm grip on the long knife.

God, I really need you now. Leah sent up a steady prayer as she cooked. After a few minutes, the man seemed satisfied she wasn't hiding a gun in one of the potato barrels, and meandered to sit in a kitchen chair.

Leah moistened her lips. She needed to know if this man was in Simon's employ, or if he was just a good-for-nothing scoundrel.

She tried to keep her voice casual yet firm. "My family will be back any minute." Despite her effort, the words quivered a bit. And he didn't need to know Gideon and Miriam weren't exactly family.

He gave her an evil smirk. "You better get cookin' faster then, sweetheart, so I can eat up and have some fun before I'm on my way."

The words triggered a shudder in Leah, but after she studied them for a moment, they were oddly comforting. It sounded like he was only a vagabond, planning to be off as soon as he'd gotten whatever he could from this place. She steeled her determination. She'd feed him because she had to. But she'd die before she'd let him do anything more than eat food. *Lord, please help.*

When the crepes were ready, she placed two on a plate and slid it to him. She kept her distance, watching for an escape. After he'd eaten two servings, the man sat back and rubbed his hand over the tattered shirt that almost covered his stomach. "I hope you're as good at other things as ye are at cookin'."

Leah inhaled, preparing herself for the next distraction. She pulled the tray of cinnamon rolls from where they'd been warming beside the stove.

"Would you like something sweet to finish with?" She forced sugar into her tone, so he wouldn't suspect anything more than Southern hospitality.

His eyes shrank into a greedy squint. Leah forked three rolls onto a plate, then carried the dish close enough to slide it toward him, making sure to stay well out of reach. He scarfed the food, licking his grubby fingers but leaving a sticky mess in his beard. Leah fought the urge to wretch at the disgusting sight, but turned away to keep her composure.

"More coffee," he barked.

Leah used her apron to protect her hand from the hot handle

of the coffee pot. She limped toward the table and filled his empty mug with the brew.

Before she knew what was happening, he grabbed her right arm and jerked. The force knocked the coffee pot from her hand, sending it flying across the table. Her weak leg couldn't support her resistance, and Leah found herself landing in the blackguard's lap. *Oh, God, please!*

Chapter Nineteen

Leah pushed hard against the man, but his hands gripped her thigh and arm. She pulled his hair with one hand and pushed against his chest with the other. Using every ounce of strength she possessed, she forced her way out of his grasp. But her right leg wouldn't bear her weight, and she couldn't get her left leg under her before she went down on the floor in a heap.

The man was there in an instant, kneeling over her, pinning both arms to the wood floor. Leah struggled, trying to kick him. But he had the benefit of a better position.

A noise drifted into her subconscious. A man's voice, far away? She screamed.

He swore, then bent low to push his elbow into Leah's mouth. The stench of it—of him—convulsed her stomach. She was fighting for air now, desperation clawing at her throat.

The words spewing out of the vile mouth above her only increased Leah's temper. He glanced at his knife on the table. She forced herself to slow her fighting, but not stop altogether. If she could get him to reach for the knife, she could get enough leverage to escape his grasp. Maybe he would think the struggle had exhausted her.

He took the bait and reached for the knife, keeping one hand locked around her right wrist. Leah screamed with all her might and scrambled hard to scoot away.

The cabin door burst open, and the villain over her froze. A man, silhouetted in the door frame, held a gun pointed directly at the dirty bum.

"Freeze or I'll blow yer brains out." The voice was a hard growl, but held an undertone Leah recognized.

She took the opportunity to scoot backward, far away from her captor. As she moved, the light from the door shifted—and she recognized Ol' Mose. Her heart overflowed with relief. *God, thank you!*

While Ol' Mose kept the gun on the man, Leah hobbled to the barn to retrieve a rope. Bless Gideon, the rope was hanging on the barn wall just where she hoped it would be. The braided twine was heavy as she hauled it back to the house. Inside, she held it out to Ol' Mose, but he jerked his head in the direction of the vagrant.

"You go 'head an' tie him while I keep this gun focused on his heart."

Leah's hands were shaking, as she moved behind the man. His body odor was enough to send her back outside, but she held her breath and set to work with the rope. When she'd tied the last knot, Leah backed away, her legs barely supporting her weight.

Ol' Mose gave her a look, his eyes softening. "Miz Townsend, you go on and git yerself situated while I take care o' this varmint."

"Are you sure?"

He moved in, nudging her out of the way. "Sure as shootin'."

The two men left the cabin, Ol' Mose pushing the perpetrator with his gun and spewing a steady streaming of insults about the man's character.

It was at least a half hour before Ol' Mose came back into the cabin. Leah had put her appearance back together, brewed another pot of coffee, steeped a cup of chamomile tea for herself, and was about to come looking for her friend, afraid the drifter might have found a way to get the upper hand.

As Ol' Mose entered, Leah rose from her chair, and hobbled with her crutch to take his hat. He must have read the expression on her face, for he gave her a wink as he handed off the felt piece.

"Don't you worry, missy. He won't be causin' you no more trouble."

She tried to offer a smile, but it was weak, at best. "Please come have a seat. I have fresh coffee and can offer you what cinnamon rolls he didn't eat."

"Can't say as I could pass up an offer like that." He pulled out a chair at the table and collapsed into it. "Where's Gideon and the li'l gal?"

Leah filled his mug as she spoke. "They're branding today." She tried to say it as if branding were the most natural thing in the world, spoken in all the society parties in Richmond—not something she'd heard of for the first time that morning. "I expect them back around dark, but I hope you'll stay until they get here. I know they'll want to see you." And the thought of being left alone was crippling.

"Wouldn't dream of missin' em." He leaned back in his chair, cradling the warm cup in both hands. "You sure are a sight fer sore eyes, Miz Townsend. When I left here a few weeks ago I weren't sure you'd be stayin' longer than it'd take ya to hike out. Meant to come back through in a couple days, but ol' Slip come down with the fever an' I had to git him to Helena lickety-split. I didn't want you takin' ill, neither."

A sober expression took over his face. "I hope it ain't been a hardship for ya to stay. The Bryants is good folk or I wouldn'ta left you so long."

His concern eased some of the tension in her shoulders. "It's not been a hardship at all, except for this little episode today."

His face took on such a grandfatherly warmth she wanted to crawl into his lap. "I'm awful sorry."

It took the rest of the afternoon, but Leah's nerves finally settled from the incident with the drifter. He was safely tied to Ol' Mose's wagon wheel in the barn, where he would stay until her friend drove him to the sheriff's office in Butte City the next morning.

While she finished final preparations for dinner, Leah kept an eye out for Gideon and Miriam's arrival. She had to catch them before they made it to the barn and saw the man tied to the wagon. But the sound of boots thumping on the front porch was her first alert of the Bryants' return.

Leah was at the cook stove and Ol' Mose sitting at the table, when the cabin door flung open. Gideon stood in the doorway, his hand clasping Miriam's elbow, while she peered around his large frame. His eyes scanned the room, stopping briefly on the old freighter, but finally settling on Leah.

"What's going on here?" Gideon growled the question.

She met his gaze with a calm that surprised her. "We had a visitor today. But Ol' Mose was nice enough to stop by and help me with him. I'm assuming you met in the barn?"

"Who is he?" Gideon directed this question to Ol' Mose, his voice still a growl. He kept his grip on Miriam's arm, as though he wouldn't release her until he had the situation under control.

"Some ol' varmint that stopped in fer a meal. Yer Miz Townsend had him prayin' fer mercy by the time I showed up, though. A feisty one, she is. No need to worry none 'bout her." His face split into the toothy grin Leah had come to love.

Gideon stepped into the cabin then, and released Miriam's arm. His face still held a wary look, like he was expecting a bobcat to spring from the loft or a man with a rifle to jump from the bedroom.

"Come on in and have a seat. Supper's nice and warm for you." Leah infused her voice with calm and the sweet Southern drawl she'd spent years perfecting.

"Sounds good to me," Miriam spoke for the first time, as she headed for the kitchen. "I'll pour the coffee."

The dinner table that night saw the liveliest conversation it had witnessed in many moons. Gideon's shoulders finally relaxed, and Leah's cheeks began to ache halfway through the meal from her continuous laughter at Ol' Mose's tales. He was a master storyteller to be sure, describing even the most commonplace account in a way that kept them on the edge of their hard oak seats.

"Did ya hear about Cap'n La Barge bein' arrested?"

A gasp escaped her at the familiar name. "What happened?"

Ol' Mose's face took on an I-knew-it-would-happen look. "He got caught sellin' whiskey to the Injuns. Seems he brought a bunch o' the stuff on the boat you were on, Miz Townsend."

Leah's heart fell in her chest at the news. "But he seemed like a respectable man."

Ol' Mose shrugged. "He's a business man. Prob'ly thought he'd found a way to earn some extra dollars. That reminds me of the time ol' Joe Meek was tryin' to save his woman from the Crow." And he was off on another one of his wild stories.

She even heard a soft chuckle come from Gideon's direction a few times through the evening. Especially when Ol' Mose told about the time he'd been traveling with a man named Marsh who continually bragged about his skills as a horseman. "We passed through a bit o' prickly pear an' a sticker musta got under the tail of Marsh's horse. Afore you could say ron-de-vu', Marsh was layin' spread out on top of a whole bed o' those prickles. It took us more'n a bit to git him out."

After adding his own grin to the general laughter that followed, Mose leaned forward to shove the last of his cinnamon roll through his whiskers. After swallowing the bite and licking his lips, Ol' Mose leaned back in his chair. "Miz Townsend, I do believe you're becomin' quite the cook. These sweet rolls are better'n I've tasted in a month o' Wednesdays."

Leah managed a "thank you" despite the heat flooding her face.

"Are you plannin' to stick around these parts then?" He jutted his chin toward the crutch leaning against the table. "Once yer healed up, that is."

"No, sir," Leah responded, making sure she kept her voice strong. She didn't want Miriam and Gideon to think she planned to sponge off of them indefinitely. "I'll be moving to Helena to find work as soon as my leg is healed."

A soft chuckle floated from the man. "Seems to me, ya won't

be workin' long. Those young bucks in Helena ain't gonna let a pretty li'l gal like you go unmarried." He gave Gideon's forearm a friendly shove. "I'll bet any red-blooded man in that town'd give his eye teeth to get a bride purty as her that can cook suppers like this." He waved a hand around the dirty dishes on the table.

Leah's defenses flared at the comment. "Sir, I can assure you, I am *not* planning to marry any time soon. All the men in Helena may rest assured their eye teeth will remain securely within their possession."

Silence met her declaration. Even Miriam's wide green eyes revealed shock. Leah kept her shoulders squared, though, and her chin raised. She meant every word.

Then a high cackle came from the direction of Ol' Mose, as he slapped the table hard enough to make his tin plate bounce. "Yer all right, girlie. I think yer gonna do just fine."

Gideon matched his steps to the old trapper's as they made their way to the barn. Drifter had been curled at Leah's feet when they'd left the cabin, enjoying a good ear scratch. He'd just as soon the dog stay with her anyway, to keep an eye on things. Besides, it seemed the animal was partial to their pretty visitor, too.

While they ambled, his eyes drifted upward to the stars glittering in the wide Montana sky. They carpeted the dark background, each competing to outshine the lights around it.

"It's awful nice tonight, ain't it?" The sky must have caught Ol' Mose's attention, too.

Gideon nodded, keeping his focus on the heavens, not caring if the man saw his response.

Finally, he spoke the question that had his mind bound tight. "You gonna tell me what happened?"

The old trapper released a sigh. "When I got here, the girl was holdin' her own." A pause. "I don't know how things woulda ended, but I know fer a fact the Maker does. And I trust what He decides."

Gideon didn't have an answer for that. Wasn't ready to open himself to the idea that God had any plan at all, much less a better plan. So he held his silence.

A moment later, the old man spoke again. "You've got a real nice piece o' land here, Bryant. Prettiest in these parts. God's given ya quite a blessing."

Something burned the back of Gideon's throat, but he swallowed it back down. "It's a lot of hard work." He felt Mose's shrewd gaze on him.

"How are things goin' for ya, son?"

Gideon swallowed again, debating on how honest he should be. He really didn't have anyone to confide in. Miriam maybe, but his sister carried so much burden already with the house and gardens. And she was just a kid still. It was good she had Leah to help with things now. For a little while, anyway. He released a breath and ran a hand through his hair. The short locks still felt strange, but kept him cooler in this hot weather.

"Well..." He paused, his mind working to string together the right words. "I'm short-handed with the stock. Not sure how things'll go through the winter."

Ol' Mose nodded. "You thinkin' to hire someone on?"

"Maybe." He'd been struggling with that idea for a while, actually. He just couldn't bring himself to replace Abel. Not until he had to. It didn't seem right for a stranger to be working alongside him where his brother should be.

The older man was quiet for a few moments, as they both stood in the middle of the yard, staring into the night sky. Gideon found his mind drifting back toward the house. For some reason, he didn't think of Leah as a stranger working on the ranch. He'd gotten used to her presence around the house, had come to enjoy it really. She seemed to fit right in. And she acted like she didn't mind the work or the remote life. She was a bit of a mystery, the way she'd come from such a wealthy background, but jumped right into work with the rest of them.

"So how're things going with your pretty houseguest?"

Had his thoughts been so transparent? Gideon kicked at a clump of oatgrass, his gaze no longer turned upward.

"Fine, I reckon."

"I see she's turnin' out to be quite a cook."

Gideon shrugged, trying to keep his manner as casual as possible. "She does all right for a city girl."

A snort erupted from the man at his side. "She might be a city gal, but she's got more gumption than most men I've seed raised in the back-country."

Gideon didn't respond and Ol' Mose allowed the silence to settle again. He knew the words were true. Leah'd shown gumption in the way she'd handled the pain of her broken leg, the way she'd pushed herself to help with every chore she could, the way she'd learned how to cook better than Miriam in just four weeks. She didn't fear this mountain life the way Jane had. No, Leah embraced it. Thinking back to his impression of Leah when he first saw her in the kitchen of their little cabin, he never would have expected it.

"Ya know," Ol' Mose's shaky voice broke through Gideon's thoughts. "A wise ole trapper I knowd once used to say 'Don't ever judge a book by its cover'. I reckon he meant to always give a person a fair chance to prove their mettle. No makin' an opinion 'cause of something that happened to you awhile back."

How exactly did this man do it? Were Gideon's thoughts that evident? He stared into the blackness in the direction of the road. He *had* assumed Leah's background would make her just as frightened of the mountain as his deceased wife had been. After one look at her in that little hat and the fancy dress with all the ruffles, he'd formed an opinion. But she was starting to convince him he may have been wrong.

He turned and pulled a hand from his pocket to clap the old man on the shoulder. "Sounds like your trapper friend was a smart man."

Ol' Mose gave him a grin that seemed to say "I'm glad you saw the light", then he nodded. "He was, at that. Now it's time for me to git these ol' bones bedded down. I'll be headed out again in the mornin'."

Chapter Twenty

Leah dried her water-pruned hands on her apron and turned away from the work counter as Miriam strode into the cabin. "Lunch dishes are done," she announced. "What's on our schedule for this afternoon?"

Miriam stepped into the kitchen, a grimace on her face, and reached for the large pot with caster feet from under the counter. "It's time to kill a chicken."

That caught Leah's attention. "Kill a chicken? You mean to eat?"

"Yes." Miriam's voice was full of reluctance. "The young roosters are old enough now, so we'll fry one for dinner tonight."

"All right." Leah had never really considered how the meat had gotten to their kitchen in Richmond, or even in Montana. Now she realized the birds she'd been helping to feed for the last few weeks were intended for more than producing eggs. She swallowed. How hard could it be? "What can I do to help?"

Miriam carried the pot toward the door. "I have everything set up beside the barn. Put on an old dress and apron and come on out. I'll show you what to do."

Leah obeyed, exchanging her apron for one from the bottom of the stack on the hook. She was already wearing the grey wool work gown she'd worn on the train from Richmond. She grabbed her crutch and followed her friend outside. Her steps were quicker now, almost as fast as before her fall.

When Leah hobbled around the corner of the barn, she found the pot sitting over a small campfire. Nearby, an ax lay on a stump. Miriam was nowhere in sight, but a sudden ruckus from the direction of the chicken coop gave Leah an idea as to her whereabouts.

Soon, Miriam rounded the barn with a determined set to her jaw and a rooster dangling by its legs in her left hand. She threw a glance in Leah's direction. "You may want to step back for this part, it gets kind of messy."

Very curious, but wanting to follow directions, Leah took a step away from the tools laid out. Miriam never hesitated, but strode right up to the sawed-off tree base, picked up the ax in her right hand, dangled the chicken over the stump so its head lay on the wood, and brought the ax down hard.

The ensuing scene was not pretty. Wings flapped and blood sprayed. Leah spun away, leaving Miriam to control the chaos. When the scuffling noises settled down, she finally worked up the nerve to look again. It's a good thing she'd never been squeamish at the sight of blood, for there was plenty of it around the chopping block. Miriam held the chicken with both hands away from her body, her face turned to the side to avoid splatters from the red that continued to pour from the carcass in her hands. She gave Leah a sympathetic look, but Leah wasn't sure if the look was really intended for her or for the poor chicken.

The next few steps were not as sad or gory, as they dipped the carcass in boiling water for a short time, then removed the feathers. After that was complete, Miriam sent another sympathetic look in Leah's direction. That expression launched a sinking feeling in Leah's gut, but surely whatever lay ahead couldn't be half as bad as killing the chicken had been.

She was wrong. The cleaning out of the bird was arguably the worst part of the whole nasty job. But she managed to keep her own lunch in her stomach, sometimes only by looking away as Miriam continued to work.

By the time they were back in the kitchen with a chicken body in the basin next to the work counter, Leah didn't think she would ever eat again. She really wanted to lie down, but one glance at Miriam's blood-covered apron and her own slightly-spattered covering brought necessity to the forefront.

"Miri, let me have your apron and I'll put it to soak. Do you have blood on your dress, too?"

Miriam examined her arms and skirt, then scrunched her nose at Leah. "I'm a mess."

And she was. From her mussed hair to her stained clothing. Love welled in Leah's chest for her vivacious friend who had the courage to do whatever was necessary. She slipped an arm around Miriam's shoulders. "Why don't you go change into something clean while I get things ready? Then you can read from *Pride and Prejudice* while I do the washing."

When Miriam turned a thankful look to her, Leah could see exhaustion tugging at the corners of her friend's eyes.

By the time Gideon came in for dinner that night, Miriam's enthusiasm seemed to have returned.

"Hello, big brother," she chirped, while Gideon hung his hat on a peg. Leah couldn't help but notice how his brown cotton shirt stretched across his broad shoulders. He resonated strength with every movement.

"Hello, Gideon." She offered a tentative, welcoming smile as she carried the plate of fried chicken to the table. Her greeting earned a nod, as his gaze snagged on hers before traveling to the plate of chicken.

"Food looks good."

Leah couldn't keep her grin inside. That was high praise from the man who didn't understand a need for words during daily interaction.

Miriam poured coffee while Leah brought the last of the food. When they were all seated, Gideon offered his typical succinct blessing, and Leah found herself adding her own silent entreaty. *Lord, please help the chicken to be good.*

The meal began in comfortable silence, with only the sounds

of eating utensils scraping tin plates. Leah wanted to sample her cooking, but just a glance at the chicken brought images to mind that turned her stomach. So, she settled for an extra biscuit and green beans. Maybe she would sneak a slice of ham later.

Gideon didn't seem to hold the same reluctance toward the meat. He piled two large pieces on his plate and dove in with gusto. In a matter of minutes, both sections were reduced to mere bones. As he loaded another wing and both legs onto his plate, Gideon's focus drifted to Leah. When their eyes met, heat rose to her cheeks, but didn't drop her gaze.

"Chicken's good." A twinkle glimmered in his emeralds, sending a flood of warmth through Leah's chest.

"Thank you." She held his gaze for a moment longer, until he dropped his to the chicken and began eating again.

Leah turned her attention to Miriam as the girl spoke. "So, Gid, how many cows are left to calve?"

"Five." His response was quick and certain. He'd obviously been keeping a tally.

"Do you have any new calves right now?" News about the stock always fascinated Leah. She hoped one day she would be able to see the animals.

"There's a couple that are a few weeks old. Both females."

"Is that good or bad?" The fact he'd called out the gender must be important.

"Good. We keep the females to grow the herd. Bull calves have to be sold off eventually."

Interesting. In a world where women were considered not as important as men, the females of the cattle species were more desired than males.

The meal finished not long after, and Leah rose to stack the dirty dishes. Miriam combined the food scraps into a plate for Drifter. She whistled as she carried the plate across the room to his usual corner, and the dog jumped up from his perch beside Gideon's chair, padding eagerly toward his dinner.

Instead of heading to finish the chores in the barn, Gideon remained seated, sipping coffee thoughtfully.

Leah kept an eye on him as she worked, wondering at his unusual behavior. "Can I refill your cup?"

Her question seemed to break through his trance, and he set the mug on the table. "Sure."

Leah went to the stove for the pot, but felt his stare follow her as she hobbled. The hard boards still strapped to her leg kept her gait stiff.

She didn't use the crutch in the kitchen anymore, but found she could limp around in the small space without wearing out her leg too quickly. As she poured the steamy liquid into Gideon's mug, he watched the dark brew rise up the sides of the light brown pottery.

"I think it's about time to take the splint off your leg."

Leah's eyes flew to his face, surprise stealing her attention. He didn't meet her gaze, but something tugged at the pot in her hands. Looking down, she found Gideon taking the handle from her, coffee overflowing from his mug to form a wide black circle on the wood table. Oh no.

"I'm so sorry." She allowed Gideon to take the coffee pot while she wiped the mess with a rag from the table. Heat crawled up her neck, but she kept her attention on her work.

When the spill was cleaned, she reached to take the pot from Gideon's hands. He didn't release it. Reluctantly, she raised her head to see if he was angry.

It wasn't anger that darkened his face, but amusement. His dark green eyes danced and his lips pursed, rising on his left side to create the most gorgeous dimple. Her insides melted just a bit. *My goodness, he was handsome.*

Before she lost herself, Leah took a step back. She needed to say something. Just then, her mind remembered the words that had brought on this little mess to begin with. Leah blinked, trying to clear the fog from her mind.

"You think I should remove the splint, then?"

"Yep." Gideon kept the dimple in his left cheek, as if he knew she was struggling to keep herself composed.

Leah released a slow breath. "All right, I'll do it tonight."

He shook his head, raising the full mug to his lips. "I need to take a look at it before we cut all the bandages, make sure the bones have joined the way they should."

The thought of his attentions sent a skitter of apprehension through her. Slowly, she nodded. Gideon seemed to know what he was doing, and Miriam had said he was the next best thing to a doctor when it came to broken bones.

Gideon nodded as well, then set his mug on the table and rose from his chair. The matter seemed to be settled in his mind.

Chapter Twenty-One

*A*fter the chores were complete, Leah found herself seated on the floor of the main room, the hem of her dress pulled up just enough to reveal the splint on her right leg. Miriam crouched on one side and Gideon's large form kneeled on the other. If Emily could see her now, she would be appalled. A man allowed to see not only Leah's ankle, but her entire lower leg.

There didn't seem to be another option, though. She would have to think of him as a doctor. That wasn't too hard to do as he removed a large knife from the pouch at his hip and carefully sliced through the outer strips of fabric. When the wood fell away from her leg, relief flooded the area where the sticks had rubbed.

Then he began to unwrap the bandage that covered her skin, and Leah found her eyes drifting to Gideon's face. His focus was intense as he studied her leg where the cloth had been. Twin lines formed between his dark brows, and her fingers itched to smooth the pucker. A shadow of stubble had grown on his face. The distinct line across his cheeks had softened, the pale skin across his jaw having turned golden.

Just then, he turned to look at her. She'd been caught staring. Heat flushed her cheeks, but he was kind enough not to react.

"From the outside, it looks like the bone healed well. You should go easy on it for a few days until it gets used to carrying weight without the splint. And use both crutches again."

Leah couldn't help but wrinkle her nose at that suggestion. As happy as she'd been to receive them, and as thankful as she was for the freedom they'd given her early on, she couldn't wait until she never had to look at the encumbering sticks again.

"If you put too much weight on the bone too soon, you'll risk a permanent limp, or even another break."

The impact of his words settled over Leah like a sobering cloak. She nodded, and Gideon rose to his feet, sheathing the knife. While Miriam gathered the sticks and dirty bandages, Leah flipped her skirt over her toes and slowly flexed her foot. The muscles burned, but it seemed to be more from disuse than the sharp ache of the broken bone.

Miriam and Gideon stood on either side to help her to her feet, then Miriam handed Leah the crutches. Leah gave them both as bright a smile as she could muster through the sting in her leg. "Thank you so much for your help. My leg feels much better now."

Gideon eyed her with a wary expression, as if he knew her words were an act.

"I think I'll take my leave for the night. We've had a busy day." Leah was ready to escape to her room where she could rest without having to maintain a strong front. It *had* been a trying day, first with the chicken lesson and now with the renewed pain in her leg.

Miriam scurried forward to give Leah a hug. "G'night, Leah. Sleep well."

Leah balanced the crutches at the crook of her arms as she squeezed her friend back, noticing Gideon watching them both. His expression was hard to read, almost a mixture of yearning and reserve, as if he were holding himself back from something he desperately wanted.

As she leaned back from Miriam's hug, Leah glanced at Gideon again and found he had turned away. She gripped her crutches and hobbled toward her room. "Goodnight all," she called over her shoulder.

A few weeks later, Gideon found himself riding toward the barn earlier in the evening than usual. A newborn calf lay across his legs, its head rocking with the rhythm of the horse's gait. Every so often, the calf would offer a sad bleat, as if mourning the fate of its mother, who had abandoned it into this cold, scary world.

He rubbed the animal's soft neck. "It'll be all right, girl. We're goin' to a place where they'll take good care of you."

Poor little thing. The birth had been hard, with the calf turned the wrong direction and coming out tail-first. His pulse kicked up a notch, remembering the struggle as he and the mama had fought to bring the calf into this new environment. It took a couple of hours, which had been more than the mama could handle. She'd died shortly after the little fighter stood to her feet, leaving Gideon to care for her offspring.

He hoped Leah and Miriam would be willing to take over, since they would be close to the barn during the day. As many times as Leah had asked to ride down to see the herd and the new calves, she would probably be excited to help care for the little heifer. For a city girl, she certainly had taken to ranch life. He still couldn't believe she'd plucked and cleaned that chicken, although it hadn't escaped him she'd not taken a bite of it. Still, she didn't complain.

For now, the most important thing was to get some milk in this calf. The mama had not been strong enough to stand and nurse, so the little one hadn't had a good meal yet.

As he rode into the ranch yard, he spotted Leah in the garden, holding a very full apron in both hands. She was regal, even covered in dirt with her hair falling in tendrils around her face. He headed that direction, and as soon as she saw him, she dumped her load at the edge of the garden and hobbled in his direction. The stubborn girl had stopped using the crutches, even though the bone probably still gave her pain when she walked.

As she neared, her pretty face lit like a lantern in a dark barn.

"You brought us a calf?" Wonder filled her voice.

He nodded. "She had a hard birthing and the mama didn't make it. I brought her up here so we can feed her until she's weaned."

A shadow crossed Leah's face when he mentioned the birth, but faded away as she reached to stroke the calf's velvety face. Its tongue snaked out to catch her wrist and Leah smiled like a child given a new toy.

He could have sat there all day and watched that smile, but the calf was already weakening. It needed nourishment soon or it would meet the same fate as its mother.

"I need to get her to the barn and feed her. Have you skimmed the milk from this morning yet?"

Leah's gaze lifted from the cow to his face, as her other hand drifted up to shade her eyes from the glare of the sun. Her face, always so easy to read, showed her mind turning as she tried to understand the reason behind his question.

"No, we were letting the cream rise to make butter."

He nodded, "Fine. Can you stir it good and bring me half of what's there? You can let the rest separate again. We'll need to split out half of Bethany's milk for this little girl for a while." He patted the soft shoulder in his lap.

Leah nodded, giving the heifer a final rub before moving toward the cabin. "I'll bring it to the barn."

By the time he had the calf settled in a stall and the saddle stripped from his horse, Leah and Miriam had made it to the barn with the half bucket of milk. Miri set it down and squealed softly when she saw the calf, then eased into the stall with her palm outstretched. The little one was wobbly on its feet, but at least it was standing.

Gideon grabbed the bucket handle and slipped into the stall next to his sister, leaving Leah to watch from the open gate. He kneeled in front of the calf, dipped his index and middle fingers in the milk, and then held them in front of the cow's nose. She sniffed for a second, and nosed his fingers, pushing them away in the process. He dipped them in the milk again, then prodded the calf's lips, slipping his fingers into her mouth. His fingers tingled as she sucked once—a good start. Once she got used to the sucking motion, he would draw her head down to the milk in the bucket and help her learn to drink.

"Can I try?" It was Leah's rich voice, drifting to him from just behind his right shoulder, not outside the stall where he'd left her. She stepped beside him and kneeled, only slightly awkward with her weak leg.

Without waiting for his response, Leah dipped her fingers in the bucket of milk and held her index and middle fingers out to the calf, the same way he had done. She'd been paying attention. The calf began to suck her milk-laced fingers, eliciting a soft giggle from the woman beside him. But she didn't pull back.

Gideon picked up the bucket by the base and held it toward the calf with both hands. "See if you can draw her mouth down into the milk."

The calf continued to suck as Leah lowered her hand into the bucket. But just before the little nose touched milk, it broke suction. Leah dipped her finger in the milk and tried again. This time, the calf's nose dipped into the liquid and it came up sputtering and blowing. Its long tongue reached out to lick the white film from its wet nose.

"Try it again," Gideon said, but Leah was already dipping her fingers in the milk. She had natural instinct around the animals, and seemed to enjoy them, if the enraptured expression on her face was any sign.

This time the calf continued to suck Leah's fingers even after its mouth dipped into the milk.

"Good," Gideon coached, keeping his voice hushed. "Now see if you can gradually pull your fingers out of her mouth and let her keep drinking the milk."

Leah moved slowly, and the trick worked like a charm. She withdrew her fingers from the milk, but the calf continued to drink, gulping like a dying man at an oasis in the desert.

Leah sat back on her heels, releasing a satisfied sigh. Gideon couldn't help but watch the woman, the view of her much more captivating than the new calf before them. Her hair was a rich caramel in the dim light of the barn, with several layers falling from their pins in loose waves on her neck and shoulders. The features on her face were fine, straight and proportioned almost perfectly. Feminine, but not fragile. Her cheeks were tinted pink, probably from the excitement of the moment.

She turned then, and he felt himself falling into the depths of her green gaze. Her eyes were windows, displaying her innermost thoughts. In them was vulnerability...and something else. Trust? Before he could be sure, she dropped her gaze, a deeper red suffusing her cheeks. His hands itched to touch her face, so soft and inviting. He would raise her chin for another look through that window. For some reason, he wanted to know what this woman thought. How she felt about this place...about her life...about *him*.

A stirring in the hay behind them brought Gideon's attention back to his surroundings. Miriam. He'd forgotten she was standing there. If she'd noticed his ogling, he was sure to hear about it later.

He turned back to the calf and found Leah scratching behind its ear, the same way she rubbed Drifter. The little animal had its neck stretched out, relishing the bliss of the massage. He couldn't help but smile at the picture they made. If she'd been raised out west and not in some fine eastern city, she would have made a good rancher's wife.

Chapter Twenty-Two

Leah dragged the bucket up the porch stairs, hanging onto the rail to aid her efforts. This was her punishment for stuffing all the produce into a single bucket instead of making multiple trips. If only her right leg wasn't so weak.

She limped into the cabin, leaning hard to balance the weight of her load. Once inside, she allowed the bucket to clatter to the floor while she stopped to remove her coat and hang it on the peg. With the close of September coming soon, the temperatures had begun to drop, requiring a coat most days.

"Looks like there was a lot left to pick." Miriam's voice carried from the rocking chair near the fire, the chair that had been her mother's. Leah knew from past conversations that it was one of Miriam's most prized possessions.

"Yes, quite a few green beans, some corn, and a couple of tomatoes." Leah puffed out a breath with her bottom lip extended, sending the flyaway hairs around her face blowing in all directions. "I got everything, though. The corn stalks are turning brown, so I think that might be the last of it this year."

Leah picked up the bucket again and hauled it awkwardly toward the kitchen, placing it next to the work counter with a thud. She stopped to catch her breath, and finally released a sigh. She turned to stare across the room where Miriam was working. "Miri, do you think I'll always have this limp?"

Miriam looked up, and Leah could see her raised eyebrows even from where she stood. "Don't be silly." A smile laced her voice. "I know it was painful, but the bone was only broken in one place. Soon it'll be completely well."

Her frustration softened. Miriam always knew how to cheer her up. Leah hobbled across the room to visit with her friend for a minute. A break might help her aching leg, as well.

She settled in her usual ladder-back chair, stretching her right leg in front of her. "What are you working on?"

Miriam looked up from the needle as she pulled it through a piece of flexible brown leather. "Gideon's buckskins." Her focus dropped back to her work, seeking out the next stitch. "I didn't get them mended last winter, so I'd better get it done before the first snow or Gideon will have my head." A smile touched her features, revealing she wasn't too concerned about the probability of that coming to pass.

"What does he use them for?" Leah leaned forward, examining the leather more closely.

Miriam's hands stopped moving and she looked up sharply, her golden brows rising. "He wears them." Curiosity took over her face. "Haven't you seen buckskins before?"

Leah raised her own brows in retort. "Not that I know of."

"Well then," Miriam secured the needle and began to shake out the leather, holding it up for Leah to see. "This is what Gideon wears in the winter, especially when the snow hits." The leather was stitched into a tunic-style shirt. "It's made from deer skin and is mostly waterproof, plus it's really insulated. Sometimes the snow can last for weeks up here, so a good set of buckskins can save a man's life when he's working outside."

Leah reached out to finger one of the sleeves. "It's softer than I expected. Now that I think about it, I saw a couple of men wearing these when I first arrived in Fort Benton."

Miriam nodded. "Most of the trappers and Indians wear these."

Leah glanced at the stack of leathers next to the rocking chair. "Can I help?"

"Sure, you'll have to use my extra glover's needle for the leather." She handed Leah another folded leather tunic and a large needle with a triangle-shaped point. "Make sure your stitches are really small like this. Anything farther apart will let out too much body heat at the seams."

Leah examined Miriam's work, seeing the miniature stitches. Much like the embroidery she used to do in Richmond. Not her favorite, but she was certainly capable.

While Leah settled into her needlework, Miriam began her usual chatter. "I noticed the corn husks are extra thick this year. That means we're gonna have a hard winter. Pretty soon Gideon will start hunting again and we'll have fresh meat, now that the weather's cool enough to store it. I can't wait to stop eating all this salted beef and pork." She wrinkled her nose, calling attention to the light dusting of freckles across her cheeks.

"Do you ever hunt with him?"

Miriam's face took on the look of a sad puppy. "I went a few times, but never could bring myself to actually shoot an animal. The boys used to tease me something awful."

"So you know how to shoot a gun?" Leah's hand slowed as she waited for Miriam's response.

The girl's face turned even softer than before, her lips curving a bit. "Papa never wanted me to do the same things the boys did. Said I was a young lady and should be treated like one." She swallowed, her voice quivering the slightest bit. "But after he was gone, Gideon taught me. He taught me how to shoot and ride and rope. He used to let me go with him to help with the cattle sometimes. But that was mostly before Mama died." Her voice trailed off.

"Can you shoot as well as your brother?" Leah asked, trying to steer the conversation in a more pleasant direction.

It worked. The sparkle began to gleam in Miriam's green eyes again. "No one can shoot as well as Gideon. I don't think he's missed what he's aimed at since he was ten years old."

Leah found herself sharing the smile that Miriam flashed. Then a thought came to her—an exciting idea. "Do you think you could teach me to shoot a gun, too?"

Miriam seemed to ponder that for a moment, then her smile took on a trickster's gleam as her gaze dropped back to the sewing in her hands. "I don't think so."

If Leah didn't know better, she would have thought Miriam had an ulterior motive. Something about the way the girl wouldn't look her in the face...

"And why not, if I may ask?"

"Oh, I think it would be better if Gideon teaches you. He always says I don't hold the gun right, and I'd hate to show you something wrong."

What was this little magpie up to? Surely she wasn't trying to play matchmaker. But the aura of feigned innocence was rolling off her in waves.

"Miriam..." Leah infused a hint of suspicion in her tone. "What are you up to?"

Before she had time to mull through answers to her questions, Miriam snipped off her thread and set the buckskin aside.

She stretched and yawned, obviously trying to change the subject. After leaning back in the chair, she gave Leah a too-perky smile. "So what are you planning for dinner?"

Later that evening, Leah stirred the beef stew in her bowl while Gideon and Miriam dove into their own servings. She certainly would be happy to have something to cook besides the soured beef or pork, especially if she didn't have to kill and gut the animal herself.

She snuck a glance at Gideon, admiring how the green in his shirt brought out the same in his eyes. Then she noticed the dark circles and lines that had formed under those amazing eyes. Hmmm...

He was scarfing down his food, and at first she had simply

thought him hungry. Now she saw the tension in his shoulders and jaw. He'd come in late for dinner tonight, too. Was something wrong with the stock?

"How are the herds today, Gideon?"

He gave her a quick glance, then ducked his head for another bite. "Good. Moved them to the south valley today so they could have some protection from the snow."

Leah's interest was piqued, and not just because Gideon had spoken more than two words. "Do you think it's going to snow soon then?"

He glanced toward the window, although it was too dark to see anything outside. "Tonight, most likely. The clouds are low n' thick, and the moon had a halo last night. Temperature's dropping fast." That seemed to be all he was going to say, for he dove back into his stew, eating with an urgency that Leah now felt, too.

When his second bowl was empty and Gideon leaned back in his chair, Leah rose and asked if he was ready for leftover apple pie.

"Not yet." His chair scraped on the floor as he scooted backward.

She turned to face him, sure the question showed on her face without needing to be voiced.

He answered as he grabbed his coat and hat from the pegs on the wall. "There's too much to do before the snow hits. Can it wait until later tonight?"

She offered a friendly smile to show she understood. "Of course. Is there anything I can help with outside?"

He finished buttoning his coat and reached for two of the lanterns on the wall that poured light into the cabin. "I guess you can come help with the animals if you want. Make sure you bundle up."

And then he was gone. Leah tried not to be offended that he hadn't waited for her to walk with him. Gideon may not say much usually, but his actions almost always reflected those of a gentleman. For him to decline apple pie and then leave her in his dust, he must really be worried about the weather.

As she limped through the barn door a few minutes later, she found Gideon with a double-armload of hay, tossing it into each stall as he walked. He saw her almost immediately, and called from half-way across the barn, "Can you let the stock in and milk Bethany?"

"Of course." It felt good that he was finally allowing her to help, to work beside him. Leah moved as quickly as possible, bringing in the horses and milk cow, then the calf from her separate corral.

While Bethany munched hay, Leah milked. She usually took time to enjoy the rhythm and peacefulness of the milking process, but the temperature seemed to be dropping fast. And the sounds of Gideon moving around in the barn drifted into the stall with an underlying urgency.

After milking, she poured half of the creamy white liquid into the bucket in the calf's stall, giving her an affectionate scratch on her glossy black neck. Next, she went in search of Gideon, finding him near the front stalls where the wagon horses were kept. He deposited the two buckets in his hands near the other three already on the ground, all full to the brim with water.

Leah watched his face as she approached, seeing the worry lines around his eyes. "What can I do next?"

He looked around, running a hand through his coffee-colored hair. "I think that's it for the barn. Head on back to the house now. I'll be in soon."

She studied him a moment longer. She hated to go into the cabin if there was more work to do outside. Gideon still stood with his hand in his hair, fingers pinching the ends of his short locks, while his mind ran through scenarios or to-do lists or who knew what.

Then he seemed to realize she was watching him, and he gave her a sheepish smile, dropping his hand to his side. "Go help Miriam. I'll be inside in a few minutes."

"Are you sure there's not anything else I can do out here?"

Gideon's gaze locked with hers and, for a moment, he

lowered the shield to allow a glimpse at his emotions. What she saw in that moment gripped her chest—fear and exhaustion and need all swirling together in those deep emerald pools.

"Gideon..." She took an impulsive step forward, holding his gaze. "Please let me help." She hoped he saw the pleading in her eyes, heard it in her voice. She wanted to help this man more than anything—and not just to prepare for the snow. She wanted to help shoulder his burdens, lighten his load, make him smile again.

And then he released a pensive breath, his eyes asking if she really meant it.

"Please." she urged.

"Leah..." With the sound of her name, she saw the tug-of-war playing in his heart. This fear of losing people had such control over him. *God, please show him Your peace.*

At last, he breathed a sigh and spoke. "All right. I need to string a rope between the house and barn, then bring a week's worth of firewood onto the porch."

She nodded. "Let's do it."

They worked together as a team, Leah doing her best to think ahead to his next step. It felt right, working beside this man.

When the last load of wood was stacked on the front porch, Leah turned to scan the yard where the light shone from the lantern Gideon had hung on a post. A few snow flurries caught her attention, sending a tingle of excitement through her.

"Look." She pointed toward the light, and he came to stand beside her. He was almost close enough for his arm to brush hers, and his nearness consumed any other thought she'd had. What would he think if she leaned into him, rested in his strength?

"It's the first snow of the winter."

"It's beautiful." She spoke softly, not wanting to break the spell created by the darkness, the snow, and his nearness. The flurries were coming thicker now.

"Yes, it is." His voice was low, husky.

She turned to look at him and found his gaze intent on her. Leah's breath caught. His amazing green eyes, looking at her that way...

The squeak of the door interrupted her thoughts, as Miriam stepped onto the porch and came to stand beside them.

Chapter Twenty-Three

$\mathcal{L}$eah plunged the head of the ax into the icy bucket, more like she was churning butter than splitting wood. The metal end was so heavy it took all her effort to raise it over her shoulder, so this method worked better for her. It was the third time today she'd cracked the ice in the buckets for the stock near the barn.

The snow from three days ago still came to her knees, and Gideon had said they might get more any time. He'd been nice enough to clear a trail between the house, barn, and outhouse. She wasn't sure she could have tromped through the deep stuff with her weak right leg. Why had she ever thought snow was fun?

When she finally heard the splash of water under her ax, Leah gave Bethany a pat and let herself out of the milk cow's stall. She surveyed the barn, going through her mental checklist. The animals all had hay and water, including the stall where Gideon would put his mount when he came back from tending the herd. He was late tonight, but that didn't surprise her. The deep snow made everything harder.

Leah leaned the ax against a wall and let herself out of the barn, moving stiffly toward the house. She couldn't feel her hands inside the leather gloves Miriam had let her borrow. It was colder out here than she'd thought possible.

She cocooned her head in her blue cloak and hood, trying to focus on the fire blazing in the warm cabin. She'd left Miriam with instructions about when to remove the rice and beef bake from the oven, but she'd feel better knowing it hadn't burned.

A whistle from behind brought Leah's head from her cocoon, and she turned to find Gideon riding into the yard. Drifter trotted through the snow behind him, following in the horse's tracks. Sitting tall in his buckskins and leather hat, Gideon made an attractive picture, with his strong jaw and clean-shaven face. Would he let the mountain man beard grow again now that cold weather had come? As practical as it was, she hoped not. It would be a shame to cover up that face.

He was headed in her direction, and Leah stood waiting for him, soaking in the sight as he approached. It wasn't until he reined in, that she saw the bulky object sitting behind his saddle.

She raised her gaze to his face. "What do you have?"

The corners of his mouth played as he dismounted, not answering her question.

She tried again. "What is it?"

He turned to her, a hint of pride playing across his face. "I brought you fresh elk meat. That's why I was late for dinner. This fellow came across my path, and I couldn't pass him up."

Leah felt her eyes widen as she followed Gideon around to the other side of the horse. Draped behind the saddle was a large leather-wrapped bundle with a rack of antlers poking through an opening. Good thing the rest of the animal was covered. A wave of sadness washed over her at the thought of the majestic animal dead. She forced herself to remember this was just the pattern of life, God providing for their needs.

Gideon seemed to notice her reticence, and touched her arm as he spoke gently, "I'd better get this guy to the barn, then I'll be in the house."

Leah inhaled a breath and turned to face him, forcing a bright smile on her face. "It will be great to have fresh meat."

Gideon's eyes flickered and the corners of his mouth pulled upward, as if he understood her struggle and was proud of her. "I'll see you in the house then."

Something about Gideon's understanding left Leah

disappointed with herself. She needed to be stronger if she was going to live in these rugged mountains. She *would* be stronger.

The next morning, Gideon found himself splitting wood at the stump beside the cabin before he headed out to check the stock for the day.

Swing. *Thwak!* The wood flew from the block, landing with the other pieces that had already collected in two neat piles. He reached for another round log and placed it upright on the stump.

Swing. *Thwak!* The steady effort kept his blood pumping and his muscles warm, despite the polar freeze that had come upon them during the last week.

Swing. *Thwak!* This time, he allowed the ax to rest on the stump as he straightened and wiped a buckskin-clad arm across his forehead.

"Are you ready for a cup of coffee?"

The sweet voice caught him off guard. He turned to find Leah at the corner of the house, looking like a real live angel. The steam wafting from the mug in her hand circled around her head in a halo, and her smile was soft, like a morning fog.

It wasn't until she stepped forward, offering the mug in both hands like the gift of the magi, that he realized he was staring. Closing his gaping jaw, he reached to receive the gift, his eyes sneaking back up for one more glimpse of her face. His gaze brushed hers, and he was pretty sure he mumbled "Thank you."

She turned to survey the wood chunks piled on the ground. "You've been working hard this morning."

What should he say to that? She hadn't asked a question, but she seemed to expect an answer. He'd always hated small talk.

Finally, he shrugged. "A little."

She turned back to him then, as if she could read his thoughts. "Would you teach me how to shoot a gun?"

The force of her question knocked him backward, and he braced his right foot for balance. "Teach *you* to shoot?"

"Yes. Miriam said you taught her, and you're the best shot in the area."

"No." He turned back to the stump and reached for his ax.

"Gideon…" The sound of his name on her lips stopped his retreat, and he pivoted slowly back toward her. He made the mistake of looking in her doe eyes, full of hope and longing. There was no way he could resist their pull.

"All right. Can you be ready in half an hour?"

The look of joy that flowed over her face sent a thrill through his chest. He would have fought a hundred Indians single-handed to bring on that expression again.

She was right on time, meeting him on the front porch with an eager smile. Gideon led the way toward the back of the cabin where they could shoot into the side of the mountain.

When they were positioned about seventy feet from the tree line, he took a deep breath and held up his gun. "This is a Winchester repeating rifle. It can fire several rounds without reloading, you just pump this handle."

She looked on with rapt attention while he demonstrated how to load the gun and use the lever action to cock it. Her presence so near was unnerving.

Finally, he got to the part where he could raise the gun and shoot, and the familiar feel of the solid wood frame soothed his fraying nerves. One shot… two… three… All right on target.

Lowering the rifle, Gideon released a breath, his emotions now firmly in hand. "You wanna try?"

She reached for the gun, green eyes sparkling like the mossy rocks in the creek. She held the rifle against her shoulder, high enough that it tucked into her collar bone. That would never do. The kick of the gun would likely dislocate or crack the bone. He took a deep breath, then moved into her space to help position the shooter.

He was careful not to touch her, but from the corner of his vision he could see Leah's wide eyes on his face. He didn't glance up, just kept his focus on the rifle. The steam from her breath warmed his icy hands.

As soon as the gun was in place, Gideon almost jumped backward, putting a good pace in between them.

"Go ahead and aim for that same tree." The breathless feeling in his chest surely came from the frigid air.

She squinted down the barrel for several seconds, and he could see her hands quiver from the weight of the piece. When the boom came, it shook her entire body, knocking her backwards. It was instinct that made him lunge forward, although he didn't have to move far to catch her.

For a long moment he held her, soft and warm in his arms as she leaned against him. His body clasped her tightly even though his brain screamed at him to let her go. His brain finally won, and he stepped back, keeping his hands on her shoulders until he was sure she was steady.

"You all right?"

"Yeah." Her voice sounded breathless. Was she hurt? Or were her insides doing flips the way his were?

She turned those wide, doe eyes on him again. "I guess I wasn't quite ready for that."

The wonder in her gaze sent a falling sensation through his chest. He blinked, forcing his focus back on the rifle.

"I should have warned you—it kicks pretty hard."

She raised one corner of her perfectly-shaped mouth. "Now you tell me."

The next time Leah raised the rifle to her shoulder, her hands were steady and she braced one foot slightly behind. When the gun fired, she swayed a bit but kept both feet planted. Without looking at him, she ratcheted the lever and fired again, repeating the process until the gun would shoot no more.

He watched, somewhat fascinated, as she reloaded the gun the same way he had, although not quite as fluidly. By the time it was empty again, she'd hit the tree five times. After the last shot, she lowered the rifle and swiveled to face him, triumph brightening her face.

"Good work." He couldn't keep the pride from his voice.

Gideon worked the oil through the bridle in his hand as he watched Leah out of the corner of his eye. She'd been standing at that window for half an hour now, staring at the snow falling in the darkness outside. What was she thinking behind those bewitching green eyes?

Ever since that day two weeks ago when he'd taught her to shoot, he'd been warring with his emotions toward this woman. The respect and admiration that had grown in him for several months was fast becoming more. He'd been fighting the feelings, but watching her now, he was tired of the battle. She was beautiful and kind and strong in ways he'd never imagined. What was so wrong with getting to know her better?

"Is everything all right, Leah?"

At the sound of Miri's voice, he glanced over at his sister. She'd dropped the quilt squares she'd been sewing and was looking at her friend expectantly.

He turned his attention to Leah, who continued to stare out the window as if she hadn't heard. His chest squeezed at the tension that radiated from her shoulders.

Finally she sighed, a long mournful sound. When she spoke, her voice was almost swallowed by the glass pane in front of her and the sea of darkness beyond.

"I was just thinking now that my leg is healed, it's time for me to move on."

All of his muscles tensed, as if fending off an attack. Before he could stop himself, the words in his heart spilled out. "You can't leave."

She turned, an unspoken question in her gaze.

He realized what he'd said, and his mind paddled quickly toward clearer waters. "The snow is too deep on the pass that goes to town. You won't make it through, even on horseback." He felt Miriam's curious gaze heating his neck, but he ignored it. He didn't need to mention that she could go the long way around through the valley. It was more than twice the distance, but was most likely navigable. Still, it wasn't worth the risk.

Leah didn't answer, but her face paled before she turned back toward the window.

Did she hate it so much here? Was she so desperate to leave? Or was she afraid of the harsh winter? Montana winters in these mountains could be something to fear, and this was looking to be a rough one. He'd watched fear kill Jane, and he'd be bound and gagged before he'd let the same thing happen to this woman.

He carefully chose his next words, watching Leah closely as he spoke. "If you really want to leave, we could probably hike out on snowshoes. It'd take at least a day, prob'ly two. It's up to you."

She didn't turn, and after a while he wondered if she'd heard him.

Her voice was small when she spoke. "No, I'd rather wait."

He didn't question too strongly the relief that flooded through him.

Chapter Twenty-Four

The next morning at breakfast, Leah bided her time through the meal, waiting for the right opening to make her request. She'd fixed warm sourdough biscuits with thick gravy and bacon—Gideon's favorite—and she hoped the food would work its magic. He seemed to be in a decent mood despite the snowfall through the night, so after she refilled his mug for the second time, Leah posed her question.

"Gideon, would you mind if I ride along and help with the cattle and the horses today?"

He had just sipped from the mug at his lips, but as soon as she got the question out, he released a loud choking noise. After several coughs, he made an effort to compose himself, turning red-rimmed eyes to her.

"Ride...with me?"

She almost giggled at the shock on his face.

"Yes. I'm dying to get out and ride again, and I thought there was something I could do to help out there. Maybe work with the horses or doctor wounds on the animals?" She turned her most brilliant smile on him, the one that had always worked with the men back in Richmond.

His pinched lips showed he wasn't convinced, and he looked almost ready to turn her down.

"I promise I'll stay out of your way. But I can work with the foals on their leading and handling. It's been so long since I've seen little Trojan, I'll bet he's growing up." If Gideon would just look at her, she had a better chance to convince him. But he kept his gaze determinedly pointed at the table.

"I think you should let her go with you." Miriam's interjection succeeded in raising Gideon's focus from the table.

He studied his sister's face for a moment, although his thoughts seemed to be far away. At last, he sighed and turned to Leah. "I guess you can go. But only until we come back for lunch, and you have to do exactly as I say."

Leah could hardly contain the rush of excitement that exploded through her nerves. "Oh, thank you, Gideon." She almost jumped up to give him a hug, but decided that may not be a proper response. She settled for quickly stacking the dirty dishes on the table. "I'll wash these really quick and be ready when you are."

Miriam rose and made a shooing motion. "Leave those alone and go get dressed for the snow. You can't take away all my fun today."

By the time Leah put on three extra petticoats, two pairs of stockings and her gloves and coat, Gideon had his horse tacked and was tightening the girth on the chestnut mare Miriam usually rode.

As Leah approached, he lowered the stirrup and turned to hand her the reins. "This is Annabelle. She's a good little riding mare, been Miriam's for about five years now."

Leah took the leather pieces and reached out to stroke the flat part between the horse's eyes. "Hey there, Anabelle. You ready for a ride?" She turned back to Gideon with a smile. "All set?"

His eyes skimmed her frame then shot over to the saddle, brows lowering in question. "You can ride, right?"

"Of course." She pushed as much assurance into her tone as she could. No need to tell him she'd never ridden astride before, only sidesaddle. Both legs around the horse could only be easier, right?

She draped the reins over the mare's neck, then turned slightly while Gideon cupped his hands to give her a leg up. She was painstakingly aware of his nearness as she placed her boot in his palms and vaulted into the saddle, the mare shifting a bit under her weight.

"Easy, girl," Leah murmured, trying to keep her befuddled nerves from making a fool of her.

Gideon placed her left foot in the stirrup while she settled her skirts, then he stepped back and glanced up at her.

"Everything all right?" The wrinkle between his brows and the seriousness in his tone reflected genuine concern.

Leah flashed what she hoped was a confident smile. "It feels good to be in the saddle again." And it did. Many long months had passed since she'd had the chance for a horseback ride. The leather hugging her lower body was comfortable and secure.

Miriam came out on the cabin's porch to wave them off, and Annabelle fell into step behind Gideon's bay gelding as they left the yard. The trail Gideon took was slightly downhill and seemed to wrap around the mountain.

Leah relished the companionable silence as she settled into the creak of her saddle and the snow-covered nature around them. This world was a mostly-undisturbed blanket of white, with ice covering the branches and evergreen needles. She spotted the crimson of a cardinal and heard its "chirrup" as they ambled past.

Leah glanced back at the ever-faithful Drifter who trotted behind, following in the tracks the horses made. The snow came to the knees of Gideon's horse, so the poor dog would have worn himself out if he'd tried to break his own trail.

After a while, Gideon raised a hand to point at tracks in the snow about thirty feet away. "See that deer trail over there? I've gotten more bucks here than any other place on the ranch. It seems to be their main path down the mountain."

A few minutes later, Gideon showed her long, deep scratch marks in the trunk of a cedar tree. "Those were made by a mountain lion, probably a female from the closeness of the claws."

His words raised goose bumps on Leah's arms. "Are there a

lot of mountain lions around here?"

He shrugged. "They come and go. There's enough wildlife to feed on in this area that they've never bothered us or the stock. You'll see their signs, though."

A rush of adrenaline flowed through her. She'd never been this close to the wilder division of God's creations. Wouldn't it be amazing to actually see some of these animals?

Not five minutes later, her wish came true when they rounded a bend in the brush and found three deer standing in the trail. The animals started when they saw the horses, then leaped into the woods, vanishing as quickly as they'd appeared.

"Wow..." Leah breathed.

She caught a smile on Gideon's face as he glanced back at her. "We're almost to the best part."

This whole ride had been the best part so far, she couldn't imagine what could be next. Soon, the trail moved out of the woods, and Leah had to blink as the brilliant sun glinted off the snow. Gideon reined in his horse, so she rode up next to him and did the same.

As Leah's eyes adjusted to the light, she sucked in a breath. Before her lay the most amazing view she'd ever seen. They were near the edge of the mountain, with small pine trees covering the steep descent. Far below lay a valley, blanketed in white with a darker line snaking through the center, which must be a stream. Beyond the valley, another range of mountains rose majestically into the clouds.

"It's beautiful." Her voice trembled with the awe in her chest.

"It's pretty amazing." Gideon's tone had taken on a timbre of pride, as if he were presenting his own offspring. "This is what I love the most about the high country. The enormity of it all, and the magnificence. The wildness. It's as close as I've been to heaven." He paused for a moment. "It's hard to put it into words."

Leah turned to him, her chest tight at the richness of it all. "What you just said sounded like poetry."

He faced her then, his verdant eyes glistening, pleading with her to understand. "It makes it all worth it, you know? Things are hard here, but it doesn't matter because you get to be surrounded with all this."

She felt the corners of her mouth lift at the beauty in his words, as she turned back to admire the splendor again. "I get it now." She'd fallen in love with the peace and solitude of life at the cabin, but the glory of this view was enough to capture her heart forever.

They sat for a while, enjoying the sight before them. "That's one of the pastures where I grow hay in the summer." Gideon pointed to the valley below. Our property line goes to the base of the other mountain, but no one owns the land on that slope so I don't worry too much about the cows wandering." He pointed out an elk at the edge of the woods far below.

Too soon, Gideon squared his shoulders and picked up his reins. "We'd better keep moving."

When they reached a large open area where the ground was relatively flat, Leah took in the huddled groups of cows and calves. The minute they saw Gideon, the animals began lowing and moving forward to greet him. He rode up to a little shed at the edge of the tree line and dismounted, speaking to the cows as he opened the door and forked hay into several piles. His voice was too low for her to understand his words, but the cows seemed to comprehend and settled in to munch on the fodder he provided.

While he worked, Leah rode over to where Gideon had tied his gelding, and secured Annabelle to a nearby branch. He had grabbed an ax from the shed and seemed to be heading for the tree line.

"What can I do?" she called, as she limped through the snow and mud toward the little barn.

Gideon stopped and turned toward her, as if just noticing he wasn't the only person there. "Can you put out a couple more piles of hay, away from the rest? The horses will be up soon."

"Where are you going?" She hated to question him, but the thought of him leaving her in this unknown place left a knot in her stomach.

His lips tipped up knowingly. "There's a creek just inside the wood line. I'm going to crack the ice."

A flood of relief washed through her. "Oh. All right."

Leah struggled with the pitchfork in the barn, but managed to build two piles of hay a little distance from where the cows munched. The loud crack of the ax sounded just as she started back to the barn.

In between blows, she heard a high whinny from the opposite direction. She turned to see several horses trotting through the snow, their legs rising high like the Tennessee Walking horses on the plantations in Virginia.

Three foals plunged through the white powder at the back of the herd, and Leah easily spotted Trojan, his long legs propelling him ahead of the other two youngsters.

The animals stopped at the hay she'd put out, and Leah made her way toward them, rubbing thick-coated shoulders and speaking softly to each.

A nudge at her waist brought Leah's attention down, and she found Trojan's soft muzzle nibbling at her lambswool skirt.

"Hey there, fellow." She reached a hand to stroke his thick chestnut coat and laughed when he rubbed his head against her.

"He remembers you." Gideon's deep voice sent a little shiver down her back, as he strode up to Trojan's other side.

She glanced up at him, once again aware of how alone they were in this barren place. "I've missed this guy." She dropped her gaze back to Trojan, who was leaning into her hand as she scratched the base of his shoulder.

Gideon didn't say anything, but stroked the colt's short mane. His gloved hands were so large compared to her own. Her gaze drifted up to his face and was captured by the expression in his striking green eyes. His thoughts were so hard to read. She didn't see the distaste that had been in his eyes when she'd first come to the ranch. Was it admiration she saw there now? Or at least friendship? Was that too much to hope for? Even if she couldn't decipher the emotions swirling there, she would have loved to spend the rest of the day trying.

Gideon was the first to look away, and Leah felt a rush of disappointment when he turned. "I have halters in the shed if you want to work with the foals." His voice drifted over his shoulder as he moved away.

Over the next few hours, Leah thoroughly enjoyed herself, working with the horses and helping Gideon where she could. When she'd finished leading each of the foals, she found Gideon carrying a bucket of black goo among the cattle. He showed her how to apply it to scratches and various wounds the cows had acquired. He explained that the medicine both healed and, in the summer, kept out the flies that would lay eggs in the wounds, producing larvae and worms that would eat the cow from the inside out.

Gideon was an excellent teacher, despite his succinct manner. He had an incredible amount of knowledge and she loved to watch the light in his eyes when he spoke of the animals. They were obviously important to him, and he cared for each as if it were a prized possession.

As she followed him through the herd, they came to a gaunt cow with a large calf nursing at her side. Gideon set the bucket down and placed a hand on the cow's head.

"See this girl? Her calf is too big to be nursing still. He's taking all the nutrients she needs. If we don't wean him soon, she'll starve to death."

Leah stood behind him, watching the pair. "What can you do to stop him?"

She watched as Gideon took a handful of the black goo and rubbed a thick coat on the cow's udder. "This stuff is actually good for the cow's skin, but the stench should help discourage the little one from nursing."

When he'd checked and doctored each animal, Leah followed Gideon back to the barn, feeling a bit like a pet dog on its master's heel. She was learning so much, though, just walking with him and asking questions. Did he mind all the queries? He didn't seem annoyed. If anything he seemed more animated as he shared his knowledge.

Gideon closed the barn door and eyed the grey sky overhead. "It's about time to head back to the house for lunch."

Disappointment pinched Leah's chest. She hated to leave, although she had long since lost all feeling in her toes. Still, she wouldn't have traded this morning for a thousand summer days.

"Gideon." She spoke hesitantly, not sure how to thank him, or even if she should try.

He swung his gaze from the sky to her face. Leah was suddenly aware of how tall he was. The width of his shoulders and his strong neck added to the feeling of strength he emanated.

"Yes?" His expression was earnest, almost concerned.

"Thank you for letting me come."

His face relaxed a bit, his eyes softening into an almost-smile. He took a step forward, bringing them just a few feet apart. His eyes had darkened into a deep emerald, stealing Leah's breath with their magnetism. His scent filled her head—the remnants of leather and pine and something spicy she couldn't put a finger on.

He was looking deep inside her now, as if searching for an answer. She felt her whole being splayed for him to see—her fears, her hopes.

He took another step, closing the distance between them. Her chin rose, her eyes locked in his. She couldn't move, couldn't breathe. He was so close.

His hand touched her cheek. She leaned into his warmth, absently wondering where his glove had gone. And then his head came down, and his lips brushed hers. Warm, gentle, and exquisite. Her eyes fluttered shut as she breathed him in.

Her kiss was so sweet, her virgin lips so soft and supple. Their touch brought Gideon back for another taste. His hand crept up to her hair, weaving his fingers through the softness, thankful he'd shucked his gloves. He deepened the kiss, feeling her melt into his hands. This woman was amazing. Beautiful, strong, and oh so sweet.

She released a little mew, sending a shiver of desire through him. She was kissing him back now, and he forced himself to keep his hands above her shoulders. He had to stay strong with her, couldn't allow himself to be vulnerable…to care.

But then he felt it, the old familiar fear rising in his gut. Clawing to his throat and souring the sweetness that was Leah's kiss.

He tore himself away, gasping. "I can't, Leah… I'm sorry…"

He couldn't look in her eyes, couldn't let them capture him, couldn't see the disappointment there. He spun around, putting his back to her. He struggled to get control of himself, breathing deeply through his mouth.

A hand touched his arm. "Gideon?"

Her voice was full of questions. He hated himself. Why had he gotten close to her? Why had he allowed her to come out here in the first place? Having her so close all morning had weakened his defenses, twisted his mind into thinking a little taste would be all right.

"We need to get back now." He didn't mean for his voice to sound as harsh as it came out, but an apology would weaken his defenses…again. Instead, he turned and marched toward the horses. A glimpse of her hurt expression as he brushed past pushed a knife into his gut. He relished the pain.

Chapter Twenty-Five

*L*eah stared out the window into the darkness, pulling the shawl tight around her shoulders.

"Worrying won't bring him back any faster, Leah. You might as well sit down and relax." Miriam's voice was motherly, with a strong hint of understanding.

Leah didn't turn away from the glass, knowing her cheeks were likely pink. The memory of the kiss flashed through her mind, unbidden. It had been amazing, better than she'd dreamed her first kiss would be. Until the end, that is… Poor Gideon. She knew it was fear he fought. She'd seen it haunt his eyes every time he looked at her since that wonderful day last week.

Lord, please help him release his fear. Show him he can rest in You. It was the mantra she'd prayed for months now, but a peace cloaked her heart as she released the prayer.

A sigh sneaked out, as she turned and moved toward the kitchen. Her limp was slight these days, although tiredness exaggerated it now. She lifted the lid off the pot on the stove and poked a fork into the venison roast simmering. It was getting tougher each time she checked it.

Leah shot another glance out the window. Gideon should have been home an hour ago. He was usually so dependable, almost never varying his timing more than a quarter hour. She had a suspicion he kept to such a rigid schedule for Miriam's sake, to give her a sense of security. Why else would he make the long ride home for lunch almost every day, when it would be much easier to pack the meal in his saddlebags and eat with the herd? That made his absence tonight so much more worrisome.

Squaring her shoulders, she turned toward Miriam. "I'm going out to look for him."

Miriam's head shot up from the quilt squares she'd been stitching. "You can't go out in the dark, Leah. You'll get lost and freeze to death."

Leah clenched her jaw. She could *not* just sit here without knowing if Gideon was all right. What if he'd fallen from his horse and been knocked unconscious, or been mauled by a mountain lion? He could be dying while she twiddled her thumbs.

"Miriam, something's wrong. I can feel it. I can't stay here when Gideon needs help."

Miriam paused for a moment, then sighed and set her sewing aside. "All right then, I'm coming with you."

It seemed to take forever to gather a rifle, blankets, lanterns, and a thermos of coffee, then saddle the horses. Images of Gideon's prone body assaulted her mind, bleeding from an Indian arrow, or swollen from a snakebite. Prayer was her only weapon against the unknown forces that may have struck Gideon, and she used it with fervor.

As they started on the trail through the woods, Miriam took the lead, calling for her brother as they went.

While Miriam's calls echoed through the quiet forest, Leah's eyes scanned the snow around them, eager for some kind of trail or marking that would point them to Gideon. The trees overhead sheltered them from moonlight, allowing her to see only about twenty feet in any direction. Each time she recognized a landmark from their ride the week before, Leah's heart gave a little leap, but there was no sign of Gideon. *Lord, please show us the way.*

After an eternity, the trees broke, and she realized they'd reached the overlook with the amazing view. The knot in her gut obliterated the pleasure that normally came with the memory of sitting here on horseback with Gideon. Her shoulders tensed even more, if that were possible.

The trail entered the woods again, the darkness soaking into Leah's skin.

"Gideon!" She added her own cry to Miriam's.

A yip sounded in the distance, grabbing Leah's attention. Every nerve in her body stood on alert, listening.

"Did you hear that?" Leah didn't wait for Miriam to respond, but pushed her mare off the trail and through the deep snow.

"Drifter!" After a few seconds, she heard another yip. It wasn't the dog's normal excited bark, but a strangled cry that raised bumps on her arms. She had a better fix on the direction now, and she kicked her mare, pushing her faster than was safe in the deep snow.

"Drifter!"

The dog continued to yelp in response to her calls, and finally she saw him, huddled under a bush. As she leaped from her horse and covered the last few feet, she realized he lay in a bed of dark snow. Blood.

"Hey, boy. That's a good boy. What's wrong with you?" She kept up a steady croon as she stroked the dog's head and struggled to determine his injuries in the dark. Long, deep scratches covered his right side, and his right front leg was soaked with blood.

"What's happened?" Miriam crouched behind her, peering around Leah. Her face was almost as white as the snow, giving her a ghostly appearance.

"He has some deep cuts and blood all over his leg. Can we put him on your horse so we can keep looking for Gideon?" Leah heard the intensity in her own voice. She didn't want to think what had caused the injuries, but Drifter's condition had planted a driving fear in her chest. She *had* to find Gideon.

Miriam remounted and Leah carefully wrapped the dog in a blanket, then handed him up to her friend. He whined when she first moved him, but as she settled him across Miriam's lap, she felt the familiar tongue across her wrist. "It's all right boy. We're gonna find Gideon and get you both fixed up."

Leah started off again on foot, leading her horse so she could follow Drifter's trail of blood. The going was slow and exhausting, with the snow mid-thigh in most areas. Finally, she mounted her horse. The crimson trail was more clear now, and time was of the essence.

They were moving uphill, wrapping around the mountain and skirting boulders that peeked out from the snow. The trees had thinned and morphed into low shrubs with occasional scruffy pine. She had a bad feeling about this.

Miriam continued to call Gideon's name, and Leah heard the fear in her tone intensify the farther they rode.

Leah looked around the area as they continued the search. Her eyes drifted back to the ground. No blood. The snow appeared solid white. Had they missed Gideon? She drew her horse to a stop and surveyed the area as far as she could see. No sign of the man. Should they continue or backtrack?

An opening in the rock side of the mountain caught her attention. A cave. She jumped from her horse and looped the mare's reins on a branch.

"Gideon?" Leah's hands shook as she struggled to unhook the lantern from her saddle horn. She proceeded cautiously into the mouth of the cave, her light almost ineffective against the deep darkness. "Gideon!"

She heard a faint moan and shuffled in that direction. The lantern gradually illuminated a body lying prone on the rock floor. Leah's heart clenched as she dropped to her knees beside him. "Gideon..."

He was a tangled mass of blood, and his rugged face had blanched to an eerie white, outlined by the red that dripped down his left cheek. Leah touched his forehead. His skin was so cold. *God, please!* She moved her hand down to his neck. A soft rhythm thumped against her fingers. *Thank you!*

"Gideon, can you hear me?" She spoke softly, the darkness casting foreign shadows around them.

A strangled cry sounded from behind her. Leah whirled to find Miriam, a look of sheer terror on her face.

"He's alive." Leah forced a measure of calm into her voice, fighting her own rapid-fire heartbeat. Miriam's eyes appeared almost crazy in the lamplight, like she would turn and run at any moment.

"He's dead..." she moaned dropping to her knees a few feet away.

Leah crawled to her friend, wrapping both arms around her shoulders. "He's not dead. His pulse is strong, but he's cold. Can you go get blankets from the saddle bags? He's going to be fine, but we need to get him warm."

Miriam nodded numbly, then rose to her feet and stumbled toward the cave entrance. Leah watched her go for only a second, praying the words she'd spoken would be true. *God, you have to keep Gideon alive. Please!*

She turned back to the injured man and held the lantern over his body, taking an inventory of his wounds. Most of the blood seemed to be around his abdomen. His buckskin was ripped, exposing cloth, pale skin, and bloody gashes under the leather. His legs seemed to be in better condition, and she cautiously straightened them, watching for irregular angles that might signal a break.

When her eyes traveled back up to his face, it wore a tortured look, and she couldn't help but brush the hair from his forehead. His skin was icy. They had to get him warm soon.

For the first time, she looked around the cave, wondering what animal had done this to him. Was it still around? She'd left her rifle tucked into the scabbard on her saddle. If the animal was still in the cave, she and Gideon both were in danger.

A scuffle sounded behind her, and Miriam appeared with a handful of blankets.

Leah focused again on Gideon and began to cocoon him in the quilts, careful not to move his head. He released another low moan when she touched the side of his abdomen.

"I'm sorry." Her chest ached at the obvious pain before her.

Should they get him back to the cabin, or try to warm him here? Was there still danger in the area? As if to answer her question, a shrill howl sounded in the distance. Not too close, but loud enough to raise bumps on her arms. *Thank you, Lord, for guidance.*

Another strangled cry came from her right, and Leah realized Miriam had wandered to the far side of the cavern.

"What is it?" She rose and moved with her lantern to where Miri was standing. The huge brown mass of a grizzly bear lay face up on the cave floor, its glazed eyes staring vacantly into the darkness. A pool of blood had puddled next to it, and the fur around its chest and neck appeared damp and mangled.

Leah fought the bile in her throat, and turned to see Miriam hugging her arms, her entire body shuddering. Leah reached for the girl's shoulders and turned her into a tight embrace.

A bear. That was the way Abel had died. Miriam's body wracked in her arms, great sobs shaking them both, while Leah held tightly and rocked from side to side.

"I'm sorry… I'm so, so sorry…" It was all Leah could think to say. Curled in her embrace, Miriam seemed no more than her sixteen years. Not the strong, capable woman she usually impersonated, but the scared adolescent she really was. Leah's heart ached with love for this girl.

As her sobbing relaxed a bit, Leah reluctantly pulled back and took Miriam's face in her hands. She infused all the certainty she could muster into her tone. "Gideon is not going to die like Abel did. Do you understand? We need to get him back to the cabin, though, to get him warm and doctored." She searched her mind for a job to occupy Miriam. "Can you help me put him on my horse? Then, I'll need you to lead the way back out of here."

Miriam nodded, her sniff echoing in the cave.

Then Leah remembered the injured dog. "Where is Drifter?"

"Wrapped in a blanket on the ground outside." Miriam's voice quivered, but at least she was talking.

Leah kept one arm draped around the girl's shoulders as she directed her back toward Gideon. At his side, Leah released her and kneeled to check Gideon's pulse again. His skin was still cold, but his heartbeat was strong.

She stroked his forehead and the thick locks that fell over it, contemplating how to get him over to the horses and actually up on one of them. Could two women lift this tall, strapping man without wounding him more? They would have to try.

"Let's see if we can lay him on a blanket. That may be easier to move without hurting him." After spreading the largest quilt next to Gideon, Leah gingerly slipped her arm under his shoulders, supporting his head with her body, while Miriam moved his legs. As they shifted him, Gideon released a moan and his eyes fluttered.

Once he was on the quilt, Leah draped the other blankets back over him, covering everything except his face.

"Leah..." His voice was raspy and his eyes were still closed, but Gideon had spoken. Leah's heart gave a little leap.

"I'm here, Gideon." She stroked his good cheek, her eyes wandering over every strong line of his face. Pain had etched grooves around his eyes.

"Prayed... you'd... come." His words reached into her chest where her heart resided and squeezed.

"I'm here, Gideon. We're going to get you home where it's warm."

Between the two of them, they half-dragged, half-carried Gideon to the edge of the cave. Miriam untied Leah's mount and led the mare to the opening.

Leah found herself chewing her bottom lip as she eyed the man on the ground and the height of the saddle. There was no way to make this easy. She bent back down to Gideon and stroked his face again. She couldn't tell if he was awake or if he'd passed out from the pain, but the rise and fall of his chest brought a measure of comfort. "Gideon, do you think you can try to mount the horse? We'll help you." She knew it was an absurd request given his condition, but any effort he could apply would help.

"Yes..." His voice was a raspy whisper and his eyes remained closed, but he was true to his word. With the women on either side, they worked together to boost him into the saddle. As soon as he landed in the leather seat, his body slumped over the horn.

Leah kept a hand on his arm lest he keel over.

With very little grace, she managed to climb on behind him. She settled in behind the saddle with an arm on each side of Gideon, and the warmth of the horse's wooly coat beneath her. She fervently hoped this was not the mare's first experience riding double.

As they started down the trail, Leah was conscious of Gideon's strong bulk in front of her. Never had she dreamed she would be saving this man's life in such a way.

Chapter Twenty-Six

$\mathcal{D}$uring the long ride, convulsive shivers wracked Gideon's body in front of Leah. Her efforts to warm him proved fruitless, for each time her arm touched his side, he would moan and flinch away from her. It seemed the only thing she could do to help was grip his shoulders so he didn't pitch from the swaying rhythm of the horse.

Finally at the cabin, Leah rode right up to the steps of the porch, then slid from her horse, careful not to knock Gideon off. She and Miriam tucked themselves under each of his arms to help him down from the mount and into the house. He made an effort to walk, but was shaking so badly, it was a stumble, at best.

Once they were inside, Leah looked around for the best place to settle him. He was too weak to sit upright in a chair, and a bed would be too far away from the fire. His violent shivers made warmth the most important need for now. Had frostbite already set in? She'd have to check for that soon.

"Let's lay him in front of the fire." Leah nodded her head in the direction of the hearth. "We can make a pallet for him and doctor his wounds while he gets warm."

As soon as they had him on the floor, wrapped in the quilts they'd used in the cave, Miriam scurried to gather more blankets, bandages, and hot water.

Leah knelt by Gideon's side. She needed to take off the

shredded buckskin so she could assess the damage underneath. But even the thought of removing this man's shirt felt like she was entering a taboo room. Maybe she should ask Miriam to remove the bloody garments and doctor his wounds. But an image flashed through Leah's mind of the girl's terrified expression when she'd first seen Gideon in the cave. It wasn't fair for Miri to go through this with Gideon like she had with Abel.

Leah inhaled a deep breath and released it, her nerves softening with the exhaled air. She glanced at Gideon's face. His eyes were closed in a grimace, his jaw quivering from the cold that still consumed him. She reached for the scissors from Miriam's sewing bag, and fingered the bottom edge of his buckskin tunic. Clenching her jaw, she began to snip, working her way up toward his neck.

As the leather fell away, it revealed a brown flannel shirt, with long tears shredding the fabric across the front. Leah followed the same process to remove this garment, cutting from the bottom up and spreading the two sides apart so they looked like an unbuttoned jacket.

Underneath the flannel layer was the white undershirt she had expected to find. The shreds of material that lay haphazardly across his abdomen were drenched with a viscous layer of crimson that squeezed Leah's gut in a nauseating grip. When bile rose into her throat, she clenched her eyes shut, gulping in steadying breaths.

Sooner than she wanted to, Leah forced her eyes open and began to slice through the undershirt, careful to raise it above his skin so she didn't knick him in the process.

Once this last layer of fabric was laid aside, his chest was exposed, displaying deep claw marks that slashed at various angles across his front and left side. A fresh wave of nausea washed through Leah, but she forced her mind to focus on what she should do next.

Miriam appeared at Leah's side, offering a welcome distraction and a pot of warm water.

"I put garlic in the water to help you clean."

Leah turned away from the gory sight to dampen several cloths in the water. She stole a glance at Miriam's face, which was as white as the snow outside. Was she about to faint? The last thing Leah needed was another patient on her hands. She touched a hand to her friend's arm.

"Go and care for Drifter now. I'll tend your brother."

Miriam's eyes flitted to Leah, then she spun and half stumbled to where the dog lay near the cook stove in the kitchen.

Leah turned back to her own patient. She wrung some of the water from the cloth in her hands, and began to gingerly dab the blood from around the gashes. His chest rose and fell harshly, his rough breathing illuminated by the lack of movement in the rest of his body. Still, it was good to see his lungs were functioning.

When her cloth touched a spot near the bottom of his ribs, Gideon groaned and his entire midsection seemed to clinch. She jerked away. Had she caused further damage by pressing on some compromised organ? His breathing had grown shallow, but then his muscles slowly released from their contraction.

"Gideon?"

His eyes flickered open. There was pain in their murky depths. Still, he met her gaze.

"I'm...all right. Just...hurts." His voice was raspy and weak, but at least he was awake.

"I need to finish cleaning your wounds." She hated the quiver in her voice, but couldn't seem to steady it.

"Go...ahead."

She worked quickly to clean the thawing blood from his abdomen, side, and cheek. Some of the gashes looked like they should be stitched. But how did one do that? Just use a sewing needle and thread? But wouldn't that cause him a great deal more pain? Hopefully, wrapping the cuts with bandages would suffice.

Next, she cut away more of Gideon's shirts, removing the bloody parts entirely. She thought about cutting the garments off at the arms, but they might help to warm him for now. When he felt better later, he could change into clean clothing.

Miriam appeared at Leah's side again with a handful of dried leaves. "Here's some Juniper. If you put it under his bandages, it will help with the healing. I always keep some on hand, just never thought I'd need it for this."

A faint memory flitted through her mind of Gideon putting leaves under her own bandages when she'd broken her leg. She nodded.

When it was time to apply the bandages, Leah hesitated, not sure how to wrap the fabric around his body while he lay flat.

"Gideon?" she called softly.

His eyes opened into slits. His breathing had deepened again—a good sign.

"Do you think you can sit up if I help you? I need to wrap bandages around you."

His chin bobbed once, and Leah released a breath. She moved to his shoulders and helped to push him up as he groaned and slowly raised himself. He stopped midway, his elbows propping him, while his measured breathing pumped in her ears.

"That's far enough." She worked quickly to wrap the long bandages around his abdomen, covering the juniper leaves she had spread over the gashes.

"Tighter." He ground the words through clinched teeth.

Leah's gaze shot to his face. Really?

"My ribs are broken...Tighter will help."

She wasn't sure of that, but obeyed, pulling the wraps a little more snuggly.

"Tighter."

This time he barked the word and Leah obeyed, pulling the cloth as tight as she dared. As soon as she was finished, she helped him lay back. When he was flat on the floor again, he released a slow breath.

Leah did the same. She reached up to brush the hair from his forehead. The lines around his mouth had softened some.

Miriam appeared at her side again. When Leah turned, the girl held out a mug to her.

"Willow tea for his pain." This girl who normally chattered like a magpie, now wore such a bleak expression. And she'd taken on her brother's succinct manner of talking.

Leah tried to offer an encouraging look. "Thank you, Miri. How's Drifter?"

Miriam's gaze had turned to Gideon, and her eyes roamed his form while she spoke. "I think he'll be fine. Has a big claw mark down his side, but it should heal if it doesn't get infected."

"Good." With her concern over Gideon, it hadn't really occurred to Leah that Drifter's wounds could be life-threatening. "Why don't you go on to bed now? I'll help Gideon drink this tea, then he'll need to rest, too."

Miriam turned frightened eyes on Leah. "But what if he needs me?"

Leah reached to take Miri's cold hand. "I'll sleep in the chair tonight. If either of them needs anything, I'll be right here."

Miriam continued to stare at her. What images were flashing behind those green eyes? "You'll come and get me if I can do anything?"

"Absolutely. But rest is what they both need for now." And it could only help Miriam, too.

"All right." Miriam rose and trudged toward the bedroom, turning when she reached the door, like a child asking whether she really had to go to bed. Leah offered another encouraging smile, and Miriam continued into her room, closing the door behind her.

Leah released a breath. Was the girl afraid something dire would happen to her brother during the night? Or just afraid to be alone? Either way, the poor thing needed sleep to help her recover from the evening's events. She needed to make sure she checked on Miriam in a little bit.

Leah turned back to Gideon. His teeth were quivering again. She took a blanket from the stack Miriam had brought and spread it across him. She added another and another, finishing with a small lap quilt—the last in the stack.

Now to get some of this warm drink into him. That would help most of all, with the cold and the pain.

"Gideon," she murmured. "I'm going to spoon tea into your

mouth. Do you think you can drink it?"

His chin bobbed again and his mouth parted, but his eyes remained closed. She spooned the liquid in. His lips were red and chapped. Maybe some aloe cream would help? As he swallowed, her eyes were drawn to his throat as his Adam's apple bobbed. The stubble that spread across his jaw and neck only accentuated his manliness. She poured another spoonful into his mouth.

While she continued spooning the tea, Leah allowed her eyes to roam his face, unhindered by witnesses or the mesmerizing stare of his emerald eyes. His features were strong and proportioned just right. She drank her fill.

Too soon, the tea was gone, and Gideon's even breathing signaled restful sleep at last.

Everything hurt.

He inhaled a deep breath and quickly regretted it, as pain burned across his chest. His muscles contracted against his will, forcing a cough through his clenched teeth. The effect of the cough was like a bullet through his ribs, and he couldn't help but clutch his gut. There was no stopping his moan.

A cool hand touched his forehead, soft and gentle. Somehow, it chased away the worst of the pain.

"Sshh, Gideon."

The voice rippled through him, like waves of warmth. Was it an angel? He lay still, basking in the feel of the hand that brushed across his forehead, stroking his hair again and again.

Was this heaven? After all he'd blamed God for over the years, had the Almighty still allowed him to pass through the pearly gates?

"Are you ready to wake up now?" The soft beauty of the angel's voice was at odds with her words. He didn't ever want to wake up. Why couldn't he stay in heaven?

The hand stopped stroking his face and hair, leaving him alone to face the throbbing in his temples. Had the pain been there before? Everything hurt, so it was hard to be sure. He needed to get up, to get away from this torment.

Gideon forced his eyes open, but the effort only created slits for him to see through. He forced his eyes to bring the picture before him into fuzzy focus. The angel smiled at him. Her delicate face framed by honey-colored wisps. Her pale green eyes twinkled when she spoke again.

"I'm glad you're awake."

And with the angel smiling at him like that, he was, too.

She moved out of his vision, and he turned his head to watch her. But the pain shooting through his temples stopped him. He blinked once. He had to stay awake. Without moving his head, he scanned the room—or at least the ceiling and upper walls. Maybe this wasn't heaven after all. It bore a striking resemblance to his cabin. But why was he lying on the floor in the main room? And why did his whole body hurt like he'd been clubbed near to death?

A figure moved into his vision—the angel had returned. When she turned to smile at him again, his fuzzy mind grabbed hold of her image.

Leah. What was she doing here with him lying on the floor? He needed to sit up.

He contracted his muscles to bring himself up, but the moment his head came off the floor, his abdomen burned with enough fire to sap the strength from his limbs. He lay back with a thud, not able to contain the groan in his throat.

"Sshh..." Leah—the angel—stroked his forehead and murmured. "Lie still for now."

He squeezed his eyes shut against the pain, breathing carefully to keep his chest still.

"I'm going to spoon more of this tea into your mouth. It will help."

Gideon forced his eyes open again.

Leah was watching him, spoon poised by his chin. He opened

his mouth obediently, but kept his focus on her face. Maybe he could lose himself in something other than the screaming of his body.

She was a welcome distraction, with her wide eyes framed by long, dark lashes. Her button nose, her full lips, and her chin with the hint of a dimple. She never met his eyes, but kept her gaze between the spoon in her hands and his mouth. At one point, she dripped a little bit of the liquid on his chin, and he almost enjoyed the pout on her lips as she dabbed him dry.

When she was finally satisfied he'd had enough tea, she still wouldn't meet his gaze, but fiddled with something in her lap. He wanted to make her talk again, to look at him.

"What happened?"

Her head shot up, her green eyes wider than normal. "You don't remember?"

He licked his lips, trying to remember anything before he'd woken up on the floor with this angel sitting next to him. "I only remember being cold."

She nodded, releasing a long breath. "You were late for dinner, so we went looking for you. We found you in a cave, near a...a dead...bear." Her voice cracked on the last word, and she paused.

But when she spoke again, her tone was strong. "You had some scratches on your front and left side, and a bump on your head, but I think you'll heal completely."

Her pretty forehead scrunched, as if she had a thought that worried her. "You said something about a broken rib, too. I cleaned the wounds with garlic water and wrapped them with juniper leaves under the bandages. I hope that was enough. I didn't know what else to do."

She bit her bottom lip, and his fingers itched to smooth the furrow in her brow. When he started to move though, his ribs and chest screamed. He would have to settle for words. "You did fine. That's all you can do for broken ribs. Just wrap them tight."

It was such an effort to speak, and he had to catch his breath after just that little bit. Leah stroked his forehead again, and his eyes drifted shut against his control.

"Sleep now." The angel's voice drifted to him across a wide chasm.

Chapter Twenty-Seven

*L*eah watched the rise and fall of the blankets across Gideon's chest while he slept. The steady rhythm soothed her nerves. Surely that was a sign he was resting well and regaining strength. She pulled the quilt tighter around her shoulders, and leaned her head back against the wood. To stay close should Gideon need her, she was sitting on the floor, nestled into the corner of the wall and the bricks that lined the fireplace. The warmth permeating through the clay was calming.

For the first time, she allowed her mind to drift back through the surreal images of traipsing through the snow, finding the cave, Gideon lying so still, his skin as cold as a mountain stream. The bear with glassy eyes lying in the pool of blood, Gideon's bulk in the saddle in front of her, his body convulsing from the cold. What had he been doing up on that mountain? Did he know the cave was there? Maybe he'd been out hunting and stopped to eat a bite, or build a fire to get warm. Had the bear surprised him? And where was his horse?

If God hadn't led them to Drifter, they never would have found Gideon before he froze to death. Leah sent another prayer of thanks to her Heavenly Father.

And, Lord, please heal his wounds quickly. Help him not to be in too much pain. And then, as if by rote, her heart spoke its mantra. *Lord, please soften his heart. Help him to heal and to forgive.*

Leah stayed in that attitude of prayer for a few more moments, praising her Father for his mercies. At last, the fire beside her had died to a small flame. She released the blanket from her shoulders and moved to place more logs on the coals.

A stirring sounded behind her, and she turned to find Gideon's eyes open. The slits were a bit wider than the last time he'd awoken, and he seemed to be more aware.

"How're you feeling?" She moved forward to touch his forehead. He'd been a little feverish during the night, but his skin didn't feel too hot now.

His eyes opened a little more, enough to show a faint twinkle as he spoke. "Like I had a fight with a bear."

A rush of relief washed through her. He was feeling strong enough to joke. She stroked a stubborn lock of hair from his forehead as her mouth found its own smile. "At least you won."

Her eyes wandered to his face and found his green gaze like a homing pigeon. There was pain there, to be sure, but also an intensity that kept her from moving.

"You didn't tell me you were an angel."

Leah's heart did a little flip at those words, and her gaze lost its hold, sliding down to notice the rakish tilt of his mouth before she looked away. What did she say to that?

He released a chuckle before a wince cut it short.

Her attention jerked back to his face. "What's wrong?"

"Nothing. Just hurts to laugh or breathe."

She reached for the kettle from the hearth, and poured another mug of willow bark tea. "Drink more of this."

She began to spoon it into his mouth as before, but he shook his head.

"If you'll lift my head, I can drink it."

Was that a good idea? But she did as he asked, lifting his head just inches from the floor while she held the cup to his lips.

He was able to down most of the stuff before slumping back in exhaustion. He kept his eyes open, though. Maybe this would be a good opportunity to get some questions answered.

"Have you been able to remember how you came to be in that

cave with the bear?"

His gaze drifted to the roof, but his focus seemed to be mostly inward, wandering to images playing in his mind. "Not really. I remember being there with the bear charging right at me. I got a shot in him, but it only made him madder."

Gideon's eyes closed and his dark brows pulled together, as if thinking was a major challenge. "Drifter charged him, but the bear knocked him away. I thought he was a goner. Then the bear had me in the air. I landed next to my gun. I remember shooting, but that's all." Gideon's eyes fluttered open again, but were dull now — exhausted and spent from reliving his nightmare.

Leah brushed the hair from his forehead again. "God saved you for something special. But now you need to rest again. It's time to sleep."

Gideon seemed to agree, for his eyelids had already drifted closed.

After watching him a moment, she crawled the few feet back to her blanket by the wall, and curled up against the bricks. But it was a long time before sleep claimed her.

Leah awoke to the sound of metal clanging across the room. She jerked her head up, but was slowed by a sharp pain in her neck. A survey of the kitchen showed Miriam bent over the work table, pressing hard on something.

As she stretched and began to untangle herself from the blanket, Leah's gaze drifted to where Gideon lay on the floor. The pain wasn't etched as deeply on his face this morning, and his breathing was steady.

She made a wide berth around him as she stepped toward the kitchen. Good thing she'd removed her noisy boots.

"How're you this morning?" she whispered to Miriam when she was close.

Miriam whirled, her red-rimmed eyes searching, preparing for the worst. Leah winced at the fear she saw, and couldn't help but pull the girl into a hug.

Miriam's body relaxed against her, and Leah stroked her back while she spoke. "He did very well last night. Woke up a couple times and I gave him tea, then he went right back to sleep. He's in a bit of pain from some broken ribs, but in a few weeks he'll be better than new."

Miriam nodded and sniffed, then pulled away, wiping her eyes with her sleeve. "I know. It's just hard to see him like that."

Leah wanted to agree, but she didn't need to make it harder on Miriam. So she didn't respond. Instead, she gave the girl's back a final pat and stepped away. "I need to go feed the animals and milk Bethany. Do you need anything while I'm out?"

"Oh, let me go, Leah. I meant to do that before you woke up but got stuck with these biscuits. I'd rather be outside, even in the cold."

It seemed the little magpie was returning to her usual demeanor. This young lady was resilient, to say the least. "Of course. I'll take over breakfast, but make sure you bundle up."

As soon as Miriam left, Leah surveyed the biscuit dough spread across the work table and the haphazard pile of dough circles that had already been cut. Miriam could do what she had to in the kitchen, but she didn't seem to have an overwhelming desire to be there. Leah caught herself smiling.

By the time Miriam blew back through the door in a flurry of wind and cold air, Leah had the oats boiled, the venison gravy keeping warm on the back of the stove, and a pan of biscuits about ready to come out of the oven.

"Brrr." Miriam stepped around her brother to put more wood on the fire. Of course, this bustling entrance awakened Gideon.

"Come on, lazy bones. It's time to get up." Miriam turned her back to the fire, apparently to warm that side of her, but it probably had more to do with watching her brother's reaction to the teasing.

He offered a weak smile. "Just waiting for you to get my

chores done, squirt."

She eyed him knowingly. "I thought that might be the—"

Her last words were drowned out by an explosive cough from Gideon. His body wracked in the combination of a wheeze and a cry.

Leah was at his side in a moment, helping him lay back and stroking the hair from his face. Her heart raced as he fought through the pain to catch his breath

"Miriam, can you please get some pillows—at least three or four. We need to get him propped up so his lungs stay clear."

Miriam—white-faced again—disappeared into her bedroom first, then Leah's. She brought two pillows to Leah and said, "I'll climb up to the loft and get the two from up there."

Leah poured some of the Echinacea tea she'd been brewing for Gideon, and added another log to the fire.

When Miriam returned with the last two pillows, Leah knelt beside Gideon again. "We're going to raise you up now and put pillows under your back." She bent down to catch his gaze. "I don't want you to do any of the work to sit up, do you understand? Just let us lift you."

He raised a dark brow at her, but only said, "All right."

With the women on either side of him, they managed to get the pillows under his upper body so he looked more comfortable. Miriam stepped back, and Leah held up the mug for him to drink. "This will keep you from getting sick."

He tried to take it from her, but Leah kept a hand at the base. His fingers were shaking a bit, and she didn't want him to dump hot tea all over himself. The last thing he needed was a scalding on top of those deep wounds.

As he drank, Leah couldn't help but notice how long his dark lashes were. How had she never noticed that before? She wanted so badly to reach out and stroke his jaw with its day-old stubble.

His eyes raised to meet hers with an intense look, as if he could read her thoughts. Heat rose up her neck, and she looked away—just in time to see Miriam watching them with a twinkle in her sassy green eyes.

Thankfully, Gideon had finished the drink. Leah took the mug and almost ran to the kitchen. She began filling plates, forcing her mind to focus on the work at hand.

"Miriam, would you mind feeding your brother?" She kept her voice as schooled as possible, praying her friend would say yes to spare Leah more embarrassment.

Leah heard Gideon mumble something she couldn't make out, but she thought it had something to do with being perfectly capable of feeding himself.

Despite the pain in his ribs every time he moved, it was driving Gideon crazy to see both women working so hard while he lay flat on his back. He had to get up. At the very least, he needed to relieve himself.

When the room was empty, with Miriam outside and Leah in her sleeping chamber, it was time to make his move. By grabbing onto a chair leg behind him, he was able to roll onto his side with minimal groans. His ribs were shooting fire, though, and it took all his power to keep from screaming. He pushed himself onto his hands and knees, squeezing his eyes tight against the spinning of the room.

"Gideon Bryant."

He jerked at the sound, his eyes flying open. The world spun again, and he fought for control. And then he was falling, at least he thought he was. The floor pulled out from under him, but a soft hand caught his shoulder, gently lowering him to the blanket. He rolled on his back to see Leah's wide eyes hovering over him, sparks flying from their green depths like a campfire when pine needles were thrown into it.

"What do you think you were doing?" She propped a hand on each hip, rose to her full height...and glared at him.

Gideon fought the urge to cower, but that was hard not to do when he was lying flat on his back with an angry she-bear standing over him.

"I need to get up."

"Why?" She didn't move, just kept her hands on her hips and her eyes sparking. Was she trying to stare him down?

"Because I have things to do."

"What?"

He could feel his ire rising. "My chores for one. Then I need to get out to the herd. They've not had anything to eat or drink today."

"Absolutely not."

Who was this woman to tell him what he could and couldn't do?

"Well somebody has to. I don't plan to lose seventy cows and seven horses because you won't let me off this floor."

That seemed to make her pause. At least the sparks stopped flying from her eyes. She seemed to be thinking on his words. Hopefully, she was coming to her senses.

At last she stepped back and nodded, as if everything had been settled. "I'll go out and take care of the herd."

If Gideon hadn't already been on the floor, her words might have knocked him down. "Absolutely not."

Her chin came up. "Why not?" Her eyes began sparking again.

"Because you can't go out there by yourself."

"Why not?"

If she'd been close enough, he might have grabbed her pretty little shoulders and shaken some sense into her. Not really, but it made him feel slightly better to think it.

"Because you'll get lost. And you won't be strong enough to break the ice. And the animals will hurt you. And there are so many more reasons why you will not go out there." He used his and-that's-final tone that had always brought instant acquiescence from his siblings. All he got from Leah, though, was a raised eyebrow. The blasted woman.

Finally, her demeanor softened and she actually knelt down

next to his pallet. Maybe that meant she was relenting.

"Gideon," her tone was soft and soothing. "Like you said, the animals won't make it very long without food and water. You need a few days to recuperate—you were attacked by a bear, for goodness sake. I've been out with you before, and you're an excellent teacher."

His mind wandered back to that day, specifically to that kiss, and by the bright pink of her cheeks it looked like her thoughts had drifted in the same direction.

He sighed. He really didn't have much choice. His body was weak as a babe. And the animals couldn't wait...

"All right, but feed them hay and crack the ice, then come right back. Do you understand? And take Drifter with you."

Leah had been all smiles until his last statement, but now she wouldn't meet his gaze. "I don't think that's a good idea."

Now he was the one to raise an eyebrow. "Why not?"

"He has a wound on his side and leg. He'll heal, but he needs to rest for a few days, at least."

His chest tightened. His old friend...and he hadn't even thought about the dog being hurt. "Where is he?"

One edge of Leah's mouth lifted in a sad smile. "In my room actually. We made a bed for him by the cook stove, but he seems to like mine better. He's comfortable, so I haven't moved him."

Gideon fought his own grin. That dog always had been a smart one.

Chapter Twenty-Eight

*L*eah trudged through the snow with another huge mound of hay in her arms. It was nice to see the obvious appreciation from the animals, as they tore into the fodder with enthusiasm. But this working in the snow was hard. She would never admit such a thing, but it wasn't nearly as much fun without Gideon there, either. Still, she was doing what needed to be done, and that in itself was rewarding.

After the hay was out, she'd finally made a decent size hole in the ice at the creek. Now she should doctor the animals the way Gideon had showed her.

She wandered around the herd, applying the black salve on injuries. Finally, she spotted the oversize calf with its scrawny mother. The cow appeared to have gained a little weight since she'd seen it last. Good. Gideon's strategy seemed to be working.

She got the black cream on the cow's udder without much trouble. The calf had a gash on the side of its nose, though, and that would need some medicine, too. The little guy was in an energetic mood.

When she first approached, it bolted away, lunging through the high snow and stirring a few other calves to escape with him.

Leah tried again, edging in his direction with her clean glove outstretched. When she neared him, she crooned, "Come on, little guy. I just need to put some medicine on you. It won't hurt, I promise."

He let her come close, but when she reached to grab his neck, the calf twisted away. With her upper body leaning forward but no calf there to catch her, she toppled into the icy snow. It covered her coat and snuck in under her collar, snatching her breath with its icy blast.

That little brat. Leah struggled to her feet and forced herself to creep toward the animal's new location. Was he sticking his tongue out at her?

After two more tries, Leah succeeded in swiping the black goo across the obstinate calf's wet muzzle. She dragged herself back toward the little barn, removed the glove she'd used for the medicine, and closed the door, barring it in place.

When she turned to the spot where she'd tied her mare by the tree line, Leah stopped and blinked. Surely her eyes were deceiving her. There, where she'd tied one horse, now stood two—both wearing saddle and bridle and nuzzling each other affectionately.

Leah stepped forward. The second horse was Gideon's gelding, the one that had been missing since his attack. She approached the animal with her hand out, and let him sniff her until he seemed satisfied. Then she ran her hands down his neck and over his body on both sides. Both the reins were torn near the bit, and the saddle was covered with snow and scratches, but the horse seemed to have escaped injury.

She attached a rope to the geldings bridle and mounted her own mare, then began the long trek home. By the time they arrived, Leah was wet, frozen, and starved. Why hadn't she packed food to sustain her under the hard work? Is this what Gideon went through every day? And on top of caring for the herds, he did all the hunting, splitting wood, repairs on the house and barn, and who knew what else.

Miriam met her in the yard, and her face lit up at the site of the weary threesome. She motioned for Leah to dismount, then took the reins and rope, stroking the gelding's wooly neck. "Where did you find him?"

"I'll tell you inside. I'm frozen."

Miriam gave her a sympathetic look. "Of course. You go in and warm up. I'll take care of these guys."

Leah didn't have the strength or desire to object. She nodded numbly and trudged toward the house.

When she opened the door, a wave of warmth hit her like a beautiful melody, bringing with it the aroma of stew. Her attention pulled toward the pallet in front of the fire, searching out Gideon's face. He was where she'd left him, propped up on pillows and a sort of roguish half-smile on his face. She removed her jacket and gloves, then moved toward the fire.

"How did it go?" Gideon's warm voice did as much as the fire to thaw her aching body. Leah turned from the flame to look at him. He'd changed into a clean shirt, the green one that always illuminated the emerald in his eyes.

"Everyone's good. I found your saddle horse, too."

His brows rose. "Really? Where at? Is he all right?"

Leah nodded, the corners of her mouth pulling at the eagerness in Gideon's voice. "He showed up next to my mare just before I left the herd. His reins were broken and a few scratches on the saddle, but other than that, he didn't seem any worse for wear."

Gideon's features relaxed as she spoke. "Good. Did you have any trouble cracking the ice in the creek?"

Memories of the half hour she'd spent hacking at the stuff with that heavy ax, flitted through Leah's mind. But no need to worry Gideon with that kind of detail. "I got it done."

She forced her frozen cheeks into a reassuring smile. "I cracked the ice and doctored the cuts, and put out hay. Which reminds me, there's not much hay left in that shed, maybe enough for another day. Is there more somewhere else?"

Gideon's brows knit and he pursed his lips. "They'll need to move to the north pasture soon. I have more hay stored there, and the grass is tall under the snow."

Leah put on her best I-don't-think-so face. "Just so you know, unless that can wait at least two weeks, you're not going to be the one moving them anywhere."

His brows left their thoughtful furrow to raise high on his forehead, lending to his suddenly-annoyed expression.

"I'll do what I need to do." He ground out the words through a tight jaw.

Perhaps discretion would be the better part of valor in this case. After all, they had at least one more day to argue about this before she moved the cows herself.

Leah moved from in front of the fire to sit in the chair near Gideon's feet. She tried to keep her posture as friendly as possible. "So tell me how you're feeling."

The muscles in his face relaxed, and his eyes softened to a friendly glow. "Some better. My ribs hurt to move or breathe, but the throbbing in my head's down to a dull roar."

"And you've been lying still all day? Not up at all?"

His easy expression changed to a dark look. "Yes, thanks to the prison guard you posted."

Leah couldn't hold back a chuckle. "Sounds like Miriam's been obeying orders. Good girl."

The sounds drifted to Gideon of Leah stacking dirty dishes on the kitchen table. The way his pallet was positioned, he couldn't see her without craning his neck—and that would make it very obvious he was watching.

So, he allowed his gaze to drift toward the fire and his mind to picture the image Leah made across the room. She was something to see, with her slender womanly frame and the elegant way she moved, even when she carried a stack of dirty dishes to the wash basin.

It was getting harder to remind himself he wasn't going to let another person close to him again. With the spunk, wisdom and sheer determination she contained in that pretty little package,

Leah could easily fit into his world like his buckskin gloves fit his hands. But he *would not* love and lose again.

"Gideon."

The musical voice behind him jerked his attention away from the fire. Leah stood beside his pallet, apprehension tightening her face and a stack of folded bandages in her hands. She really did look like an angel.

"Yes." His voice caught on the word, probably because his mouth had gone dry.

She wouldn't look him in the eye. "I...need to change your bandages."

It took a moment for the meaning of her words to sink in, then his mind ran ahead to what it would be like for this woman to tend his wounds. He wasn't sure he could handle that. She would be very close. Close enough to weaken his willpower.

"Miriam can do it." He could hear the harshness in his tone, so he tried to moderate it. "When she gets back from the barn."

Leah nibbled on her lower lip. She looked nervous, but maybe that was uncertainty instead.

She took a deep breath, her pretty little nostrils flaring with the action. "I... I don't think that's a good idea. Miri, well..." She released the breath and finally met his gaze. "Your wounds are pretty bad. It was really hard for Miriam, with the bear and you hurt. She didn't do so well. I... I just thought it would be a good idea if she didn't have to see it again until you'd healed some."

He was a selfish heel. All he'd been thinking about was himself, but Leah was trying to save his baby sister from more pain. He nodded, heat seeping up his neck.

While Leah settled herself on the floor next to him, Gideon unbuttoned his shirt and steeled his nerves.

She looked at his bandages for a moment, then said, "Do you think you can raise up on your elbows so I can remove the dressing?"

This was going to be tricky. Any time he used his stomach muscles, his rib felt like a hot branding iron searing his insides. Still, he'd have to do this and not let on he was in pain, or Leah would never let him out of this confounded cabin.

Gideon leveraged first one elbow, then the next, clenching his jaw against the fire inside. Thankfully, she worked fast, and the pain almost kept him from noticing when she wrapped her hands around his chest to pass the roll of bandage from one side to the other under his back. Almost.

"There, you can lie back now."

Good thing, too, 'cause his muscles were one breath away from turning to jelly from the pain.

He focused on keeping his breathing slow and even, while Leah examined his cuts and dabbed them with a wet rag. Then she laid clean Juniper leaves and cloth squares over his wounds, and picked up another long bandage. He bit his lip, mentally preparing for what was coming next.

"Do you think you can raise up again?"

If only he could say no. But instead, he forced his elbows underneath his body again and squeezed his eyes shut against the agony.

It seemed like a very long time before she said, "I'm done."

Gideon fell back, exhausted, and measured each breath so as not to stress his ribs. Something tugged on his shirt, and he opened his eyes. There was his angel—the one who had just put him through so much agony—sweetly fastening the buttons on his shirt.

Gideon reached a hand to stop her. Doing his own buttons was the least he could do. When he touched her, she froze, her eyes drifting up to meet his. His gut squeezed at her tortured expression.

"I'm sorry," she whispered.

It was all he could do not to pull her to him and kiss her until all the pain in his body and soul was gone. Instead, he slipped his hand around her soft, slender one, then raised it to his lips.

He meant to kiss the tops of her fingers, like a knight greeting his princess. But his mouth found its way to the soft, fleshy part of her palm. He savored a single kiss, then his eyes found her gaze again. "You've nothing to be sorry for."

"And don't forget to take the supplies to the north pasture first before you move the animals."

A smile tugged Leah's face at Gideon's fourth reminder. She straightened the oversize buckskin tunic over her coat and turned to give him an impish grin. "Yes, sir."

The lines on his face fell. He ran a hand through his hair, and her heart tugged at the frustration on his face. He released a sigh. "I hate being stuck here while you do all the work."

Leah knelt beside Gideon's pallet where he was propped on pillows. His earnest green eyes drew her like always. "I know you do, Gideon, but you'll be out there sooner if you let yourself heal now. Besides," she sat back on her heels, giving him a sweet smile, "I'm finally getting the chance to really help around here. Please don't spoil my fun."

His lips twitched at that, and Leah rose to her feet and wrapped the scarf around her head. The thickness of her layers made it harder to move, but she relished the softness of Gideon's buckskin. Just the fact that it was *his,* heated her insides much more than the abundance of clothing she wore.

The cabin door opened, and Miriam stomped in, shaking the snow from her skirt. "Brrr. Leah, your horse is saddled and ready for ya."

"And I'm ready, too." She pulled on her last glove.

"You're taking Drifter, right?" Gideon asked. "Where is that dog?"

On cue, the click of toenails on wood sounded the animal's presence as he trotted from the direction of Leah's bedchamber. She reached a hand to him and he came willingly, his tongue lolling as she stroked his head.

"It appears he's chosen a new master these days." Gideon's tone was grumpy, reminding Leah of that first day when he'd been so angry about Drifter's friendliness toward her.

She studied his face now to gauge his temperament. Through the four-day stubble around his mouth, it pinched in a firm line. Her gaze drifted up to his eyes. Would she find a storm brewing there? Or worse—the impassive expression he used to mask his fears. Instead, there was the faintest glimmer of a twinkle, and it sent her heartbeat into double time.

Leah turned toward the door. She needed to leave now if she was going to. "I guess I'm off then."

Miriam followed Leah onto the porch, and Leah turned to face her. "Please make sure he doesn't get up today, Miri, unless he absolutely must. His color is looking better, but he could injure the rib bones again if he moves around too much."

Her friend placed a hand on Leah's arm. The pressure felt slight under all her clothing. "I'll take good care of him, Leah. Don't worry. Just take care of yourself out there."

Miriam's clear green eyes were so kind and her concerned smile so sweet, Leah couldn't stop an impulsive hug. "I know you will. I'll be back before dark."

Chapter Twenty-Nine

The sky was a clear blue as Leah followed the trail through the woods, with Drifter trotting in her horse's tracks. The quiet time was perfect to thank her Father for the beauty all around. And, of course, she sent up her usual prayers for Gideon and Miriam back at the cabin. She was careful to stay away from the topic of her future in her prayer, though. She would need to face reality once the snow melted, but no need to push things yet. For now, she could enjoy this peaceful haven in the mountains.

When the trees broke and she arrived at the overlook, Leah paused for a moment to enjoy the view. It still took her breath away—the wild beauty of this scene. The white valley far below, rising into majestic peaks in the distance. She knew how Gideon felt when he'd said the land was a part of him. Her chest hurt at just the thought of leaving this place.

What would it be like to marry a mountain man and stay here forever? Images of Gideon flashed through her mind. First the strong, hardened, emotionless man she'd met when she arrived at the ranch, then the tender strength he'd shown after she changed his bandage the other night. There had been emotion in that face, to be sure. But could Gideon ever allow himself to love her? He'd been through so much. Would he let his defenses down again? Only God could make that happen...but would He?

Leah kneed the mare forward, heading toward the pasture

where the stock milled about. She did a quick visual inspection of the animals as she rode to the tree where she usually tied her mare. All seemed to be in good shape, although they started mooing as soon as they saw her.

"Sorry, guys. I don't have hay for you today. I'll get you water, though, before I move the supplies." A nicker from the horses at the far side of the field answered her.

Once she'd cracked the ice, loaded most of the supplies from the little barn into her saddle bags, and tied the bucket of medicine onto her saddle, Leah mounted and rode toward the tree line at the higher end of the pasture. She found the deer trail right where Gideon had described it. Then she followed the tiny hoof marks in the snow as the trail wound ever higher up the mountain. At last, she came out into an open area, smaller than the lower pasture where the cows were now. Her eyes were drawn to a rocky overhang that jutted out of the mountainside, creating a shelter underneath. The snow was a serene blanket, unbroken by the tumult of hooves.

A place under the tree canopy looked like a good spot to secure the supplies. After securing them, it was time to mount her mare and headed back to the lower pasture for the hard part— moving the herd.

Gideon was a good teacher, to be sure, and his methods worked. She found the lead cow he'd described, then worked to separate her from the herd.

"Come on girl, let's go."

Nothing. The cow just glared at her.

Leah nudged her horse forward a step. "Hey there, let's show the others what to do. Come on."

With much coaxing, and after several tries, she finally had the old girl moving down the deer trail. Drifter circled the remainder of the herd, yipping and nipping at their legs. Wonder of wonders, the animals began to amble after their leader.

Leah stayed about fifteen feet behind the animal, as Gideon had instructed, letting her move at her own pace. The cow seemed smart, though, and stayed on the trail. As they neared the higher clearing, she picked up her pace, as if she'd done this particular routine more than once, and knew good things were coming.

Once the animals broke into the clearing, they spread out, stomping and pawing through the snow around the tree line where it wasn't as deep. Leah couldn't hold back a wide grin. She'd made it. At least with most of the herd. A few cattle still drifted into the clearing from the trail, but she would make sure all the animals were in the new pasture when she went to get the horses.

The elation at moving a herd of seventy cows on her own—with Drifter, that is—soon faded as she tried to break through the ice in the stream. This virgin ice was thicker than most tree trunks, and Leah began to wonder if there was any running water underneath after all. After half an hour of sheer determination, she finally collapsed against a pine, the gurgle of water her reward for the incredible effort. If only Emily could see her now...

The deeper chill of late afternoon had taken over when Leah finally mounted her mare and scanned the animals in the clearing for the last time. A warm feeling of accomplishment drifted over her, infusing strength into her weary muscles.

Gideon had described a shorter trail she could take which would meet up with the main path going back to the cabin, and Leah found it easily enough. She relaxed as they made their way home. She was almost a real rancheress, with her horse and her dog.

A menacing growl from behind raised the hairs on Leah's arms. She twisted in the saddle to see Drifter, frozen in place, with his attention pinned to something off the trail to their right. Her horse seemed to see it now, too, as the mare's ears pricked and muscles tensed.

Leah squinted in the direction the animals pointed, but had trouble seeing anything against the blinding white of the snow. There it was. A movement through the trees. It could have been a branch swaying in the wind, but the tension in her chest told her it was not.

Should she run? Or approach to see if it was one of the cattle?

But if it wasn't one of the herd, the movement could have been from a mountain lion, a bear, or who knew what else.

Before she could decide, the object moved again, this time morphing into two men on horses. But they weren't just any men. As they rode closer, her skin tingled and she froze. The men had brown skin, sharp cheekbones, and long black braids. Indians.

The horses stopped about thirty feet away from her, the Indians staring stone-faced under their heavy furs. They seemed to be taking her measure, but all Leah could do was stare. If she turned away, would they chase her?

For what seemed an eternity, they all stood and watched each other. Then the taller Indian spoke to his partner, his voice rising and falling in a lively cadence. It was all gibberish to Leah. The shorter Indian responded with a single guttural sound.

Would they understand English? Just when she had worked up the courage to speak to them, the Indians turned their horses in unison, like a well-rehearsed ballet, and rode back the way they'd come.

Had she really just seen Indians? It had all happened so quickly, it now seemed surreal. But no, the tracks were there, plain as day. And Drifter still sat by her horse's hooves, emitting a low growl every few minutes. For a long moment, Leah didn't move, but her mind whirled in ten directions.

Her horse stamped in the snow and jerked on the reins in her hand, pulling Leah from her reverie. She urged her mare forward. They needed to get away from here. What she wouldn't give to be tucked safely inside the warm cabin right now.

Leah saved her dramatic Indian story for after dinner, when they were all gathered around the fireplace. Leah and Miriam sat in chairs, while Gideon was still propped against pillows on the floor.

He listened to her recounting in silence, a wrinkle between his brows. At last he spoke. "Were they wearing any paint on their faces or horses?"

Leah brought back the image of the men in her mind. "I don't think so. One of them wore a fur hood, but I could still see his face. I don't remember any paint, though."

He nodded, the wrinkle lessening a bit. "Sounds like they were Apsaroke, probably a hunting party passing through. They sometimes have a winter camp a couple of mountains over, but I haven't seen them yet this year."

Leah raised her brows. "I've never heard of Apsaroke before. Are they friendly Indians?"

Gideon shrugged, then winced at the movement. "The white men call them Crow, but they call themselves Apsaroke. They're usually friendly, especially in these parts where there aren't that many white men. If they were wearing war paint, I might be worried. But they usually try to stay on good terms with us. We don't bother them, they don't bother us, and we all take care of the land."

A shiver ran down Leah's spine. From fear or excitement?

Gideon relished the sharpness of the icy air on his face and the feel of horseflesh beneath him. It had been almost two weeks since his encounter with the bear, and *Doctor Leah* had finally released him to accompany her as she went out to care for the herd. Of course, she'd only agreed after he promised not to carry anything heavy or do anything dangerous. His lips twitched at the memory of the plucky little woman with her hands on her hips, her chin locked in determination, and both green eyes shooting fire.

The truth was, between his ribs and his head, he'd just now gotten to where he could stand up without groaning and reaching for a chair to keep himself vertical. He'd acted miffed with Leah for playing the part of his jailor, but he probably wouldn't have been able to mount his horse without help before now.

Getting back out on the trail though, that was what he

needed. The world was right. And for some reason, the woman riding on the bay mare behind him seemed to fit perfectly in this right world.

When they reached the upper pasture, Gideon tied both of their horses while Leah grabbed the ax and headed toward the creek. He made his way through the cattle, eyeballing them as he rubbed itchy spots. It was hard to relax, though, with the echo of the ax ricocheting in the clearing. He gripped his hands into fists to fight the guilt. She shouldn't be doing the hard work while he stood there useless.

He moved toward the sound, the frustration building as she came into view. Leah's slight body heaved the heavy ax over her head, then drove it into the frozen creek. It seemed to take every ounce of her strength, and she paused to take a breath after each blow. He stopped himself about ten feet away, gripping the bottom edge of his buckskin so his hands didn't jerk the ax away from her. This was not right.

After an eternity, she broke through to water. Three more whacks and she had a decent sized hole. Leah allowed the metal end of the ax to fall to the ground, holding onto the handle like a cane. She leaned against it, her shoulders rising and falling with heavy breaths.

He couldn't stand it anymore. In two long strides, he reached her, then pulled her elbow so she turned to face him. Gideon gripped both of her arms, the ax handle falling to the ground. "Are you all right?"

He could see the exhaustion in her eyes, her chest still heaving under the thickness of his buckskin. *His* buckskin. A possessive heat flared through him, and his right hand crept up to stroke the leather where it rested on her shoulder.

His gaze found hers again and rested there. "Thank you, Leah. For everything. You've been amazing." If only he could tell her how amazing.

Her mouth opened, as if she wanted to speak, but no sound came out. His attention was drawn to that mouth, though, her full lips flushed red from the cold. He couldn't pull his attention away, and before he could stop himself, he lowered his mouth to hers.

Oh, she tasted good. Her lips warmed his own with their sureness. She didn't hesitate, didn't pull back. He forced himself to keep it gentle, but couldn't wholly stop the desire she raised in him. He didn't remember it being like this with Jane. He had no sense of duty with Leah, just this feeling of elation that soared through him. He wanted to be all she desired, wanted to be worthy of her. So much it scared him...

The old familiar fear rose in his chest, but he forced it down, deepening the kiss. He would fight this, he had to. Images flashed through his mind. Abel's blood on the snow... Four crosses in the little graveyard...

He tore his mouth away from Leah's and dropped his forehead to rest on hers, squeezing his eyes against the images. He struggled to catch his breath. A gentle hand touched his cheek, but he couldn't lift his lids, couldn't meet her gaze.

"Gideon?" Her voice was soft, uncertain.

"I'm sorry..." It was all he could say. He pressed his eyes tighter, hating the pain he knew he was causing. "I can't do this, Leah. I'm sorry..."

Her head pulled away, and he let his fall, feeling so much the failure. Then something touched his chin—warm and soft and a bit moist. His eyes jerked open and met Leah's shimmering green pools.

"It's going to be all right, Gideon." The earnestness in her expression stopped his breath. Oh how he wanted to believe her. He wanted to trust her. But the fear twisting his gut held him back.

Chapter Thirty

Leah folded the bread dough in half as she worked it, kneading and squeezing to mix the ingredients. Her mind wandered back to Gideon, as it usually did these days. Was he still thinking about their kiss last week, too? The pure anguish that had been in his eyes, in the slump of his shoulders, made her chest ache with a physical pain. *Lord, please. Help him. Show him Your perfect love casts out all fear.*

"So when are you going to tell me what happened?" Miriam's voice pulled Leah from her prayer, as the younger woman sliced meat beside her.

"What happened when?"

Miri rolled her eyes. "When you and Gideon went out to take care of the herd last week. You've both been acting strange ever since."

Leah's brows pinched. "I've not been acting funny." At least she hoped she hadn't. She couldn't stop worrying about Gideon—or praying for him.

A "humph" from Miriam brought Leah's attention back. "I may be younger than you, Leah Townsend, but don't think I was born yesterday. You look at him like you've lost your best friend, and he won't look you in the eye. On top of that, you've let him go out by himself every day since that first one. And you knew good as I did he wasn't strong enough. And you're worryin' yourself sick." Miriam sliced through the meat with an extra strong force as if to illustrate her disgust.

Leah chose to ignore most of what Miriam said and focus on the last. She gave her best look of offended innocence. "I'm not worrying."

A snort broke forth from Miriam. "You mean that wasn't worry that made you put the biscuits in the pie safe instead of the oven yesterday, so they were mounds of goo when we found them at dinner time? Or how about when you were doing washing on Monday and you scrubbed Gideon's shirt so hard three buttons popped off, and you pulled a hole in the arm seam?"

The heat coming off Leah's cheeks could have baked the bread dough she had now smashed to a thin layer.

"So are you gonna tell me what happened?" Miriam stopped cutting meat and turned to face Leah, her right hip cocked against the work counter and her left fist propped on the other one.

Leah desperately wanted to tell her. There wasn't much she hadn't told Miriam over the last few months. But Gideon was her brother. Her *older* brother whom she respected and adored. It wouldn't be right to talk about the deep roots of his fears to his baby sister.

Miriam threw her hands off her hips in frustration and turned back to the meat. "I know you love the man, although why I'm not always sure."

The embarrassment radiated from Leah's ears now. "Why in the world do you say that?"

Miriam gave her a longsuffering look. "You look at him the same way Mama used to look at Pa. And they were more in love than anyone I've ever seen."

Leah fought the burn of tears, and looked down at the dough in her hands. "It really doesn't matter anyway."

A hand touched her back and rubbed gently. It was almost Leah's undoing, but she bit her lip and blinked back the moisture.

"Don't worry, honey. He'll wake up and see things straight one of these days. He just needs to find a way to get through the past."

Leah nodded, not trusting herself to speak.

The warm sunrays were heavenly on Leah's back as she scrubbed Miriam's brown wool skirt in the wash water. The frigid pattern of snow and cold grey skies had finally ceased, and the sun had forced its way through the clouds for three days now. The sound of cracking ice had changed into dripping water through the trees, and bare patches were even beginning to show on the ground in the sunny spots.

It was time to leave the ranch.

She knew it in her head, but her heart fought violently against the notion. She'd finally admitted to herself she loved Gideon Bryant, but it was obvious he wasn't going to let himself love her back. And being so close to him, knowing he wouldn't love her, was driving her mad. Even if the snow hadn't begun melting, it was still time to leave. Staying would only be painful for them both.

Lord, please show me where You would have me go. Butte City? Helena? The Washington Territory? With each name, she waited for a feeling of peace or that gentle prodding she used to be able to recognize so well. Nothing.

Leah wrung out the skirt and laid it with the other damp clothes in the basket. Then she rose to her feet with the hamper, squaring her shoulders with the determination that comes from desperation.

At the dinner table that night, the bile in Leah's stomach kept her from forcing down much of her Shepherd's Pie. Halfway through the meal, she finally set her fork on the plate and squared her shoulders. It was now or never. She had to do this.

"Gideon, do you think the pass has melted enough to get

through to Helena or Butte?"

His head jerked up and his hand froze, suspended midway to his mouth with gravy dripping from the chunk of bread in his grasp. For a split second, the emotion in his eyes looked almost like hurt, then it was gone. Covered by that awful impassive expression he used to wear so well.

For a long moment, he didn't move, didn't chew, didn't say a word. Just studied her, his emerald eyes turning too cloudy to read.

And then he spoke. "Prob'ly so."

Two words. Just two words that had the ability to blow up her hopes like a bullet exploding a glass bottle. But what had she expected? That he would drop to one knee and beg her not to leave?

Leah expelled her hurt slowly, forcing her mind to move on. "I guess I'll be leaving then. I think I'll start in Butte City since it's closest. Surely one of the stores or restaurants is hiring." She was rambling, although she couldn't have repeated anything she'd said if her life depended on it. She had to get control of herself.

"Would you mind if I borrowed one of the horses to ride to town? I'm sure I can send her back with Ol' Mose next time he comes through, or else I can have a messenger bring her." Although where she'd get the money for that, she hadn't a clue.

"I'll take you." He said it with a snarl, as if she'd just called him a no-count, mule-brained, horse thief.

It was obvious he didn't want to. Probably because he had too much work to do on the ranch, and likely wasn't feeling up to a full-day's ride in the wagon. She opened her mouth to object, a muscle flexed in his jaw revealing how tightly it was clenched. She couldn't read a thing in his eyes, but the rest of his body language said it all. He was going to do this.

"Thank you." Leah's gaze dropped to her plate. The casserole there had been just short of mutilated. There was only one more question she desperately *didn't* want to ask. But she had to know.

She raised her eyes to Gideon's face again, then forced her dry mouth to swallow. "When do you think we can go?"

"I'm only taking this one trunk, Miri. I want you to keep the rest of my gowns." Leah forced an almost unnatural cheeriness into her voice, and looked up to see if her words brought a smile to her friend's face.

No, Miriam looked like she might burst into tears at any second. She was supposed to be transferring undergarments from the bureau to Leah's trunk, but her progress was slow.

The weight that had pressed on Leah's chest for two days now—since Gideon agreed to take her to Butte—was close to smothering. And Miriam's persistent melancholy had Leah's nerves on edge. She would not cry, though. *God, please keep me strong through this.*

"Leah, you just can't leave. It isn't right!"

Leah turned at the outburst from her friend.

Miriam's pale green eyes were shrouded in red, her bottom lip quivering.

Leah dropped the brown traveling suit she'd been about to pack, and strode across the room. She took Miriam's hands in her own and lowered her head to peer into the girl's face.

"Miriam, I wish I didn't have to leave you. I really do. But I need to move on with my life, and find what God would have me do. You and your brother have been so kind to take me in these last months, but I can't depend on your hospitality forever. I need to make my own way." Leah's voice cracked at the end, and her eyes burned with tears that would fall any minute. She turned away so Miriam wouldn't see her heart breaking.

Miriam pulled her hands. "But you belong *here*, Leah. Don't you see? You belong with us. Gideon will marry you, I know he will!" Miriam's voice rose to a high pitch, laced with desperation.

Leah's heart clenched at the words. She searched Miriam's face to see if it showed any foreshadowing of truth in her words.

But no, she spoke only the desperate longings of a lonely young woman.

Leah released one of Miriam's hands and reached to cup her cheek, wiping a tear with her thumb. "I don't think Gideon will ever marry again. And my presence here is just making things harder for him. It's better if I go."

"But Leah!" Miriam's voice was an avalanche of pleading. Then it fell to almost a whisper. "Don't you know *I* need you?"

Leah couldn't stand it any longer. She pulled the girl into a fierce embrace and let the tears stream down her face. Oh, God, why did this have to be so hard? After a few minutes, she worked to control her weeping, but Miriam's shuddering sobs continued. Leah kept the girl in the hug, gently stroking her back while she searched for the words in her heart.

"God has amazing things planned for your life, Miriam Bryant. I don't want you to forget that, do you hear me?" Leah paused to sniff. "You just have to make sure you lean on Him no matter what. And always be seeking His will."

She leaned back enough to see Miriam's face, but kept one arm wrapped around the girl. "God will take you to better places than you could ever imagine. But wherever you go, make sure you stay in touch with me, do you hear? And if you're ever nearby, I expect a visit. Understood?"

Leah paused as Miriam sniffed loudly and wiped her eyes with a sleeve, then nodded.

"All right, then. I think this trunk is ready to go. Would you mind helping me carry it to the wagon?"

She received another nod, then released Miriam and the women each took an end of the crate.

The wagon and horses were waiting by the front porch, and they were able to load the trunk with no problems.

"I suppose Gideon must be in the barn. I'll go let him know I'm ready." The last thing Leah wanted to do was find Gideon. But the morning was passing quickly and they needed to get on the trail. Besides, he'd been avoiding her for days now, so it wasn't likely he'd want to talk.

As she entered the dim light of the barn, Gideon came out of Bethany's stall. A few pieces of hay still clung to his navy wool shirt. When he approached, Leah found herself looking anywhere but at him. "I...I wanted to let you know I'm ready when you are."

She expected a gruff response, or maybe just a growl of acknowledgment. That was about the only words he spoke these days. But he didn't make any sound.

After a few moments of silence, Leah's curiosity got the better of her and she allowed her eyes to drift to him. He had his hands behind his back, his attention focused on the ground where he was kicking at a dirt clod.

"You know." His voice was deep, almost raspy, as if he hadn't used it in a while. "You don't have to go. You can stay on here as long as you want."

Leah's chest burned all the way down, and her heart convulsed at the vise that was squeezing the life out of her. *Lord, You're giving me more than I can bear. If You want me to leave, You have to help me.*

She swallowed hard and turned her gaze to look at the stall door, anything so she didn't have to see the man in front of her. "I...I don't think..." *Lord, please!* "I think I need to go." The words came out in a tumble, as if they knew she would never let them out if they didn't speak now.

Her disobedient eyes trailed up to Gideon's face in time to see his expression change to the impassive look she knew so well. His eyes shuttered, sending painful memories of the way he'd looked when she first arrived at the cabin.

"Let's go then." It was an order, like what he'd say to Drifter. And he marched past her out of the barn.

Chapter Thirty-One

After three long, awkward hours in the wagon, Leah could finally see rows of buildings sprawling in the valley below. This must be Butte City. She tried not to wrinkle her nose at the sight. The town looked dirty, even from this distance, although it was a bit larger than she had imagined.

A wave of longing hit Leah for the peaceful cabin she'd left, and the wide-open beauty of the mountains. What was she doing here? Her eyes burned. She could turn back now, ask Gideon to let her return with him to the cabin. They'd let her stay, she was sure of it. She could work to earn her room and board. Heaven knew, they could use the help.

Leah stopped herself just before raising a hand to touch Gideon's arm. She'd never considered herself a coward before. She needed to straighten her spine and face this next step head-on. She squared her shoulders.

Gideon drove the wagon down first one street, then another. Past plain, unattractive buildings. There was none of the elegant architecture of Richmond or St Louis. At least most of these buildings were covered in whitewash, although a lot of that was peeling and in need of a fresh coat.

Finally he pulled up in front of a two-story structure with a sign over the door that read *Watson's Boarding House*. Leah climbed from the wagon before Gideon could assist, although judging from his stiff movements and the sharp set of his jaw, he may not have offered.

She followed him into the building and paused at the threshold to get her bearings. The room was not large, more like an oversize foyer. Just big enough to hold a fireplace, a coat stand, and a small desk. The staircase rose in front of her, with a narrow hall beside it.

Gideon had approached the desk and was speaking to a middle-aged man with long fuzzy sideburns. "This should cover room and board for a couple of months. If she decides to leave before then, I'll expect you to return whatever wasn't used. Do I make myself clear?"

The man gave a sober nod. "Of course, sir. Any gold dust not used for Miss Townsend's stay will be returned upon her departure." He spoke in a sophisticated accent, at odds to the plain appearance of his hotel.

Leah peeked around Gideon's shoulder and saw a small leather bag on the desk. Were they talking about gold dust in that bag? And room and board for two months? Even though he'd originally offered to reimburse her steamboat trip, it didn't sit right for Gideon to put out so much money for her.

The man behind the desk closed the book in which he'd been scribbling, picked up the leather bag, and said, "If you'll wait a moment, I'll get someone to carry her luggage up." The man retreated through a doorway.

This was her chance. "Gideon, I don't like you giving me that much money. I should have a job within a week and can pay my own expenses. Please take most of it back." He'd turned to face her when she started speaking, but Leah couldn't meet his gaze. Her eyes fluttered to his arm, the desk, the wall—anything but his face.

"No."

It was such a strong word, spoken with quiet authority. Her wayward eyes darted to his deep green gaze, searching for the hidden meaning behind that answer. There was stubbornness there, for sure. And was that longing?

Her own heart tugged at her, pushing her body forward to run to him, but her feet wouldn't move. They were planted like the huge rocks up on the mountain. He took a step toward her, and opened his mouth to speak.

"Okay, Miss Townsend. If you'll follow me to your room." The obtrusive voice of the hotel clerk chased away whatever Gideon had been about to say. "Mr. Bryant, if you'll show Michael the luggage, he'll be happy to carry it to Miss Townsend's room."

And just like that, the moment was gone.

Gideon turned and strode through the outside door. Leah numbly followed the clerk toward the stairs. At the bottom, she turned for one final glimpse of Gideon, vain as it was.

There he was, through the open door. He gestured toward her trunk and spoke words she couldn't hear to someone she couldn't see.

And then he looked up, as if he could feel her gaze on him. But his eyes didn't hold the same expression they had moments before. She would recognize that impenetrable mask anywhere, and it made the distance that now separated them stretch as wide as a canyon.

Leah forced herself to turn away and trudge up the stairs. Her teeth found her lower lip as she struggled to keep the moisture in her eyes at bay. *Lord, please help me.*

Gideon jerked on the wagon's brake harder than necessary, but he barely heard the groan of the wood in his hand. He forced himself not to stomp into the dry goods store, and then to punish his impatient heart, he allowed another man to step up to the counter in front of him. While Gideon waited behind the man, his mind fumed.

Of all the nerve. Leave it to a city woman from back East to run around wherever she pleased, ignoring the feelings of others. And now his baby sister was going to pay the price. Miriam didn't have many friends, and he'd never seen her bond with a woman the way she had with Leah. But that didn't seem to matter to the selfish lady.

Finally, the grubby man in front of him moved away from the counter, and Gideon stepped forward. He slid his list toward the clerk. "Can I pick these up first thing tomorrow morning?"

The balding man picked up the paper and squinted through his spectacles. "Should be fine. We open at seven thirty."

Gideon nodded and turned toward the door. He'd make it through his errands this afternoon, then get out of town first thing tomorrow.

When he pulled the wagon to a stop in front of the blacksmith's shed, the burly smithy was beating the heat out of a strip of metal. Gideon's hands itched for a turn. Why was he letting this get to him? Letting *her* get to him? But she hadn't gotten to *him*, it was Miriam she was hurting by leaving. If that was the case, though, why did he feel the pain so deep in his own chest? Leah's image flashed through his mind and he clenched his fists to keep from clawing it away.

"What can I help you with?"

Gideon blinked at the smithy standing next to the wagon, his face smeared with dirt and sweat clinging his brown shirt to his shoulders.

"Have a couple wheels that need fixin'."

The man nodded, and helped Gideon unload the two broken wagon wheels he'd brought along. He nodded again as Gideon pointed out the flaws in the metal. It was nice to meet another man who didn't have to use up words to communicate.

"I'll have 'em ready tomorrow before noon."

Gideon schooled his face against the disappointment. He'd hoped to be back at the cabin in time to eat lunch with Miriam. "The earlier the better." He turned to climb back on the wagon, tamping down his frustration.

Maybe food would put him in a better frame of mind. He turned the team down Granite Street toward Pearl's Café. She served the best cinnamon rolls in town, almost as good as the ones Leah had made last week. In front of the building, he allowed the team of horses a drink from the water trough, then tied them to a rail.

Inside, he found a spot at one of the two long tables that spanned the room. A waitress placed a cup of coffee in front of him, and he nodded his thanks.

"You want dinner?"

He looked up to see the woman eyeing him expectantly. She was middle-aged with a good bit of grey filling in her dull brown hair. The lines around her face made her look worn out, and she likely was from serving this crowd.

"Yes, thanks."

Satisfied with his answer, she moved on to pick up a stack of dishes from the end of the table, then disappeared through a doorway.

Gideon scanned the faces around him, finding a motley bunch ranging from miners with their dirty flannel sleeves rolled to the elbow, to businessmen in suits and bowler hats. As he scanned, one of the men across the table met Gideon's gaze and gave a polite nod. The man was small, with spectacles illuminating his tiny features and giving him the appearance of an owl.

Before Gideon could answer with his own nod, a burly man beside the man with the spectacles reached for a coffee pot, knocking over the salt shaker in the process.

"Oh, dear," said Spectacles. But the big man didn't seem to notice his own clumsiness, just refilled his cup and clunked the pot back on the table. Spectacles reached over to right the fallen shaker, pushing his glasses higher on his face as he did so.

"You from around here?" Burly had gone back to his meal with gusto, but asked the question between bites, tilting his head to look at Spectacles as he spoke.

Spectacles cleared his throat and pushed his glasses up again.

"Ah, yes. I'm the telegraph operator here in Butte City." The man's voice came out raspy, as if he needed to clear his throat, and occasionally it pitched high. Either he was suffering from a throat ailment, or he was nervous. "And you, sir. Are you from this area?"

"Naw, got business here." Burly spoke through a mouth full of chicken.

Spectacles took a dainty sip of his coffee. "And what is your business, Mister..." He paused for Burly to fill in the name.

"Name's Jenson, an' I'm here lookin' fer my wife."

Spectacles' eyes grew even larger, if that was possible. "Your wife? Is she visiting our fair city?"

Gideon bit back a snort. Butte was a dirty, vice-ridden mining town. Not much *fair* about this city.

He watched Jenson, waiting for a reply. For a quick second, the man's eyes held a hard glint, before his thick brows merged to form a concerned expression. "The woman done took the crazy notion to run away. Her ma passed on an' I think it touched her in the head a bit, 'cause she weren't thinkin' straight. I'm worried she'll get mixed up with the wrong folks an' git herself hurt."

Something about the man didn't seem on the up and up. His concern for his wife appeared forced, and he told the story almost like an actor at the theater Gideon's parents had taken him to back in Kentucky—dramatic and well-rehearsed.

"Maybe you've seen her," Jenson continued, his eyes squinting as he studied Spectacles. "She's middlin' height, brown hair, green eyes. Her people had money in Richmond so she walks an' talks like high society."

Every nerve in Gideon's body came to life as the man's description resonated in his mind. *Her people had money in Richmond.* The description matched Leah exactly, although it was vague enough to match at least a dozen women in this mining town, and hundreds more throughout the Territory.

Gideon studied the man who'd called himself Jenson, trying to recall everything Leah had said about the fiancé who'd threatened her life. He'd been a business associate of her father's, but Gideon couldn't imagine this grubby man in Richmond's business world. But maybe this man had been hired by the blackguard in Richmond. He was probably too yellow to do his own dirty work.

He struggled to pull back Leah's words. Her fiancé had sent a man to follow her to St. Louis. Had that been this man? Had he followed her all the way up the Missouri River? If so, it was clear he hadn't found her yet. Probably because she'd been hidden away in Gideon's cabin for all these months.

But now she was in town, and planning to ask around for a job. It was very likely this Jenson would find her. And then what would he do? Could they force her to marry the rat against her will? Leah had obviously thought that was possible, or she wouldn't have fled across the country to escape him.

"Here you go, sugar."

Gideon snapped out of his thoughts at the woman's voice behind him. She placed a steaming plate on the table. The fried chicken, whipped potatoes, and canned apples looked like they should be good, but his appetite had left. The knot forming in his stomach made him want to jump up and run from this place, find Leah and make her go back to the ranch with him.

But he needed to keep an eye on this Jenson fellow, too. For now, the man had turned his full focus back to the plate in front of him, so Gideon forced himself to eat as well. He would probably need the sustenance for strength soon.

While Gideon ate, his mind wandered back through the story Jenson had given. Was there any chance it was true? Could Leah really have been married to this man, and in her delusion made up the story about a fiancé trying to kill her? Images played through his mind—of Leah serving dinner, Leah patiently teaching Trojan to lead, Leah tending his wounds from the bear. There's no way she was crazy. She was too brave and strong and caring. And she'd always been honest with Miriam and him. She brought out the best in them—in him.

His eyes trailed to Jenson again. The man shoved a cinnamon roll into his open jaw with both dirty hands. He had glaze smeared on his beard and a streak of something brown on his cheek that Gideon hoped was cinnamon. No, there was no way his kind, genteel Leah had been married to this man.

Gideon could take the sitting no longer. He rose, climbed over the bench, placed a coin on the table for the meal, and strode out the door.

Chapter Thirty-Two

Gideon had to ring the little bell at the desk twice before the clerk came through the doorway, covering a yawn. It was the same man from earlier, the one with the thick hair on the sides of his face, but clean-shaven around his mouth.

"Is Miss Townsend in her room?" He didn't mean his voice to sound as harsh as it came out, but the urgency of her situation had him wound tighter than a mountain lion before attack.

"Yes, sir, but she's already retired for the night, and asked not to be disturbed."

Retired for the night? It couldn't be seven o'clock yet. He placed both of his hands on the desk and looked the man square in the eyes. "I need to speak with her, and it can't wait."

The clerk's chin jutted out as he coolly returned Gideon's glare. "I'm afraid I can't allow that. As I assured you earlier, Mr. Bryant, the safety and comfort of our guests is of the utmost importance to us. Miss Townsend has requested privacy, and that, sir, is what she will receive."

Gideon held the man's gaze as he thought through the situation. The actions of this clerk were exactly why he'd brought Leah to this boarding house instead of the larger City Hotel. He'd heard this was a family-run place where they put great stock in caring for their guests. It looked like Wooly here wouldn't let anyone close to Leah for tonight, at least. And Gideon would be here first thing in the morning to fetch her, whether this man "allowed" him to or not.

At the breakfast table the next morning, Leah perused the scene around her. The boarding house clerk had recommended this eatery as "quality food and service", and it appeared many other people agreed with him. All tables were occupied, and the aroma of sausage and fried potatoes wafted through the room.

"Can I sit here?"

She looked up to see a large man standing behind the empty chair across from her. His hair was mussed and his beard shaggy, but he wore a suit—although it was at least two sizes too small, and the buttons pulled across his burly abdomen.

"I suppose so." With so many people around, the man was surely harmless enough.

He plopped into the ladder-back chair and motioned toward a waiter across the room. Leah took a sip of her tea while he ordered coffee and food. His manners were rough, at best, and his gentleman's clothes seem to fit his personality as poorly as they fit his body. Her gaze drifted to his hands. They were huge and calloused, but at least dirt wasn't caked under his nails.

When the waiter moved away, the big man turned to her with a scrutinizing look. The hairs on her neck tingled. Maybe it wasn't such a good idea to allow a strange man to share her table.

"So are you from these parts?"

Why did that question make her cheeks heat. Maybe it was the way he studied her. "No, sir. I'm from the state of Virginia originally, although I've been traveling in recent months."

Oh, no. She shouldn't have told so much about her background. The months at the cabin had given her a false sense of security, but she was back in the real world now. But would Simon really be able to track her to the Montana Territory? She shouldn't take any chances.

The man's interest showed on his face. "Virginia, huh. I have friends there. Where're ya from in Virginia?"

Uh, oh. She'd said way more than she should have. But how to get out of the question? "I'm from the eastern side of the state." And that was all he would get out of her.

"An' what'd ya say yer name was?"

She had to find a way to reroute this conversation away from herself. And what if his friends were from Richmond? The Townsend name was well-known in that city. "My name is Leah. And yours?"

It was almost unheard of for a woman to allow a strange man to use her Christian name, but if word got back to Simon that a Miss Townsend was in Butte City, the outcome would be much worse than an improper manner of address. And the chances of her meeting this man again were slim. She hoped.

"Name's Jenson."

"Well, Mr. Jenson. Do you live here in Butte City?"

She was spared his answer by the arrival of their breakfast plates, and Jenson dove into his like he hadn't eaten in a week. His table manners left much to be desired.

Leah averted her eyes and nibbled at her own food. She needed to begin looking for work today, but the thought held no appeal. Where should she start? It didn't seem likely she'd find a governess position in this town. Maybe she could visit a mercantile and see if they had any jobs for women.

Her breakfast companion finally raised his head and sat back in his chair, wiping his face and hands with the napkin. The cloth came away quite dirty.

Maybe he could tell her where to find the local businesses. "Mr. Jenson, would you be able to give me directions to the mercantiles in this town, and the dress shops or other clothing stores?"

He crossed his arms over his gut and leaned back in the chair so it rested on its two rear legs. "Don't know about no shops for fancy duds, but Lanyard's Dry Goods is over on Washington.

They've got decent stock of most things."

"Thank you. Do you happen to know if they're hiring additional employees?"

His eyes narrowed to slits as they perused her face. She shouldn't have asked that question. When would she learn when to keep her mouth shut?

"Seems like I did hear somethin' about them lookin' fer a new sales clerk."

The words grabbed her attention. "Really? Can you tell me how to find the store?"

Less than thirty minutes later, Leah strode down Park Street as Mr. Jenson had instructed. She crossed over Arizona Street, then turned right on Gaylord. It was a longer walk than she'd expected, but the roads were exactly as he'd said they would be.

The buildings she passed, though, were increasingly more run-down. Collections of wood shacks were scattered between the places of business, although the dwellings didn't look like much more than lean-tos built onto each other.

Loud, energetic piano music drifted from one of the limestone buildings. Surely any business in this part of town would not be a proper place for her to work. Should she turn back? Find a woman or a respectable man to ask for better directions? She should have known better than to take advice from a rough-looking man like Mr. Jenson.

Her feet had begun to protest against the leather of her good boots, and a bench called to her from the corner of the two-story restaurant she was passing. A few minutes' rest before turning back would be nice, and it shouldn't be too hard to follow her directions in reverse.

Just as Leah relaxed onto the seat, something strong came around her waist and pulled her backward. She screamed, but the sound was muffled as a cloth covered her mouth. It smothered all noise and breath. Her hands flailed, trying to grab something, anything to keep her upright.

It happened so fast. The strong arm around her waist drug

her backward, farther into an alley. A sharp antiseptic odor permeated the fabric on her face, and she struggled to think through what was happening. She clawed at the arms, but they were so strong. And she was so tired…

Gideon stood outside the café and ran both hands through his hair, pinching it at the tips and pulling. Hard. Maybe pain would keep him from screaming at this intense frustration.

How had he let this happen? He'd tossed and turned and worried for so many hours last night, it had been the early part of the morning before he'd drifted to sleep. And then, for the first time since he was a little boy, he'd actually slept past dawn. And now Leah had left her room, eaten breakfast, and headed out into this rough town where at least one man was ready to pounce the moment he saw her. He growled at his stupidity.

So what should he do now? The matron inside remembered showing Leah to a table, but had no idea when she'd left or where she'd gone. Should he start by looking for her at the local businesses? Hope he could pick up her trail?

His mind drifted back to the man Jenson. He was a shady character, no doubt about that. Up to no good. Maybe he could find the man and trail him. Learn who had hired him. A man like that probably spent his days on the southeast side of town, near the rough area the locals called the Cabbage Patch. The thought of a lowlife like that looking for Leah, forced him into a jog as he headed in the direction of Arizona Street.

When he crossed over Gaylord, he slowed to a walk, scanning the road and the open doorways for a sign of Jenson. Maybe he should go into some of the bars to ask about the man. He didn't have far to walk, because jaunty music spilled out of the next building he passed. It wasn't even noon yet and the liquor houses were doing a lively business in this slum.

He approached the bar, trying not to be too obvious about scanning the faces in the room.

"What'll ye have?" The man behind the counter with the apron eyed him expectantly. A beard covered the man's face, and tired lines around his eyes showed he was most likely old enough to be Gideon's father.

"Whiskey's fine." Anything was fine, really, because he wouldn't be drinking a drop. It would stick out too much if he didn't order, though.

The bartender poured a shot and placed it in front of Gideon. Now was the time.

"I'm lookin' for an acquaintance of mine. Maybe you've seen him before?"

The man raised a salt-and-pepper brow. "Maybe."

"His name's Jenson and he's a big man, tall and thick."

The bartender's lips pinched. "Yeah, I have the *pleasure* of his company most ev'ry night." The man's sarcastic twist on the word *pleasure* told Gideon it was anything but. "He comes in here with a couple o' roughstock to drink and cheat at cards. I get to break up their fights when the other players aren't too drunk to notice he's takin' all their gold dust."

He had Gideon's full attention. "Has he ever said what he does during the day?"

The man behind the bar shrugged and wiped out glasses. "Don't recall. I know he talks about how he's tryin' to find his wife an' take her back home. I don't blame the old lady, myself. I'd leave the scum, too, if I had to live with him."

Gideon couldn't help a wry smile. "Do you know who his friends are?"

The bartender squinted into the distance, as if that would help him remember. "I usually see him with Walters an' Ashe. Walters was just in here before you came. Gettin' his daily bottle."

Gideon forced himself to use slow, casual movements as he rose and pulled a coin from his pocket for the drink. "What does he look like? Do you know where he was headed?"

"Tall and skinny, brown hair. Wears a full beard to cover up a scar on his left cheek, but you can still see it. He was headed south when he left, but don't know where he was going. Said somethin' about the boss was waiting."

"Much obliged for everything." Gideon slid an extra coin on the counter and strode from the building.

As much as he wanted to sprint, he had to move slow enough to check each building he passed. He was on the right trail, he could taste it in the wind.

A couple of blocks down, a tall, slender man exited a shanty and headed in the same direction Gideon was going. The man wore a floppy brown hat, and suspenders holding up grey wool pants that were a couple inches too short for him. He had a beard, but the man was at least a hundred feet ahead so he couldn't see about the scar yet. What he could see clearly, though, was the gun belt around the man's lean waist and the glass bottle in his hand.

Gideon lengthened his stride and crossed to the opposite side of the road. After a few minutes he was able to gain enough ground to pull ahead of the man. He shot an inconspicuous glance over his shoulder and could have sworn he saw a mark on the man's left cheek. This had to be Walters. He matched the bartender's description exactly, and instinct told Gideon this was him.

He slowed his pace again and continued to follow. The buildings had thinned and they were moving into the foothills, with heavier foliage and boulders that kept him sheltered. About a mile outside of town, Walters turned off the road onto a short driveway. As they continued forward, it led to an open area with a large hole into the side of the mountain.

An old mine shaft.

$\mathcal{C}hapter$ $\mathcal{T}hirty$-$\mathcal{T}hree$

Gideon watched from behind a cedar as Walters disappeared into the opening. Should he follow? Most of the smaller mines only had one entrance, but did Walters know of another way out? The grass and remnants of snow in the area didn't show enough activity for this to be an active mine with workers coming and going daily. Must be abandoned. Then why had Walters gone in? If he was involved in something unscrupulous with Jenson, which Gideon was pretty sure was the case, could this be their headquarters?

Or maybe he was on the wrong track altogether. Maybe they had nothing to do with Leah, and Jenson really was searching for his crazy wife. Gideon had never felt so unsure of how to handle a situation. Always before, he'd been able to trust his instincts and watch the signs to make the right decision. But nothing was clear here. This cave could be only a drunk's hideaway.

A sound from the road pulled his attention. He moved behind a large rock just before a wagon pulled down the little trail. The man driving wore a straw hat pulled low, so Gideon could only make out an eye patch and an unkempt beard. The driver reined the horses to a stop in front of the mine entrance, set the brake, and strode into the black hole.

Who was he? Possibly the other man the bartender had mentioned? Avery or Anson...or maybe Ashe? Yes, Ashe. Gideon hadn't gotten a clear view of the back of the wagon, but he'd seen a few odds and ends—a coil of rope, a couple of bottles, and some other things he couldn't see clearly.

Now he needed to find out what the men were up to in the abandoned mine. Was it merely free lodging? Surely the nights were too cold for that to be the case. He would wait for a little while and see if anyone came or went. As long as he could see the wagon, they wouldn't be leaving without his notice.

The wait was driving him mad. But about ten minutes later, his heartbeat kicked up a notch when Walters appeared at the opening carrying two wood crates, which he loaded into the back of the wagon. The other man wasn't far behind, carrying another two boxes. The containers weren't identical in size, but all were the kind used to package canned goods and other supplies.

Both men went back in the cave, and Gideon crept closer to get a look in the crates. He'd only moved about ten feet, when he heard voices from the opening. Walters appeared again carrying a wooden barrel. The man he assumed was Ashe came right behind with another crate. Again they placed the items in the wagon, and disappeared back in the cave.

What were they loading? Were they packing up their hideout to leave? Or did the containers have stolen objects? He needed to get a look in them, but with all the activity around the wagon, it was going to be hard to get close without being seen.

Then Jenson emerged from the mine carrying a woman over his shoulder. Gideon's blood ran cold. He'd recognize that elegant body anywhere, even hanging almost upside down from an oaf like Jenson. The man tossed her into the wagon like a bag of sugar. Anger coursed through his veins.

Leah wiggled around until she sat upright. She was gagged and her arms bound. Likely her feet, too, since Jenson had been carrying her. The dirty dogs thought they had to tie up a woman like a calf at branding. Her hair was wild and had mostly fallen from its tie, and she looked worn out. What had they done to her?

Every muscle in him wanted to attack. Shoot every one of 'em and ride with Leah straight back to the ranch.

He took a breath and released it. He had to be smart about this. He had the six-shooter on his hip he usually wore while in town, his hunting knife, and a smaller knife in his boot. Too bad he'd not thought to bring his rifle, or a horse, for that matter.

If only he weren't alone. An ache hit his chest like he hadn't experienced in months. If Abel were here, they could take on the men together. With his sidekick, he could handle anything. *Why, God? Why did you take him away?*

Jenson's sharp command pulled Gideon's focus back to the scene in front of him, but he was too far away to understand the words. Walter climbed in the back of the wagon next to Leah, and the other men took seats in the front. Jenson sat with a Sharps Carbine in his lap, and was a much more imposing figure than the smaller Ashe who held the reins. The little man snapped the leather hard, though, and the horses lurched forward.

Gideon's heart galloped through his chest. The men were leaving and he still didn't have a plan.

He moved from rock to tree to bush, staying inside the line of foliage. The wagon followed the driveway, then turned left on the road toward Helena. Away from Butte City.

Were they taking her all the way to Fort Benton, then on to Richmond? Panic pulled his muscles tighter than a deer hide on a stretcher. No denying it. These men were taking her back to that louse. The man who planned to kill her.

Through the trees, he saw Jenson turn in the wagon seat and speak. Then Walters reached up to jerk the gag from Leah's mouth. Were they setting her free? But no, Walters raised a pistol from his lap so Leah—and Gideon—had a clear view of it. So help him, if any one of them hurt a hair on her head…

The horses pulling the wagon settled into a steady gait, and the landmarks became more familiar as they went. This was the main trail between Butte and Helena, the Mullan Road they called it. At one point it traveled through the edge of a property that neighbored the Bryant Ranch.

Should he take the time to find his old friend John Stands-alone and recruit help? With only himself against three men, he could deal with but one person at a time, while the others would have ample opportunity to hurt Leah. He couldn't risk attacking without more manpower or a smart strategy.

But it could take an hour to hike up to John's cabin, then the time to ride back. And what if Jenson and his men didn't stay on the road? What if they had another hideout somewhere close? Or what if they *did something* to Leah while he was gone? He swore under his breath. He would never forgive himself.

Through the trees ahead, Gideon glimpsed a wooden structure. Another wagon? But it was the opposite direction from the road. On the defensive, Gideon crept through the woods toward the building, still keeping the wagon in sight between the trees.

It was an old cabin, not more than a shack, really. There was no sign of inhabitants. Should he ignore it to keep the wagon in his sights? But what if there was something or someone inside that could help him? He couldn't risk the chance for reinforcements, and he could easily make up ground after a quick search.

The old wood door stuck at first, then the hinges released a shrill complaint as he tugged it open. There was no movement inside, just a dank odor and a mostly barren room.

Gideon stepped in, scanning the space. A pile of furs lay in a corner near the fireplace. A table, bowl, and pipe sat against the opposite wall. But his gaze zeroed in on what hung on the wall beside the door—a bow and quiver of arrows. It must be Sioux, from the decorative paint on the bow and the beadwork on the quiver. Matching feathers hung from the ends of both pieces.

And then his eyes drifted to something he hadn't noticed before. A rattlesnake skin, complete with the head and rattles. Not the almost translucent kind a snake sheds naturally, but the kind of hide that was killed, skinned, and cured.

Urgency gripped him again, and Gideon tore his eyes from the hide. He grabbed the bow and arrows, and headed out the door. Hopefully, they hadn't rotted from age. They needed to be strong and sharp enough to find their mark—quickly and silently.

He now had a plan, and lost no time in weaving through the woods to catch up to the wagon. All those days he'd spent as a boy with John Stands-alone came back to him in an exhilarating rush. With the native weapons slung over his shoulder, he melted into the land, each step landing on the balls of his feet so his boots were silent against the damp ground.

Soon, he found his target—the wagon—and slunk past it until he found a thick tree with a fork in the branches at eye-level. He touched his Colt revolver to make sure it was loose in the holster. Good.

Then examined the arrows and selected the straightest. Placing it against the string, he drew it back and forced his mind to filter through long-ago memories. *String between thumb and forefinger, chin tucked, nose almost touching the string.* He closed his eye farthest from the string, and focused on the wagon in front of him.

For a moment, he followed the wagon with the bow, gauging its speed and how far ahead of his target he would need to aim. Then he centered the wide flint tip of the arrow about a foot in front of Walter, just above the man's chest. Without allowing the bow to move even a fraction, he released the arrow and watched it fly toward its mark.

He didn't have time to waste, but drew his Colt and dodged to a closer tree. Taking aim on Jenson, he saw from the corner of his eye that Walters was doubled over in the wagon. Looked like the arrow hit its target. A surge of pride washed through him, but he didn't have time to glory.

He refocused his aim on the big man in the front of the wagon and squeezed the trigger.

Time slowed before him. He heard the report, smelled the acrid smoke, watched Jenson jerk, then reach for his left shoulder and turn in Gideon's direction.

Time regained its speed in a fury, as Jenson and Ashe both began shooting at him. He used his shots sparingly, only when he had clear aim. He just had five bullets left. A scream pierced the gun fire, but Gideon didn't have time to lose his focus from the three men. They had ducked low in the wagon now, using the wood as cover. Did Jenson jerk after Gideon's next shot? Maybe, but the man kept sending fire in his direction.

They seemed to have an unlimited supply of bullets, unlike his situation. He was down to one shot, if he'd counted correctly, and still had three bad guys to deal with. Surely he'd wounded Walters and Jenson, but the men continued to open fire on him

What else could he do? Where could he turn? *God, I need some help here!* His gaze moved to where Leah had been sitting, but she had sunk low in the wagon, too, and he could only see the top of her brown hair. *God, please!*

He sank back out of sight, fully covered by the tree. Panic choked out his breath, but he was powerless to stop it. What now?

Chapter Thirty-Four

The sound of gunfire continued on the other side of his tree, but Gideon squeezed his eyes against the noise. Then he heard a cry, the sound of a man in pain. Had they turned the guns on each other? He peeked around the rough bark to get a look.

Walters had turned in the wagon so he faced toward the front, but his firearm was nowhere in sight. Jenson was curled almost in a fetal position, arms wrapped around his stomach. And strangest of all, Ashe had set down his rifle and raised both hands over his head.

Gideon's gaze moved forward to a vision he'd never imagined. Ol' Mose stood in the road, a short, stubby gun in his hand. He fired a last round over the heads of those in the wagon, then lowered the firearm.

"There, ye varmints. Keep yer hands out where I kin see 'em. You, too, Goliath."

Jenson groaned as he unwrapped his hands from around his abdomen and raised them toward the sky. Pain twisted his already ugly face.

A movement in the back of the wagon caught Gideon's attention. Walters had one hand raised in obedience to Ol' Mose's command, but the other was stretching toward a rifle just a few feet away.

"Don't move." Gideon barked the command as he left the

woods and sprinted toward the back of the wagon. He kept his gun loosely pointed in Walters' direction, until he could move far enough over so Leah wouldn't be in front of his bullet. He hadn't let himself look at her yet. He would lose all the focus he needed to keep on these criminals.

Walters must have thought his loose aim was an open door, because in a quick movement, he jerked forward to grab the rifle. Gideon shot without allowing himself to think. Walters dropped the rifle and screamed as he reached for his right shoulder.

"There's more where that came from if you can't follow directions." Gideon ground out the words while he kept the Colt focused on the man. The scoundrel didn't need to know there wasn't any more where that had come from. He was out of bullets.

Walters moaned as he leaned back against the side of the wagon, gripping his shoulder still.

"I think they're understandin' things a mite better now," said Ol' Mose, still holding a gun on the two men in the front of the wagon. "Why don't ya see if ya can find some rope to tie 'em up? If ya don't find it in their wagon, I've got some in mine just over yonder hill." He nodded behind him where the road disappeared over a knoll.

Still keeping his empty revolver on the moaning Walters, Gideon finally turned to look at Leah. "You okay?" He hated the quaver in his voice, but he couldn't control the reaction that flooded him at the sight of her.

"I'm fine." Her voice flowed out like music, a little breathless, but the perfect melody. She was disheveled, but appeared to be blessedly whole. His chest might just explode from emotion that he couldn't have explained. Then he noticed her hands and feet still bound, and it pushed him into action.

With his left hand, he removed his hunting knife and moved toward Leah, keeping a wary eye on the wounded man beside her. "Let me cut your ropes." He kept his voice soft, his words meant only for her. He took his gaze from Walters long enough to slice the rope around Leah's wrists. Raw, red flesh glared at him before she flipped her sleeves down. It was enough to release a flood of anger through his veins.

"I can cut the rope at my ankles, just let me hold your knife."

Leah must have seen his expression, or else she wanted him to focus on pointing the gun at the men. Either way, he relinquished the antler handle of his hunting knife and reached forward to grab Walter's rifle. He holstered his own pistol and aimed the Winchester at the man.

As soon as Leah cut the rope around her ankles, she stretched her legs forward and rubbed her wrists.

"Leah, get out of the wagon and come over here."

He stepped back ten feet, and waited for her to hobble to him. "I want you to hold this gun on Walters while I tie him up. Hold it just like I showed you, and don't be afraid to shoot him if he moves. Just pretend you're hunting, and he's a deer." Gideon said the last part loud enough for all the men to hear, even though Leah had never actually shot a deer. What the men didn't know could only help him.

As Leah took the rifle from him, her hands shook. He glanced at her face, and saw a mixture of fear and uncertainty there, but also a fierce determination. He gave her an encouraging smile and brushed her upper arm with his hand. "You'll be fine." And she would. She was the bravest woman he'd ever met.

It took a few minutes to get all three men tied securely and loaded in the bed of the wagon. Ol' Mose and Leah both kept their respective guns aimed until he had the ruffians settled. The minute that was done, Gideon strode to Leah and took the gun from her hands.

For a moment, he drank her in. There were so many things he wanted to do and say, but what first? She made the decision for him when she flew into his arms, wrapping herself around him like a leaf blown against a tree trunk. It was what he'd wanted her to do, and he clutched her with all of his might.

He breathed in the sweet scent of her, savoring the feel of her wrapped in the shelter of his body. Moisture burned his eyes, but he closed them against the sensation. They stood there for several moments, and he would have gladly stayed like that all day, holding Leah, gently stroking her shoulders. But she finally leaned back in his arms, turning her beautiful face up to him.

"I'm so glad you saved me." She spoke the words softly, as if handing him a gift.

Gideon swallowed the knot in his chest. "Me, too."

A throat cleared not too far away from them. Gideon hated to, but he turned away from Leah to face Ol' Mose, keeping an arm around her waist. There was no way he was letting her get away again, whether his friend was standing there or not.

"Wooo-wee!" The old man's face split into a toothy grin. "Weren't it somethin' the way God took care o' that little mess?"

The words caught Gideon off guard. "God?"

"Yessiree. Jest when you was outnumbered three to one, I got to be the army of angels to fight off the Midianites."

What in the world was he rambling about? Poor ol' fellow must finally be losing it. "Been out in the sun too long, have ya, old man?"

Ol' Mose gave him a look full of mystery, like he knew a secret. "I'm talkin' about yer namesake from the Bible, son."

Then the man's gaze drifted to Leah and a fatherly smile touched his face. "What say you two young folks drive this wagon o' vermin into town, and I'll follow in my rig with me ol' Blunderbuss trained on 'em."

Gideon nodded. "Is that what that thing is? I've never seen a gun quite like it."

Mose held the squatty gun out like a royal crown. "Yep, my pa passed it down to me, and it's served me well all these years. It sprays lead so it's not so good fer huntin' dinner, but awful good fer huntin' vermin like these." He gestured toward the three men tied in the wagon.

"Let's get 'em back to the sheriff, then." Gideon kept his arm around Leah's tiny waist as he moved her forward to the front seat of the wagon. She fit so perfectly next to him. He lifted her up, then climbed beside her while she scrambled over to make room. She didn't move very far, though. Good thing.

He gathered the reins in one hand, flicked them to move the horses forward, then slipped his arm back around Leah.

Leah would have been content to ride nestled under Gideon's arm until the wagon drove off the face of the earth. Her hands had finally stopped shaking, but her muscles still hadn't regained their strength.

"You up to tellin' me what happened?"

The vibrato of Gideon's voice rumbled against her ear, sending a purr of contentment through her. Leah drew in a deep breath, then released it in an unsteady whoosh. A little of the tension left her chest with the spent air. At last, her mind drifted back to the beginning of the terror.

"I was on my way to inquire about a job, but Mr. Jenson gave me bad directions." She told about the run-down part of town she'd been sent to, and Gideon asked several questions about the specific location.

"When I woke up, I was already in the cave. It was so dark and cold, and they kept me tied and gagged the whole time."

Gideon's shoulder tensed under her cheek. "They didn't...hurt you or...anything else, did they?"

She knew what he was asking. She pushed the memories back. "No, they didn't touch me like that. The other men wanted to, but Jenson kept saying the boss wanted me clean." She snuggled deeper into Gideon, and he wrapped his arm tighter.

"Did they say who the boss was?" His voice held a touch of steel, like he was trying to keep it corralled.

"Simon." If the man had been there, she would have spat in his face.

"The man you were going to marry?"

"Yes." Was that bitter voice really hers?

Gideon's thumb stroked her side, and the coarse stubble on

his chin brushed her forehead as his lips touched her skin. "I'm sorry, love. I won't let him hurt you again."

Snuggled under his protective arm, Leah could almost believe him.

They rode that way for several minutes while her nerves loosened. Then they began to pass a few buildings, and the town filled in around them. Gideon seemed to know where he was going, though, and the wagon soon pulled to a stop in front of a single-story block building. It had bars on the windows, and a hand-painted sign overhead proclaiming it as the sheriff's office.

Gideon climbed from the wagon and reached for her with both hands. "We can go in and talk to the sheriff first. He'll probably send someone out to get these three."

Leah gripped Gideon's shoulders and allowed him to lift her down. The craving to lean into his chest and feel his powerful arms around her again was so strong, she had to grip the side of the wagon to hold herself back.

With a hand at the small of her back, Gideon guided her around the horses and up the few stairs to the wood door. He stuck his head in the building first, before steering her inside. It had been so long since she'd been able to simply follow—have someone else lead and make decisions and do all the talking.

She allowed Gideon to take over now, speaking to the sheriff, relaying the day's events—including the run-in he'd apparently had with Jenson the night before. She didn't have to say much until the end, when the sheriff turned his bushy grey brows on her.

"And, Miss Townsend, do you have any idea why these men kidnapped you?"

She hated this part of the story, but it had to be told. Nodding, she summoned moisture into her dry mouth and started from the beginning—when her father signed a contract to marry her off to seal a business partnership with Simon Talbert, the owner of the largest oil distillery in the southeast.

It felt good, really, telling her side of the story at last. She'd not even told Gideon or Miriam all the details before now. A glance at Gideon as she finished, though, revealed a firm jaw and a prominent blue vein running down his temple.

"If you need to confirm my story, Sheriff, you can wire my father's steward in Richmond." She paused. "I'd rather you not do that unless you must, though. I'm sure Simon knows I'm in Butte City from his friends, but I'd rather not open the possibility for any more info about me to get back to him."

"I don't think that'll be necessary. I should be able to get what I need from the sheriff in Richmond. He'll be takin' Talbert into custody soon, I'm sure."

He turned to another man sitting behind the wood desk. "Tommy, you wanna help me get these jailbirds unloaded?"

The sheriff turned and reached for his hat from a peg on the wall.

Leah spoke up. "You'll be needing a doctor for them. All three men have bullet wounds, and Mr. Walters has an arrow in his leg."

The sheriff turned to her with one brow arched. "I'm afraid that won't matter, ma'am. There's not a doctor within four hours ride of here. We'll take care of 'em, though."

Leah froze, her mind flashing back to the blood oozing from Jenson's shoulder. "But they need medical care. Are you trained to sterilize wounds and stop bleeding?"

The man shrugged. "No formal training, but we've had plenty of practice." With that, he settled his hat on his head, and left the building with the man Tommy close on his heels.

Chapter Thirty-Five

"You sure you won't eat supper with us?"

Leah leaned against the wagon while Gideon clasped Ol' Mose's hand. "The least I can do is buy you dinner."

"No, sirree. I need to get this wagon over to the dry goods store so they can unload before closin' time."

Gideon stepped back beside Leah and slipped his arm around her waist again. He'd not let her stray more than three or four feet since he'd first tied the men in the woods. She wasn't complaining, though.

"All right then. But make sure you stop by the cabin next time you come through, and we'll make sure you get a good meal."

Ol' Mose's toothy grin flashed. "If Miss Leah's cookin', I'll take you up on that one."

The old man turned to climb back in his wagon, and Gideon guided her toward the café. Inside, the homey aroma of beef and gravy almost took the last bit of energy from Leah's limbs. She was more famished than she'd been aware.

Gideon spoke to a man near the door, who showed them to a table, then he helped her collapse into a chair. What she wouldn't do to lay her head on the table right here. But that wasn't an option, even in this uncivilized town.

Gideon ordered for them both. She needed to put forth some effort, but she was so very tired... Her mind slipped into a daze as their voices hummed.

"Leah." Gideon's voice poured over her like honey on a sore throat. "Leah." His hand nudged her shoulder. It was more of a push, really, and not as gentle as she would have expected. She raised her head to frown at him. Why was her cheek wet? With effort, she forced her eyes open. What in the world?

Gideon stared at her, his emerald gaze sympathetic. She touched her cheek. Her hand came away covered with white goo and some kind of brown gelatinous substance. She looked back at Gideon. What was going on? The sympathy was gone from his eyes, replaced by a twinkle, accentuated by the quirk of his mouth.

"It's mashed potatoes and gravy. Try it."

She had no idea what he was talking about, but she gave him a dark look anyway. He pulled his hand away and leaned back in his chair.

"You fell asleep at dinner. I was going to let you rest for a while, but then your head landed in your plate." He leaned forward again and swiped a finger across her cheek, then slipped the lump of fluffy potatoes into his mouth. "Mmmm... You should have a bite."

The corners of her mouth pulled. Was Gideon actually teasing her? She scooped her own finger-full of potatoes from her face, then tasted. They were still warm, and reminded her stomach she'd not eaten since breakfast.

Leah wiped her warm cheeks with the cloth, keeping her gaze averted from Gideon's face. What must he think? She ate the rest of the food in front of her, forcing her eyes to focus on her plate so she didn't doze again.

When all remnants of the meal had disappeared, Leah sat back in her chair and touched the napkin to her lips a final time.

Gideon watched her, his face a mixture of emotions.

Amusement mixed with…intensity? She would love to know what was going through that mysterious mind of his. Another day. When she was strong enough to hold her head up.

"Let's get you back to your room for the night." Gideon rose and helped her from her chair. Pulled her up, really. The walk from the café to the boarding house was a long two blocks, and she was ever so thankful he kept a strong arm under her elbow.

They stopped to speak to Mr. Watson at the desk in the foyer, but they could have been discussing her gravestone, and she wouldn't have cared. Not right now. She was so tired…

Gideon watched the door to Leah's room close, listening for the latch to click in place. The wall opposite the door beckoned, so he sank against it for a minute. He needed some time to process.

Leah had been so exhausted. Had she heard him say not to leave her chamber until he came to get her? It was a huge relief that the boarding house had another room available for him, right at the end of this hall.

He released a long breath of pent-up air, then ran a hand down the front of his face, stopping to rub his chin. Three days' growth of beard was starting to itch in full force.

What was happening to him? He'd been gone from the ranch for a day and a half now. Miriam was by herself at the cabin. No one had checked on the cattle and horses. And here he was in Butte, not about to leave town until he could talk this Easterner into going back to the ranch with him. Had he lost his mind? How had his priorities shifted so sharply? He pushed off from the wall and headed down the hall to room five. He needed to figure some things out tonight.

After slipping out of his boots and cleaning up a bit, Gideon should have gone to bed. But he went to stand at the window. The streets were dark on this side of town, which was a good thing considering what bright lights meant at this time of night. The view only brought back memories of the fear he'd felt watching Jenson toss Leah into the wagon outside the old mine. Gideon turned from the window and began to pace.

He'd fallen hard for her, there was no denying that now. When he'd been married to Jane, his love had been sturdy and wholesome. He had provided for her and protected her—at least until the end, when he'd failed miserably at the protecting part. The vision of her swollen and blackened arm flashed through his mind again, pressing on his chest the way it usually did. He pushed it aside—hard.

Why had he married Jane, though? He surely had a good reason, at the time. It must have been for Miriam. Yes, that's right. To be a companion for Miriam, and help her with the cabin and ranch. Jane had done a decent job at that. She'd been generally helpful, if a bit timid, but the two girls had never gotten really close. Not like Leah and Miriam.

In truth, everything was different about Leah. She consumed him. She was part of every thought, drove most of his actions, made him want to do better, *be* better. It scared him how important she had become.

And now he'd almost lost her. Just like everyone else who had been important in his life.

A sob began somewhere deep inside and burned through his chest until it escaped. He dropped to his knees on the wood floor, laying his head in his hands. The desperate helplessness he'd felt in the woods cloaked him like a heavy fog. It ate up the air around him, replacing it with images. Abel's bloody body. Jane's disfigured arm. His mother, frail and delirious from the fever. His father's corpse, frozen stiff in the snow and already missing fingers.

The sobs wracked him, and he was helpless against them. The memories, the images, the pain—it all played out before him now. Like a nightmare he couldn't escape.

God, please! His mind cried out. It was the same cry he'd sent up in the woods. *God, I need Your help here.* His soul pleading.

Please take this burden. I can't carry it any more.

The peace was slow and silent. It had come before he even knew it was there. But his spirit sensed the change.

"God?" The word echoed in the room, and the response drifted over him like a comforting blanket. A warmth touched his soul, then radiated out to his skin. He wrapped his arms around himself, cradling the peace.

"God, I want You back. Please." The warmth expanded, and he turned his face heavenward, relishing the joy.

Gideon had no idea how long he remained in that posture, his mind finally at peace. No more visions, no nightmares. Just rest.

And then his mind came to life again.

Leah always said God had a plan for her, and she wanted to be where He put her. But she had been through so much—fleeing Richmond, boarding the steam boat in St. Louis, arriving in Fort Benton penniless, meeting Ol' Mose so she had a safe way to travel, then Mose bringing her straight to the ranch. Had God been guiding her all along?

Then a new thought drifted into his awareness. Was it just Leah that God was looking out for? He thought back through his own life, but saw it through a different lens this time. Life had been great while his parents were alive. Then after Mama had died, he'd been old enough to take care of Abel and Miriam, helping them grow to be strong, competent adults.

When Jane came, she'd never been happy on the mountain, but she *had* taught Miriam a lot about cooking and sewing and crocheting. After Jane's death, he'd put his strength into the cattle and the ranch, nurturing the animals and growing hay for the winters. Abel had been his right hand through it all.

That was what made his death so much harder to deal with, though. But then Leah had come along and helped distract him. It wasn't that he didn't miss Abel, but Leah had kept him from wallowing in guilt and sadness. And she had been the best thing for Miriam. The girl had blossomed with Leah around. She had been what they both needed. And Leah had said God brought her there.

Ol' Mose's words drifted back to him. *Weren't it somethin' the way God took care o' that little mess?* The picture came clear in his mind like a map, the way God had led him to the mine shaft, put him exactly where he needed to be to find Leah. Then brought reinforcements in the form of a cantankerous old trapper with a hundred-year-old shotgun. He'd guided them all, and most importantly, kept them *safe*.

Gideon turned to the window and saw the glitter of the stars. "God, thank you for bringing Leah to us. I think I see what she means about You taking care of us. I'd be obliged if you'd keep on doing that with her, and Miriam, too. And help me be the man You want me to be. And if it's Your will…please help her stay."

Leah leaned into the stretch as the tension in her muscles released. She relaxed back on the bed, taking in her surroundings. The room was clean, if a bit basic, with cream-colored curtains in the windows being the only real ornamentation. The sunlight filtering through the fabric brought a rush of awareness to clear the fog in her mind.

Daylight meant she'd overslept.

Leah lurched from the bed, the groaning of her body becoming audible as she forced herself to stand. She allowed herself a little extra time to wash before dressing. What she wouldn't do for a warm bath.

Soon, she slipped the final pin into her hat, and opened the door to the hallway. Sitting against the opposite wall, was Gideon. His arms rested on bent knees, and the strong features on his face clean and freshly shaven. So different from the ragged man who'd said goodnight to her.

"You feeling better?" His emerald eyes were clearer than she'd ever seen them, as if illuminated by a light from behind. The skin around them creased with a hint of a smile.

"Yes, much. How are you this morning?"

"Better than I've been in a long time." The creases grew deeper around his eyes, and the deep green twinkled. Actually twinkled. He rose to his feet, and motioned for her to proceed him toward the staircase.

What was going on with him? She'd never seen him look so...happy. Or peaceful. The brooding demeanor that had always characterized him was gone, replaced by a calmness. It was like joy and peace covered him in layers.

"You hungry?"

Leah fought the urge to look back at him. To see if she could get a hint as to why he was so different. "I guess."

"Hungry enough to stay awake?"

Leah raised an eyebrow as the heat crept into her cheeks. "I'll try."

As they descended the final stairs, the front door opened and the sheriff entered. He removed his hat as soon as he saw them.

"Miss Townsend, yer lookin' much better this mornin'. Mr. Bryant." He nodded at Gideon as they both came to stand at the landing.

"Thank you, Sheriff. Everything all right?" Seeing the man brought a flood of memories from yesterday.

"Yes, ma'am. I received a response from my wire to Richmond. The sheriff there confirmed your background. He's arrested Simon Talbert. For now, he's holding him for threatenin' yer life and for payin' to have you kidnapped. They're lookin' into the death of his former wife, too. It's my guess he'll be hanged before it's said and done."

A ball of tension tightened in Leah's stomach as the man spoke. Was it over? Could things really end this quickly? Why wasn't she relieved?

Gideon placed a hand at the small of her back as he spoke. "Thank you, Sheriff. That's the best news you could've brought. We were just headed to breakfast, will you join us?"

The man squeezed his hat brim—an uncomfortable action. "No, thank ye. I ate with the boys at the jail. An' I should prob'ly get back. Got a cell full of prisoners." His mouth parted to reveal a coffee-stained smile.

"Well, we're much obliged for the update." Gideon reached out a hand, and the men shook.

When the door closed behind the sheriff, silence took over the room. When Leah turned, Gideon was watching her, raised brows speaking his question before he did.

"You don't seem as happy as I thought you'd be with that news." His green eyes were caring, prodding into her soul in a way she couldn't evade.

She swallowed a lump in her throat. "It's just that Simon is so well-connected. He could probably buy his way out of jail, or at least send people after me while he's there." She tried to resist the panic needling her chest. "And now he'll have an even stronger motivation to find me—revenge."

Chapter Thirty-Six

She expected to see anger in Gideon's posture, or protectiveness, or *something*. But his gaze stayed soft. He kept one hand at the small of her back, and with his other, touched her shoulder, trailing his fingers all the way down her arm until he slipped his hand into hers. His warmth left tingles everywhere it touched, and she had to work hard not to shiver at the effect.

"Leah." His voice was deep, husky. "Don't you think God can take care of you?"

Between his touch and the intensity of his gaze, she was so mesmerized that it took a moment for his words to register. God?

"Yes, of course." What else could she say? Was this Gideon talking about God? Nothing made sense, and the pull of his touch was almost overwhelming.

His eyes crinkled at the corners. "Don't worry, then."

A door opened behind them, breaking into the spell that ensconced her. As the clerk entered the room, Gideon squeezed her fingers, then released them. He gave her a wink, and turned to nod at the man.

"Morning, Watson."

They took breakfast at the same little café where they'd eaten dinner the night before. For some reason, Leah struggled to carry on a casual conversation. She couldn't make sense of this new, happier Gideon.

She picked at the eggs on her plate, spearing a few onto her fork. She raised her eyes to sneak a glance at him. He was watching her, unashamed. He didn't look away, didn't say anything, but the tips of his mouth quirked upward in a grin. Who was this man?

She scrambled for something to say. Something to break the awkwardness and uncover a hint of reason for the change in him. "Are you planning to head back up the mountain today?"

His expression became ambiguous. Not the stoic, impassive look he used to wear, but more like he had a secret he wasn't about to reveal.

"Maybe. Not sure yet."

Not able to hold his gaze any longer, Leah dropped her focus back to the food on her plate. She took a bite of the eggs. They were lukewarm now, not appealing with the knot in her stomach. She tried the fried potatoes. They were probably good, but she really had no appetite. Leah set her fork on the plate and leaned back in her chair.

Gideon watched her, as before. This time, though, he raised a brow. "You get enough to eat?"

She dabbed at her mouth with a napkin. Why was she so nervous? "Yes, thank you."

He flashed a dimple. "Good. I was hoping you'd like to take a walk."

Why wasn't he already in the wagon heading back toward the ranch? He'd been gone for two days. Surely he was worried about Miriam and the animals. For goodness sakes, *she* was getting worried about Miriam and the animals. Still, she wasn't about to pass up a chance to spend time with Gideon, as much as she needed to focus on finding a job.

"That would be nice."

Gideon paid for their meals, helped her with her chair, and then escorted her out the door and onto the dusty street. The breeze played with the tendrils of hair she'd left loose around her face, its freshness releasing some of the tension in her nerves.

"I asked Ol' Mose to stop in and check on Miriam on his way

back through the mountains." Gideon's baritone washed through her like a soothing balm.

"Oh, good. I was starting to worry about her being alone for so long. I'm sure she was concerned when you didn't come home yesterday."

"Maybe, but my sister's a tough one. She knows these mountains and how to take care of things." He paused. "I don't want her to worry, though."

They seemed to be walking toward the outskirts of town, and her nervousness slid away as she focused on simply enjoying this time with Gideon. It would likely be her last, but no need to think about that.

He spoke of the supplies he needed to pick-up that day, of the wagon wheels he'd left for repair at the smithy, and other bits of small-talk. The buildings had thinned by now, and they came upon a pretty white structure, with a meadow stretching behind it.

"What a lovely place. What is it?"

"This is the church. Thought you might like to see it."

"Really?"

He must have heard the surprise in her tone, for he looked at her with a single raised brow. "You don't want to see it?"

"No...I mean, yes. I mean...I guess I'm surprised Butte has a church. The town doesn't even have a doctor, and it's so...rough here."

His chuckle was deep. They walked a few more moments until they entered the church yard.

Gideon stopped and turned to face her. She glanced up under the cover of her lashes, and the look in his eyes took her breath.

"Leah, I was crazy to let you leave. Will you ever forgive me?"

What? His face was earnest, waiting for an answer. But what was he asking? "Forgive you?"

His emerald eyes twinkled, and a dimple flashed in his right cheek. "Yes, and marry me?"

She might have been knocked senseless...seeing

stars…almost incoherent. "Ww…what?"

He stepped forward and reached up to cradle her cheek. His touch was warm and inviting.

"I'm sorry, Leah. I'm not very good at this."

Her chest hammered. Her breath still wouldn't come. "Good at what?"

"At saying what's in my heart. At telling you how much I love you."

It was what she'd been hoping for, praying for. Her breath came rushing back in one fell swoop. "Oh, Gideon."

She took his face in her hands, rose up on tip-toes, and answered his question with her lips.

It was the sweetest kiss Leah had ever imagined. A breathtaking exchange of the promise of love. Gideon pulled her to his chest and nuzzled her ear. Leah basked in his nearness, his breath on her skin, his love.

"So does that mean you'll marry me?" His voice was husky.

"Yes." She could barely think to string words together.

He leaned back to look her in the eyes, and Leah drank in the sight of him. She ran her hand over his smooth jaw, admiring the strong angles.

"You belong in a mansion somewhere back East."

Her gaze shot to his. What? No. She wanted to be with *him*.

"That's what you deserve, Leah. So much more than that." His arms tightened around her waist. "But do you think you can see yourself on a ranch in the Rockies?"

She released her breath and snuggled into his chest. "I couldn't stand it anywhere else." She felt his breath exhale, and his heartbeat grew strong under her ear.

"I was hoping you'd say that."

Leah could spend the rest of her life listening to his deep voice.

He held her close for a few moments, then spoke again. "So, since we're here at the church, shall we go see the preacher now?"

It took a moment for the words to register, then Leah sprang back. "Get married now?"

He raised a brow, a devilish grin on his face. "Only if you want to."

"But what about Miriam?"

He lifted a shoulder. "She'll be happy."

"She'll never forgive you. Nor me. She might even skin you alive."

Both brows rose now.

Leah brought a hand to her hip. She could see she would have to shake some sense into him. "Gideon Bryant, if you think your sister would ever forgive you for getting married without her there—without her even knowing you were engaged—you must not have met her yet."

He revealed a rakish grin as he gathered Leah back into his arms. "I don't think she'd mind so much. As long as I let her say 'I told you so.'"

Leah stood with Miriam in front of the little white church. They were to wait for the cue from the harmonica before entering for the ceremony. A smile pushed through her nerves. Who would have thought Ol' Mose knew how to play the Wedding March on his harmonica? He was certainly a man of many talents.

"You don't have to be nervous."

She glanced at Miriam, whose smile could barely fit on her cute little face. "I'm not nervous."

One of the girl's brown eyebrows rose. "If you smooth your dress one more time, you're going to wear the shine off."

Leah looked down at her dark green gown. It was one of the few she hadn't altered to make more practical. And it was her favorite. She rubbed a hand to smooth the fabric.

A chuckle drifted from Miriam. "See?"

Miriam's giddiness was infectious, but Leah tried to keep her own giggle inside. This was her *wedding day*, she wasn't a school girl anymore.

"Really, Leah. I've never seen a more beautiful bride."

Leah raised her eyes to take in Miriam's face, now as serious as her words. She was such a dear friend. God had blessed her, indeed.

She wrapped Miri in a quick hug. Anything more might bring on tears, and that was not to be allowed right before her wedding. "I'm so glad I have you here," she whispered. The tears threatened, so Leah stepped back and dabbed her eyes.

Miriam sniffed, her own eyes pools of jade. "I didn't mean to make you cry on your wedding day. You're gonna have your work cut out for you with that brother of mine." Her face broke into a wobbly smile. "But if anyone can handle him, it's you."

The clear note of a harmonica drifted through the church door, saving Leah from another teary hug. She inhaled a deep breath and then released it, ran a hand down her dress, and moved through the doorway behind Miriam.

Miriam strolled down the aisle in front of Leah, blocking Gideon from her view at first. Leah released another breath, trying to force down the butterflies flitting about in her stomach.

And then she saw Gideon.

He stood between the preacher and Ol' Mose, wearing a long-sleeve green shirt that matched the emerald in his eyes. His hair was trimmed short, his clean-shaven face accentuating every amazing feature. Leah couldn't take her eyes from him. Didn't want to. Was she really about to marry this man? Her dreams finally coming true? Moisture threatened her eyes again. But when Gideon took her hands, she forgot about everything but him.

The pastor addressed them, but Leah couldn't pull her focus to his words. And then Gideon began to speak in his rich baritone.

"I, Gideon Jacob Bryant, take thee, Leah Marie Townsend, to be my lawful wedded wife. To have and to hold from this day forward, for better for worse, for richer for poorer, in sickness and in health, to love and to cherish, till death us do part, according to God's holy ordinance, and thereto I plight thee my troth."

The love in his eyes took her breath away.

She made it through her part of the vows. A sense of peace and rightness overwhelmed her as she promised to love, cherish, and obey this man.

"I now pronounce you man and wife. Gideon, you can kiss her now."

Heat flooded Leah's face before she found the nerve to meet Gideon's grin. He brought his lips to hers in a sweet kiss, but the promise of passion was there. A hoot from Ol' Mose ended the moment sooner than Leah wanted.

Gideon slipped a hand around her waist and turned to their little party. "What say we celebrate? Lunch at Aunt Pearl's for us all?"

Ol' Mose only chuckled and slapped him on the back.

Chapter Thirty-Seven

Leah snuggled deeper into Gideon's side, relishing his warmth as the wagon wound up the mountain road. How different this trip was from the stony silence of their ride down to Butte. On this return trip, not only was Gideon speaking to her, but she was his *wife*. She was Leah Bryant. Mrs. Gideon Bryant. Her dream had come true.

"When did Ol' Mose say he would bring Miriam home?" She raised her face to catch her husband's expression.

"Tomorrow before lunch."

Since they weren't planning a wedding trip, Ol' Mose and Gideon's sister had conspired to give them time alone at the cabin. But the thought of the night ahead set off the butterflies in her stomach. It would be nice to have Gideon all to herself, if only for a day. Better not to let her mind drift too far into that topic.

"Did I tell you what the sheriff said when you were gone to get the wagon?"

Gideon shifted his weight to look at her. "No, I didn't know you saw him."

"He came by to tell us about the wire he received from Richmond."

"Another one?"

"Yes. They found Simon hanging in his cell at the prison...dead." Leah swallowed. As much as she'd feared the man, it was hard to think about anyone ending their life in such a way.

Gideon's hand tightened on her knee.

"Oh." The word came out in a rasp. Was he angry? Or sad?

"Such a tragedy. The whole situation. I just keep thinking it could have turned out so differently." Leah watched Gideon's face, willing him to understand her words. His Adam's apple bobbed. She kept going. "If he hadn't been so selfish, none of this would have happened."

They rode in silence for a long moment, then Gideon finally spoke. "You're right about it being sad the way he ended. I can't say I like anything I've heard about the man, but no one should get to the point he takes his own life.

"But Leah," he turned so he could look her square in the eyes. His gaze was soft, but fervent. "If he hadn't threatened your life, you never would have left Richmond. You wouldn't have made it to our ranch."

Leah allowed that to sink in. It wasn't a theory she'd examined before. "So you think God gave Simon such an evil heart in order to bring us together?"

His gaze was intense. "I think God used the situation to bring you into my life, but he didn't make Simon evil. If that man hadn't threatened you, God would have brought us together in a different way."

How had Gideon become so wise? Leah sent up another prayer of thanks for this husband the Lord had given her. And then she remembered the final part of her conversation with the sheriff.

"I also asked him to send a telegram to my father's steward, letting him know my location and news of our marriage."

Gideon nodded. "That's good."

"I asked him to keep running the business for now, but we'll need to decide what to do with everything."

Gideon's body jerked. "What do you mean?"

"I'll turn twenty-three in a couple months. Since you're my husband, you'll own Townsend Oil, and the rest of my father's holdings. They'll need to know what you plan to do with them."

The muscles in his jaw worked. The silence grew thick between them, but she couldn't tell what he was thinking.

"I don't want it."

She blinked. To be honest, she didn't want the business either, but did he realize how much money he was worth now? "But you have to. It was my inheritence. I heard our steward say one time the oil company makes over three hundred thousand a year."

Gideon raised a brow at her, then turned his face back to the road. It was hard to read his emotions. Although not quite the impassive expression he used to wear as a mask, this was the closest she'd seen to his old façade. She knew better than to rush him, though. Better to settle in and watch the scenery change as they made their way up the mountain.

After a few minutes that felt like an hour, Gideon finally spoke again. "I don't know the first thing about oil."

Leah wanted to interject to say the Directors would teach him all he needed to know. He didn't look like he was finished, though, so she held her tongue.

"And I really don't want the money. I kinda had in mind I would support my wife, not the other way around." He shot her a sideways glance, then focused on the trail again.

But then he released a sigh and turned to face her, threading his fingers through hers. His eyes were kind. "But it was your father's legacy, what he spent his life building. You decide what you'd like to do with it. If you want us to go back to Richmond, for temporary or for permanent, well…we can talk about it."

Leah allowed his words to soak in. She didn't want to move back to Richmond any more than he did, but the fact he would even consider it… Consider leaving the ranch and all he had poured his life into… He would leave it all if she asked him? She brought Gideon's hand up to her cheek and met his gaze with blurry vision. "No, love. I don't want to go back to Richmond. I want to stay right here with you."

He gave her a soft smile, then wrapped an arm around her and pulled her against his side. "We'll figure it out then."

A few moments later, he asked, "Does the company have good leadership?"

Leah scanned the recesses of her memory. "I think so. Papa always said good things about the Board of Directors. I guess I could send a wire to the steward to make sure."

He nodded. "Let's do that. Then we can wait for God to make our direction clear."

Leah's heart squeezed, and she stretched up to kiss his cheek. He quirked an eyebrow. "What was that for?"

Leah didn't try to hold back her smile. "Just because I'm thankful God gave me such a wise husband."

He gave her a hooded look. "It's a good thing we're home now."

Leah tore her gaze from him long enough to see they were, indeed, pulling into the ranch yard. Her stomach did another flip at the thought of what lay ahead, but she squashed the emotions.

Gideon reined the team in front of the house, climbed down, then reached up for Leah. Instead of helping her down, though, he swept her into his arms and headed for the stairs. She squealed, then wrapped her hands around his neck, giggling.

"I don't think you've carried me since you broke my leg," she said, not able to resist a little teasing.

He raised an eyebrow. "You had to go and bring that up, did ya?" An impish grin came over his face. "I guess it was the only thing I could think of at the time to keep you here."

"Oh!" Leah blustered, then caught the twinkle in his emerald eyes. "You rascal."

He carried her over the cabin threshold and lowered her feet to the floor. Leah turned to face him, a small distance and a strong awareness filling the air between them.

Gideon's mouth twitched. "Why don't you set out a bit of dinner while I put the horses away?"

Leah turned away from him, grateful for the job. "All right."

After he left the cabin, she scanned the jars and barrels of food in their little kitchen, but everything there would take hours to cook. Her eyes hovered over the salted ham. That'd be perfect with the biscuits she'd brought from Aunt Pearl's café. Surely she could do something with these.

By the time Gideon was back from the barn, she had the table set and a fire taking hold inside the stone hearth. And her nerves were wound tighter than a concert violinist's strings. For the first time in a while, she longed for her mother. Or even Emily. Someone who would tell her what to expect and what to do.

Gideon settled his hat on the peg by the door, and turned to survey the table. "Looks good."

"It's not much, but it's ready." She moved to the stove for the coffee pot, then poured the steaming brew into Gideon's mug first, and then her own.

Gideon helped her with her chair, then sat and spoke a blessing over their food. The gusto with which he consumed the ham, biscuits, plum preserves, and dried apples, was more than the simple meal deserved.

Leah picked at her own food, mostly to keep her hands from twisting knots in her skirt. There was no way she could eat.

After finishing the last bite of his apples, Gideon set down his fork with a contented sigh. "I didn't realize how much I've missed your cooking." Smile lines formed around his eyes.

Leah raised her brows. "It's only been three days. And I didn't really cook this." She motioned toward the empty dishes in front of them. "The biscuits were from Aunt Pearl's."

The twinkle in Gideon's eyes darkened. He placed his napkin on the table and rose to his feet, deliberation cloaking each movement. He locked his gaze with Leah's, holding her attention so tight she couldn't breathe.

She watched his every step as he came around to her chair, took both her hands, and pulled her up and to his chest in a fluid motion, like a magnet to iron. He cradled her hands between his own, then raised them to his mouth, planting a kiss on her fingertips. Her whole body trembled.

"You're cold." Concern shadowed his face. He turned,

leading her toward the large fireplace. When they reached the hearth, Gideon wrapped his arms around her and pulled her tight against him. The heat of the fire soaked into her, and the warmth of Gideon's hold pushed her nervousness away. She absorbed the strong beat of his heart.

How many times had they been in front of this fire together? But never like this. Never with this glorious feeling of melding together. Her mind drifted back to other times they'd been here, when she'd doctored Gideon's wounds from the bear attack. She'd been so frightened then. Not really knowing what to do. Afraid she'd miss an important step that would kill him.

And then the idea came, like a bullet striking its target. She leaned back to watch Gideon's face while she spoke. "I know what we should do with the money."

His expression registered confusion, but his hands kept their grip at her back. "The money?"

"From my inheritance."

His confusion shifted into amusement. "What should we do with it?"

Excitement started to build in Leah's mind. "We should bring a doctor to Butte City, so the people here can have real medical care. And maybe an assistant, too, so he can make house calls into the mountain country." She paused, eager for Gideon's response.

His face softened, and he raised a hand to cup her cheek. The love in his gaze tightened her chest so she couldn't have spoken if she wanted. "I think it's a wonderful idea. That's one of the things I love about you. How much you care about other people."

Leah drew a breath, lost in the emotion in his deep emerald gaze. "Really?"

His eyes twinkled. "Yes. But there are so many other things I love, too." And then he drew closer, bringing his lips to hers. His kiss was soft and light and filled with love. He pulled back to look in her eyes, the twinkles taking on a rakish gleam. "Can I tell you about them?"

Did you enjoy this book? I hope so!

Would you take a quick minute to leave a review on Amazon.com?
HTTP://AMZN.TO/1BFTGYD

It doesn't have to be long. Just a sentence or two telling what you liked
about the book!

About the Author

Misty M. Beller writes romantic mountain stories, set in the 1800s and woven with the message of God's love.

She was raised on a farm in South Carolina, so her Southern roots run deep. Growing up, her family was close, and they continue to keep that priority today. Her husband and children now add another dimension to her life, keeping her both grounded and crazy.

God has placed a desire in Misty's heart to combine her love for Christian fiction and the simpler ranch life, writing historical novels that display God's abundant love through the twists and turns in the lives of her characters.

Sign up for e-mail updates when future books are available!
MistyMBeller.com

Don't miss the other books by
Misty M. Beller

The Mountain Series
The Lady and the Mountain Man
The Lady and the Mountain Doctor
The Lady and the Mountain Fire
The Lady and the Mountain Promise
The Lady and the Mountain Call
This Treacherous Journey
This Wilderness Journey
This Freedom Journey (novella)
This Courageous Journey
This Homeward Journey
This Daring Journey
This Healing Journey

Texas Rancher Trilogy
The Rancher Takes a Cook
The Ranger Takes a Bride
The Rancher Takes a Cowgirl

Wyoming Mountain Tales
A Pony Express Romance
A Rocky Mountain Romance
A Sweetwater River Romance
A Mountain Christmas Romance

Hearts of Montana
Hope's Highest Mountain
Love's Mountain Quest
Faith's Mountain Home

Call of the Rockies
Freedom in the Mountain Wind
Hope in the Mountain River
Light in the Mountain Sky

Made in the USA
Coppell, TX
09 March 2021